WRONGED IN PARADISE

PARADISE SERIES

BOOK 19

DEBORAH BROWN

WRONGED IN PARADISE
All Rights Reserved
Copyright © 2019 Deborah Brown

ISBN-13: 978-1-7334807-0-3

Cover: Natasha Brown

PRINTED IN THE UNITED STATES OF AMERICA

WRONGED IN PARADISE

Chapter One

That morning, Creole and I met our best friends, Fab and Didier, at our favorite restaurant, a local haunt called the Bakery Café. Fab snagged our usual table at the far end of the sidewalk, prime for people watching. We'd finished our breakfast and were lingering over coffee, making plans for the day, when a cop car careened up and illegally parked diagonally in front, blocking in a couple of cars, ours included.

I shuddered.

"What?" Fab demanded.

"I don't have a good feeling about this." I attempted to rub away my tingling neck hair, which everyone who knew me knew was a bad sign."Maybe someone attempted to rob the restaurant again."

Fab's blue eyes scanned every corner of the open-air patio.

The car doors opened, and two officers got out.

They weren't local. I was on a first-name basis with most of the officers on the force.

Creole straightened in his chair.

One cop approached our table; the other hung back, hand on his weapon.

"Fabiana Merceau?" the officer asked.

"Yes." She nodded.

"Stand, please. You're under arrest for the murder of Aurora Bissett." The officer stood over her, cuffs in hand.

Fab stood slowly in her designer heels, smoothing down her skinny jeans and silk blouse. "I don't know that person, and I've never murdered anyone." She tucked her long brown hair over her shoulder.

"Hands behind your back."

"Where are you taking her?" Didier asked. He also stood, towering over her. Her husband's dark hair managed to fall perfectly against his face, exposing intense blue eyes, growing darker as his worry grew.

"Not a word without your attorney present." I sat up straighter and made a "zip-lip and throw away the key" motion. I reached under the table for Creole's hand and squeezed, happy he was by my side. He put his arm around my shoulders, pulling me close and threading his fingers through my wild red mane. Thank you, humidity.

"Everyone, stay seated," the other officer who'd stepped forward said, accentuating his command with a stern stare around our table and the one next to us.

The rest of the customers seated outside had

ceased their conversations and turned their chairs for a better view, all ears, their attention on the unfolding drama. Patrons and employees that had been inside filled the doorways.

The first officer slapped the cuffs on Fab and led her to the car, assisting her into the backseat. Seconds later, he signaled to the other officer, who climbed in, and the two pulled back into traffic.

"I'm going to follow them." Didier ran and jumped in his Mercedes, not noticing the women who turned to stare. He squealed out of his parking spot and followed the cops down the street.

The waiter came over, and Creole settled the bill.

Shifting in my chair to face Creole, I told him, "I want to go to the station. Fab's going to need a friend."

"Fab has her husband, and he'd never let anything happen to her," Creole said, as though I needed to be reminded. "He'll get her the best representation." He pulled me to my feet.

I stood on my tiptoes and kissed him. "I'm going. Fab would be there for me."

"Not by yourself." Creole grabbed my arm and walked me to the Hummer, opening the door. I slid in. "I recognized one of the officers, and Fab's on her way to Miami. Whatever went down happened in their jurisdiction."

Creole had been an undercover cop until he

got shot up and, after a long recuperation, decided he'd had enough. Now, he, Didier, and my brother, Brad, had formed a real estate partnership—a family affair, as every member was an investor, all of us silent until a vote was needed on the next venture.

I retrieved my phone from my pocket and paused as Creole fired one question after another at me about Aurora Bissett. The biggest one being who was she? I had to tell him several times that, like Fab, I had no clue who the woman was and thus didn't have any idea why someone would want her dead or why Fab was a suspect.

It never got old living in Tarpon Cove, ideally located at the top of the Florida Keys. The sun shone brightly that morning and glittered off the blue-green water. But I was having a hard time enjoying the warm weather this morning. I turned my face upward and soaked in the warm rays.

Creole had shot up the Overseas Highway and took the curve north, headed to Miami, when his phone rang. I knew from his vague answers that it was Didier and he wasn't happy with the direction of the conversation. Fab and I, for the most part, shared phone calls on speakerphone; the guys refused.

"Didier doesn't want you involved," Creole said after he hung up. "He already called Tank, who's out of town, so Didier called in a favor from a friend. He promised to call when they get back home."

Fab had met Tank during a jail visitation— he'd professed his innocence, and apparently he wasn't full of it, as he'd retained his license and set up a law office in the Cove.

"What? What are you talking about? Fab needs a lawyer. And a good one. Who better than me to help?" Didier knew that without having to be reminded.

"Didier's got that covered. He has a friend who's a lawyer. He's already contacted him, and the man is meeting them at the station. So Fab's got representation." He pulled into a left turn lane to hang a u-turn and head back south.

I struggled to suck down a loud groan. "Fine, take me home," I said militantly. "Once we get there, I won't be getting out. I'll drive myself. If you think I would sit back and do nothing, you'd be mistaken. Fab would be there for me and has proven so in the past, and I'm not letting her down."

"Madison Westin," Creole growled, "you are the stubbornest woman ever."

I turned my head slightly, sucking in a calming breath, which rarely worked to relax my nerves. "That was disclosed before the I-dos, and you signed off," I reminded him in a superior tone. "Too late now. I don't want to hear about marryer's remorse."

"You're aggravating." He signaled and pulled

back into traffic.

"Another irritating trait already disclosed," I snapped, biting back a smile, happy that I didn't have to drive myself. It would be worth any favors I had to pony up later.

In the Westin family, we traded favors like hard currency, and the idea had spread to our friends, catching on and becoming popular. It came with the stipulation that when asked to pay up on said favor, you had to do it without complaining.

I decided I'd had enough of the silence. "I know that you know this is a death penalty state. No offense to Didier's friend, whoever he is, but he's not the best criminal attorney in the state. That would be Cruz Campion. Fab needs the best, and he's it. I'll bet that she'd agree with me."

"Didier is her husband; don't you think he knows what's best for her?"

I caught my snort in time. "No, I don't. Not in this case," I said in a huff. "Didier's a businessman and has zero experience with the law." I underscored that by holding up my fingers, forming an O. "You know I'm right, Mr. Ex-Undercover Badass." I stabbed my finger at him. "Who would you want? Some priss Didier probably met hobnobbing at a South Beach party when he was a highly sought-after model, or a lawyer with an excellent win record in criminal court?"

I'd put off making the call to Cruz's office long enough, assailed by an attack of nerves. Our relationship was tenuous at best. I flicked through the contacts in my phone and called the man in question. It surprised me when his snooty assistant, Susie, didn't answer and the call was instead transferred to the receptionist. "May I speak with Mr. Campion?" I hesitated to give my name, in case I was on a banned list. I knew that if Susie had answered, she'd never have put the call through. I'd bypassed her a couple of times to get to her boss, and she'd never forgiven me.

"Mr. Campion is gone for the day," a young voice said in a harried tone. Susie would've hung up.

"When would be a good time to call back?"

"Tomorrow afternoon. He has court in the morning."

"Thank you." I hung up. That was the best news next to his taking the call.

Cruz blamed me for his grandmother getting her bump and grind on while on vacation. He'd had to be reminded that I owned vacation cottage rentals and wasn't in the business of regulating my guests' sex lives. It had fallen on deaf ears. I'd thought about banning every one of his nine hundred relatives from ever getting another reservation. Good thing I hadn't because it gave me enough of an edge for this conversation, or so I hoped. How long it lasted would depend on his mood.

I called the next person on my list, hanging up after a minute. "That's irritating and a first — calling the chief of police and getting an answering machine." I called the main number for the Miami police department.

"He's no longer here," said the man who answered, then hung up.

"Did you know that the chief ditched his job?" I asked Creole, staring at the screen.

"I guess you need to be reminded that you have a much better relationship with the man than I ever did."

I laughed, which earned me a raised eyebrow. "I can't help that I'm charming."

He snorted and asked in a suspicion-laced tone, "Who are you calling now?"

I ignored him as the call was diverted to a message box. "I hope you didn't blow the area without so much as a good-bye. I need a favor, if you're so inclined. If not, I've got criminal friends I can call." I hung up.

Creole shook his head.

"That was Spoon, and he knows I'm kidding. Why do you suppose he didn't answer?" Jimmy Spoon was married to my mother and was seldom averse to doing me a favor.

"I'm sure that friendly message you just left will get you a return call."

"Sarcasm is unbecoming."

"You should be very nice to me. I may be the only one speaking to you when you're done with your behind-the-scenes machinations, which you've been asked nicely not to do, and oh look, you're doing anyway." Creole knew a shortcut to the station, having worked there for years, and he pulled into the parking garage from a back road. He picked up his phone, making a call. "Where are you? Madison didn't take no for an answer, so we're here to hold your hand until you run us off." He laughed and hung up, then got out and went around to help me out, grabbing my hand in a tight hold as though I might make a run for it. We hiked across the street.

Didier was easy to find. He was the only person in the reception area other than the man at the front desk answering the phones. We sat in uncomfortable chairs next to him.

Didier looked at me and held up his hand. "Before you get started, I called Cruz first and was told that he's not taking new clients."

"Did you identify yourself as Fab's husband?"

He nodded.

We waited for what seemed like forever. Two hours, to be exact. Finally, a man wearing an expensive suit, not a strand of his sun-bleached hair out of place, strolled in, gave the lobby an arrogant once-over, and headed straight to Didier, who introduced him as Kurt Byron, South Miami criminal lawyer. He acknowledged Creole and me with the briefest of glances and directed Didier to join him off to one side. When they finished their short conversation, he went to the desk, and Didier motioned Creole over. I knew it was another "you can take your wife home" conversation, assuring us that he had the situation handled.

They exchanged a few words, and Creole strolled back, a determined glint in his eyes. Recognizing he was about to fling his arm around me, I didn't step out of his reach and also didn't offer up another argument about not leaving, which he was clearly expecting. "We're going home." He escorted me out of the building and back to the car.

Back on the highway, I got my phone back out and called Gunz, one of Fab's longtime friends and business associate, who had far-reaching connections. He answered on the first ring. I'd improved in his esteem after successfully working with Fab on a couple of jobs for him. "Fab is being held at the police station in Miami on a murder charge. I don't know anything other than that she was arrested. Any update you could get would be helpful. And if necessary, could you also have someone on standby, ready to make bail?"

"I'm on it," Gunz grunted and hung up.

I scrolled through my phone and made another call. "Huge favor," I said to Xander when he answered. If you asked him, he'd tell you he was VP of the first business that Fab and I had started together, which was nothing more than a phone number on a business card since we couldn't agree on a name. Of course, no one knew that. It wouldn't be professional. "Fab's been arrested for murder," I blurted when he answered. "She didn't do it. I need you to run a check on Kurt Byron; he's a lawyer friend of Didier's. What I want to know is what his reputation is and, more importantly, has he had any murder cases and what's his win record? You can bill me triple if you get the information back to me before tomorrow morning." I gave him the few scant details about Byron that I'd garnered from Creole. "One more job. This isn't a rush but don't dawdle." I pinched Creole's thigh.

"Ouch, dammit."

I shot him a cheeky grin. "The dead woman's name?"

"Aurora Bissett," he snapped.

I repeated it to Xander. "I want to know everything there is to know about the woman and any connection you can find to Fab."

Xander was our information specialist, and he was damn good at his job. While finishing his last year of college at the University of Miami, he'd eagerly agreed to work remotely. It was rare now for him to make an appearance at the office and lounge on the couch, which was his first choice for a seat, mainly for the advantage of seeing everything going on. It surprised me to find that I missed having him underfoot.

"It's impressive to watch you in action." Creole smiled at me as I shoved my phone back in my pocket. "Fab's lucky to have you as a friend."

Chapter Two

Creole eyed me over the rim of his coffee cup as I accented an above-the-knee black dress with an onyx watch, earrings, and low heels. "I'm afraid to ask what you're up to, but you look hot and I'm more than a little annoyed that I haven't been invited."

"I'm on my way to court," I said in a tone with an undercurrent of "let's not argue."

Didier had called the night before with an update, which was scant on details. Fab was still being held for questioning, which they had the legal right to do for seventy-two hours without charging her. His hotshot attorney friend wasn't optimistic about her getting released anytime soon, and it was just a matter of time before she was booked and fingerprinted.

As soon as I got Xander's report on Byron, I'd emailed it to Didier, highlighting his lawyer friend's win record, which wasn't all that impressive. No need to add an extra comment regarding the client that got the death penalty, as I'd bolded it in a different color.

"I relayed every word to Madison," Creole had told Didier. "'Leave the case to the professional you hired' went in one ear and out the other." He'd blown out an exasperated sigh. After that, he'd done more listening than commenting. He ended the call with a grouchy, "You tell her." I'd expected my phone to ring, but it didn't. "He's worried about his wife, and he thinks he's doing what's best for her."

I picked up my purse and tote bag and crossed to the kitchen to stand in front of Creole, leaning in and kissing him. "Try to stay out of trouble." I smiled cheekily. "I'll do the same."

"Are you going to give me any details about your day, or perhaps I'm to wait until I get a call for bail? You do know that just because you get booked into the same jail as your friend doesn't mean you get to share the same cell. Never happens."

"You're not funny." I ignored Creole's sad face. "Cruz is in court this morning. There's no better time to run into him and badger him until he agrees to represent Fab."

"You've got some nerve." Creole shook his head. "If I could move my meeting, I'd go for the show."

"I'd go to his office like a normal client if I thought I had a chance of getting past his ferocious guard assistant." I made a growling noise.

"You're exaggerating."

"No, I'm not. If Susie had the power to banish me to another world, I'd be gone." I laid a long, lingering kiss on Creole. "You behave."

"You need to take your own advice." He jerked me back to his chest and kissed me again, then took my hand and walked me to my SUV.

I blew through the coffee drive-thru and ordered an extra-large caramel coffee, extra whipped cream. I sucked down half the cup and morphed into Fab, hitting the gas and sending the Hummer speeding down the highway, only sticking to the speed limit around known speed traps. Thanks to light traffic, it made for a fast trip to Miami. I needed to make a note and boast to Fab later about what a badass I was behind the wheel. It would give us something to laugh about over cold alcoholic drinks.

I lucked out, and a car pulled out as I drove up, making me the beneficiary of a great parking spot. I ran up the stairs, hoping I wasn't going to have to cool my heels for hours waiting for Cruz to get a break. I cleared the metal detector, unlike the man in front of me, who I went around when he backed up for a redo, and easily found the bulletin board where court assignments were posted.

The last time I trotted out this trick, I'd pretended shock: "Imagine running into one another." Now that we were old acquaintances, I would corner him, explain the situation, and beg if I had to. The elevator doors opened, and fifty people wanted to squeeze in and stand shoulder to shoulder. No thanks. I took the stairway to the third floor.

There were a handful of people scattered along the benches that lined the walls outside the courtrooms. I peered through the window in the door of the courtroom Cruz was in and spotted him at the defense table. I knew it would be a while, with the judge on the bench and a woman in the witness box. I opened the door and slid into a seat in the back row with a quick glance at the prosecution table. Thankfully, the prosecutor rustling through a mountain of paperwork and looking aggravated was no one I knew.

After about five minutes, I wanted to jump up and down when the judge excused the witness and called for a break. I waited until the courtroom cleared, with the exception of a handful of people, one of whom had nodded off, then walked to the railing and leaned forward, whispering, "Mr. Campion."

The dark-haired, dark-eyed attorney turned in his seat, did a double-take, and smirked. "I should've warned my assistant that some phonied-up excuse wouldn't be enough to shake you if you wanted something, but she was so proud of her ability to keep you at bay, I couldn't bring myself to burst her bubble."

It wasn't his assistant that let the details of his whereabouts leak out, and I wasn't about to out the receptionist. "If you weren't the best attorney in the universe, as you like to tell all and sundry, I'd be dogging someone else. The way I see it is we both have interests, and I'm sure we can come up with something mutually beneficial."

"Wait for me in the hallway." Cruz didn't bother to hide his eyeroll. "You've got five minutes. Three would be better."

I nodded and slipped out to sit on the bench next to the door.

Cruz didn't make me wait; he came out the door, scanned the hall, and sat next to me. "You're here but your appendage isn't, for once. So what is it you want?"

"Fab was arrested yesterday for the murder of a woman she doesn't know. Currently, she's being held at the jail across the street."

He shook his head. "There are other capable attorneys in town; call one of them."

"Did you know that your Aunt Carmine is visiting from somewhere and currently in residence at The Cottages for a month-long stay?"

Cruz gave me a *who?* look. "You mean Carmela?"

"I guess you didn't know that she prefers Carmine—sounds more mafia, and those are her words," I related in a superior tone, ignoring his look of disgust. "I'd hate to toss Carmela to the curb and, of course, blame you. In case you're unaware, you have other relatives with upcoming reservations that are about to swoop in. I'll cancel them. All of them. You certainly have a passel of relations."

"That's blackmail," Cruz snapped.

"By the time a judge agrees with you, vacation time will be over."

"I'll own that dump."

"I've ignored your surly attitude over that unfortunate fiasco with your grandmother long enough. Time for you to forgive and forget. I don't know why you blame me for her sleeping with a retired college professor. On the bright side, as my employees constantly tell me, it's a happy ending—he's not a beach bum.

"You could've fooled me."

I didn't have to look at my watch, which I'd never set the time on, to know that I was running out of time before either the break was over or Cruz lost patience and left me sitting there. "Please, oh please." I put my hands together in a prayerful gesture. "Represent Fab. Get her off. Then we'll all be happy. Maybe not you, but your family will be ecstatic, and that's a win."

"I should call security on you, have you thrown out."

"Do you think I'd track you down at the courthouse and practically beg for your services if I wasn't desperate? Fab's my best friend."

Cruz glared at me like a lying witness he had on the hook. I held my own, but it was wearing on me. "I'll go over to the jail after lunch," he finally said. "Next time, and I'm sure there'll be one, try a straight-out request and skip the blackmail."

"You're the best."

"We both know that to be true." Cruz stood and straightened his tie, which wouldn't have the nerve to be out of place, then strode into the courtroom without a backward glance.

It took a stern scolding to myself not to happy dance my way to the elevator and instead manage to walk down the stairs and out of the courthouse in a dignified manner. I walked back to my SUV and slid inside, cranking the engine for some cool air on the hot, sultry day. Instead of calling Didier, I hit the speed dial for Creole; he could be the bearer of good news.

"Hi, honey," I said in an overly sweet tone when he answered.

"What?"

"Your wife calls mid-morning, you could at least pretend to be happy to hear from her."

"I'm always happy to hear from wifey, even when she wants something. Just so you know, I'm taking your mother's advice and asking for details before agreeing to anything." Mother had issued an edict to her husband, which had made the rounds of the family, and now most asked before offering a blanket "yes."

"I spoke with Mr. Campion, and he's agreed to talk to Fab and will be there after lunch. I'm certain he'll agree to represent her. So, mediocre attorney—whatever his name is; I've forgotten—needs to move on, nice guy that I'm sure he is. I need you to convey the happy news to Didier."

Creole snorted a laugh. "Don't tell me you lost all your nerve. After cornering the esteemed lawyer and badgering him into agreeing, now you can't make a simple call? How did you pull that one off?" He hissed an agitated breath through the phone. "Another thing. I don't appreciate being the go-between, passing messages that both of you ignore. Neither of you wants to be the bad guy, but it's okay that I am? That stops now."

"Pleez…"

"You're in luck. I'll do it this one time because Didier's attorney friend isn't a shark, which became apparent at Didier's first sit-down with the man, and it bothered him. He's going to be relieved. I'm going to pass along the good news and take total credit."

"Love you."

Chapter Three

Fab got released that night after Cruz managed to get her out on bail. The night of the murder, she'd gone to a party with Didier's friends in South Beach and had been seen by more than two dozen people; they were still checking to see if there was security footage of the event. She'd called on the way home from Miami.

"What evidence did they have against you?" I asked.

"A journal with one phony entry after another about how I accosted her in public and threatened her. And here's a good one. Aurora had numerous text messages from "Fab Merceau," but they were from a number I didn't recognize."

None of that made sense since they didn't have a relationship.

"Thank you so much for getting Cruz. Don't care how you got him to agree, just that you did," Fab said.

"It wasn't as hard as I'd thought it would be."

"Didier and I are going to spend some alone time together; then I'll call you."

Three nights later, I got another call. Creole and I were sitting on the couch, working on our laptops.

"You need to spring me tomorrow," Fab said in a whisper. "I'm supposed to meet with a client in the morning, and Didier swears that if I try to leave the house, he'll handcuff me to his wrist, which is why I hid them."

"How am I supposed to break you out?"

Creole's ears perked up, and he stared at me. I smiled lamely.

"Don't let me down." She hung up.

I pocketed my phone and turned my attention back to my laptop.

"What's going on?" Creole asked.

"That was Fab. Checking in."

I knew he was staring, but I wasn't going to look up and have him do one of his mind-reading tricks.

"As if she doesn't get in enough trouble. Now she has to go looking for it?" Creole said, fishing around.

"I'm right here and not going anywhere, so you don't have to worry." I glanced up with a quick smile.

"Yeah, sure."

* * *

I woke up before the birds, unable to sleep, and lay there concocting a bold plan. What other kind was there? I did my best not to toss and turn so the husband wouldn't wake up and ask questions. I'd have to guess at the timing and hope I could get it right. Finally, I slid out of bed, showered, and put on a black full skirt and a sleeveless top. Since this had something to do with a client of Fab's, I chose a pair of low heels and strapped on my thigh holster.

"It's been daylight for five minutes, and you're taking your gun... where?" Creole punched up the pillow, shoving it under his head.

"It's been light for about an hour."

His glare conveyed that it was too early for any antics, and I agreed.

I picked up my purse and slung it over my shoulder, staying away from the bed. "I'll be back in half an hour to pick you up." I tapped my wrist. "So be ready with your smile on. And some clothes."

"Details?"

"It's a surprise." I shot him a lame smile.

"It'll be a surprise all right. I'm not going wherever." His lips quirked, which ruined the glare he had going.

"Be ready," I said in a foreboding tone. "Don't think I won't drag you out of here."

He laughed as I marched to the door.

I pulled it open and turned. "Then I'll hurt my back and have to go to the hospital and ask Mother to move in and nurse me." I shut the door, jumped in my SUV, and raced out of the compound.

Creole and I lived in a cozy beach house on one end of a dead-end street. He'd bought the house on the cheap from an investor looking for a quick sale, then turned around and kicked out all the walls, renovating it into an open-concept plan with high-end finishes. Fab and Didier lived in the manse at the other end of the street. In between were two empty houses. As a wedding gift, Fab's papa, Caspian, bought the whole block, excluding our house, and had ten-foot fencing installed around the whole area.

I slid my phone out my pocket and called Mother.

"It's early," she said upon answering.

"Fab's got me involved in some kind of convoluted scheme that requires spiriting her out of the house under Didier's watchful eye, and I need help or backup, depending on how it turns out."

"I'm in," Mother agreed without a thought, excitement in her voice. "What do you need me to do?"

I gave her instructions and hung up, then parked in front of the Bakery Café. Since they hadn't been open long, I was able to breeze in and out with two large boxes of baked goods. I sped back home and cruised through the gate, pausing as I waited for it to close, a long-established rule to prevent anyone from sneaking in behind one of us unnoticed. I texted Creole: "Your ride is here."

To my surprise, Creole was coming out of the front gate as I made the curve. I u-turned and pulled up alongside him.

"You're the best husband," I said as he slid into the passenger seat. "I'm so going to reward your cooperative behavior."

"I don't get the neck hair thing like you, but something told me I didn't want to miss out on whatever you've concocted."

I flew down the street, pulled into Fab's driveway, and parked in front of her door. I slid out and opened the lift gate, pointing to the boxes when Creole joined me, then grabbed a large brown shopping bag.

I entered a code into the security pad at Fab's front door. I'd pilfered it by looking over her shoulder.

"When did you get your own code?"

"I didn't."

I slid through the entry before Creole could ask more questions, but I knew that wouldn't be the end of it—the subject would come up again. The house was so quiet you could hear a pin drop. We went into the kitchen and put everything on the counter.

"Do they know we're here?" Creole asked in a hushed tone, looking concerned.

"I'm about to announce our arrival." I pulled a bullhorn from the bag, walked over to the hallway leading to the master bedroom, and yelled, "Rise and shine!" through it.

Creole laughed, much to his disgust, judging from the look on his face.

"Come on, I don't have all day," I yelled again.

"Give me that thing." Creole rushed over, hand out.

I hid it behind my back. "A girl's gotta have a horn. My last one was stolen, so I'm taking special care of this one."

"It was my bullhorn." Fab padded in from the hallway in a silk robe, Didier behind her in pajama pants, broad-shouldered with eight-pack abs, all sexy, his hair disheveled and sticking on end.

"What the devil?"

I was spared from answering when the doorbell rang. "Someone's at the door." I made a startled face and pointed, in case Didier had forgotten the way.

Too much of a gentleman to tell me off, he strode out of the kitchen to answer the door and came back with Mother and Spoon. Mother had a silly smile on her face, and I knew she was enjoying a peek at morning-Didier. It had been a while—back in the days when we lived together, she'd stop by with one excuse or another to share a cup of coffee or leer. What woman would pass on that opportunity? The women in the family were lucky; all our men were hot in the morning.

Mother joked about having married a younger man, but it was a good match. They'd bonded over their love of cigars and were living happily ever after. I was ecstatic for her, as my father died when Brad and I were pre-teens and she'd raised us as a single mom; oftentimes, we didn't make it easy.

Spoon hooked his arm around Mother's shoulders, holding her close. He didn't care what kind of antics his wife got involved in, as long as he was in the know. He must have thought my urgent call was too good to pass up, much like Creole. I noticed the dude smirk they traded.

"Bon jurio," I called and turned to the task at hand, opening the cupboard and lining up the coffee mugs, then going to the refrigerator and pulling out the coffee. "I'm going to need help working these coffeemakers."

"What is going on?" Didier demanded and settled a glare on me.

Fab sidled up next to him, put her arm around him, and flashed me a "showtime" look.

"As we all know, Fab has been out of commission," I said. Good thing Creole had made calls and informed the family about the murder so no one could gripe about being the last to know, a big pet peeve in the family. "She's got clients that need tending." Hopefully, this wasn't an animal case. "Big-hearted me," Mother rolled her eyes, "I'm going to channel my inner

Fab and serve her clients until she's back full-time."

"No, you're not," Creole barked.

"I meant find out what ails them and find a fix. Better?" I smiled at him. Not waiting for an answer, I said, "So I called Mother in as sidekick, and she readily agreed. What better way to get the assignment details than over breakfast and, of course, coffee?"

Spoon flicked up the lid on one of the signature pink bakery boxes. "Smells good."

"Coffee first," Didier grumbled and walked over to fill the machines. "I could use a couple of cups before we get started on this discussion."

"We might as well sit at the island," Fab directed and got out plates.

Spoon dragged over two additional barstools.

I hugged Mother and whispered in her ear, "The plan is for it to be Didier's idea that Fab goes with us."

After all the coffee mugs were filled, we took seats around the island and filled our plates.

"What kind of job is this?" Mother asked.

"Cyrus Mane, an old acquaintance, called and requested a meeting, and that's all I know," Fab said.

"Are you going to call and let him know you're sending me? You better upgrade me to partner, since I'll be showing up in your stead." I stared, doing my best not to smile or, worse, laugh.

"If he's expecting Fab, how's he going to feel when someone he doesn't know shows up?" Mother asked.

"I know what this is." Didier smacked his hand down on the counter. "Make Didier feel bad for being worried about his wife."

Fab leaned over and kissed his cheek.

"You're the best husband," I said.

Creole cleared his throat. "Excuse me."

"You're the very best." I winked.

Fab gagged, which had us laughing.

"So you're driving where?" Creole asked. "Meeting with who? And once you find out what *ails* him, you're going to do what exactly?"

"South Beach," Fab answered. "Cyrus is an investment strategist and has waterfront offices on Ocean Drive. Once Madison arrives, she'll call, and I'll talk her through what to do next."

"I know when I've been set up." Didier glared down at Fab. "I don't want you losing your clients, but I also want you to be safe. The three of you together, maybe, hopefully, can stay out of trouble. Do you think that's a possibility?"

"That's why I'm tagging along, to give everyone peace of mind," Mother said. "Who would have any objection?"

The men groaned but didn't say anything.

"I can't stay cooped up in the house; I'll go crazy," Fab said. "We need to get back to our everyday lives. Business as usual. We've got one less worry since Cruz signed on. We hole up, and someone other than us wins."

"In exchange, I get the bullhorn." Didier's eyes narrowed.

I clasped my chest. "That's too much."

Chapter Four

The drive north into Miami had been uneventful and quiet and a wasted opportunity to figure out what the plan was. Whatever Fab had in mind would need to be tweaked; her plans always did. Instead, she and Mother had gossiped like schoolgirls and dished on some new store that had opened.

Fab cut down to the beach and circled the block. It was unclear what she was scoping out in the business district. I turned my head and ignored the water lapping the white sand, which was hard for me to do.

"Why are you parking in a loading zone?" I asked as she pulled up in front of a glass-and-chrome office building.

"You're going to get behind the wheel, keep the engine running, and wait patiently," Fab said in a snooty tone that had Mother smirking at her. "If you spot a meter cop in your side mirror, pull around the block. You know I hate the parking garage."

"Mother, this is an educational opportunity." I moved forward and poked my head between the seats. "Always park where you can maneuver a fast getaway."

Mother turned and looked at me. "Thank you, dear."

Then I blew out an irritated, "No," and clipped Fab in the back of the head. "My mother is the one that you're going to leave lollygagging in the zone because I'm coming with you. You need supervision to prevent you from agreeing to whatever convoluted job rich dude has cooked up."

"Don't worry about me; I've got this handled," Mother said. "I'll u-turn, pull down the street, and park by the beach, then roll down the window and whistle at the young surfers." She smiled at a group of them crossing the street. "On your way back to the car, give me a call, and I'll be waiting."

"Madeline is more of a team player than you are," Fab pronounced.

I snorted. "Wait until Spoon finds out you're drooling over youngsters."

Mother laughed. "That would just lead to… never mind. Listen up, you two, aren't you supposed to have a plan, and if so, what is it?"

I cut Fab off. "We're going to find out what old Cyrus wants. That's his name, isn't it?"

"Mr. Mane sounds more businesslike, don't you think?" Mother said, a tone of reprimand in her voice.

"Anyway…" I tapped my cheek. "Fab is going

to find out what Mr. Mane wants while I hang on every word. If it's not an outright felony, then she'll agree and we'll be back down. Under no circumstances, considering your current predicament, do you agree to anything remotely illegal. Got it?" I shook my finger at Fab, who was staring at me in the rearview mirror.

"You're outnumbered." Mother patted Fab's shoulder. "I agree with Madison. The last thing you want to do is give the police any additional ammo to use against you."

Fab opened her door, her silent way of agreeing, and Mother and I followed and crossed paths. "You behave yourself." I kissed Mother's cheek.

"You can't suck the fun out of everything," Mother said in a faux huff.

"The day's not over yet." I hurried to catch up to Fab, who'd headed for the entrance. "Don't look so down. Mr. Mane might surprise us, and it will be something easy that we can dispense with in short order."

On the ride up in the glass elevator, I turned and stared out at the ocean. "Introduce me however you want; I'll hang back and keep quiet. Don't think I won't jump into the middle of the conversation if he mentions a felony or anything harmful to our health and tell him to go to hell."

Fab mimicked Mother: "Behave yourself."

The doors opened into a large, empty reception area. The sign read "Mane and

Associates." Fab approached the desk and announced herself.

"Mr. Mane's expecting you." The woman directed her down the hall. She gave me a once-over but didn't say anything.

Fab moved down the quiet hall, where most of the doors were closed, and easily spotted his name plate. The door stood open, but she knocked and he waved her in. I followed and hung back, gazing around at the lackluster surroundings. Black and chrome and a couple of cheap reprints of abstract paintings. The only personal item was a small frame on his desk.

The sixtyish grey-haired man, who clearly spent a lot of time in the sun, sauntered around his desk in a custom-made suit and closed the door. "Take a seat," he directed Fab, giving me a brief glance. I took a seat next to the wall.

Mane settled back behind his desk, opened a drawer, and pulled out a jewelry box, which he set in front of Fab. "I need this returned to the jeweler."

Fab opened it and inspected the diamond bracelet that sparkled back.

"Here's the address." Mane pushed a piece of paper at Fab.

Fab stood and grabbed the paper, putting it and the box in her purse.

"Why not send your secretary?" I asked, wondering why he'd pay Fab's fee to make a return. Mane ignored me.

"A receipt?" Fab asked, and Mane shook his head. "Is there someone specific I should ask for that would be familiar with this transaction?"

"There is a slight anomaly to this job." Mane cleared his throat.

Here it comes.

"The bracelet was stolen, and I'd like it returned," Mane said matter-of-factly.

Now I had a dozen questions and jumped to my feet, barely restraining myself from barking one after another at him. "Why don't you cough up the details on this *anomaly*?"

His gaze lingered on me longer than before, actually acknowledging my presence. I was now an actual person and not a bug that wandered in.

Fab opened her purse and took the box back out. "Without the details, I'll have to decline the job."

"Sit," Mane commanded, letting out a long, drawn-out sigh. "My wife stole the bracelet. She has... issues and was doing so well, and then had a relapse."

I'd heard that rich women liked to shoplift but didn't personally know any. You'd think the humiliation of potentially being caught would be a deterrent.

Fab motioned for him to continue.

"The owner of the jewelry store spotted the theft on the security camera, recognized my wife, and called, demanding its return. I offered to pay for it. He's demanding the money *and* the bracelet back or he'll have my wife arrested. I'm not caving to blackmail."

"The Society section will have a field day," Fab said sympathetically. "I imagine your clients wouldn't like the bad publicity."

"For a number of reasons, this situation needs to be taken care of in the most discreet fashion possible."

Fab put the box and paper back in her purse. "I'll call when it's taken care of."

We walked out and didn't say anything until we left the building.

I pulled out my phone and texted Mother as we walked to the curb. "I'm not certain of the legal ramifications of returning a stolen item that you didn't steal, but I'm of the opinion that you should foist it off on me, just to be on the safe side." Creole would kill me if I ended up in cuffs.

Mother squealed to the curb and hit the brakes; she'd been hanging with teenagers too long. She jumped out, relinquishing the wheel to Fab, and hopped in the passenger seat. I got in the back.

"Well?" Mother asked.

Fab related the visit as she pulled away from the curb and, without the benefit of GPS, drove straight to the jewelry store, a small upscale boutique in the outer courtyard of a five-star hotel.

I threw out my hastily concocted plan—Fab stays in the car, Mother and I handle the return.

Mother squirmed at the idea but didn't say anything.

"Wink at the valet guy," Mother nudged Fab, "and he'll probably let you loiter in the no-parking zone until we're finished." She turned in her seat and faced me. "When the owner asks your relationship to Mr. Mane, I'd suggest being truthful; you were hired to expedite the return."

"And I point to you and say, 'This is bring your mother to work day.' Hence your presence."

Fab frowned, not happy with the plan. "I think I need to get a 'temporarily out of business' sign. I can't foist my jobs off on the two of you."

"Who else? Another perk: you can trust us not to screw you." I was struggling not to snap at her. "I'm of the opinion that Mane knows you're in deep trouble already, so what's a headline about being involved with stolen jewelry? Any mention of his name after that and people will think you're shuffling the blame off on some other poor soul."

"He'd say it's nothing personal," Fab responded with a tinge of bitterness.

I caught her eye in the rearview mirror and attempted to lighten the mood. "It gives Mother and me something to brag about at the next family dinner. You know best story wins. We should have a prize—a trophy or something."

"Madison, get out of the car," Mother said in exasperation.

Fab handed the box to me. "Owner's name is Gunner. Only one name. We're used to that."

I wanted to laugh; our husbands both used only one name. I stuck the box in my purse and joined Mother. We walked over to the store and rang the bell for entrance. "I don't like that you're my backup." I kissed her cheek. "But I'm happy that I'm not doing this job by myself. I'm already feeling guilty for returning a stolen item, and I didn't steal it."

A middle-aged woman with a severe bun at the nap of her neck opened the door and gave us a twice-over with her intense brown eyes as she ushered us inside. "Welcome. How can I help you today?"

"I'd like to speak with Gunner." I pasted on my friendly smile, which I still continued to practice in the bathroom mirror. "I'm here on behalf of Mr. Mane."

There was a flash of recognition at the mention of Mane's name, and she walked over to an antique desk in the corner, picked up the phone, and spoke in a low tone.

"Don't touch anything," I whispered to Mother. "No leaving your fingerprints."

A shaggy grey-haired man, well over six foot, opened a door with a peephole and strode out. "How can I help you?" he boomed in a deep voice.

I reached in my purse and pulled out the box. "I'm here to return this on behalf of Mr. Mane." I held it out and was surprised when he didn't take it; in fact, he stepped back.

"Naomi," he snapped. Naomi's head popped up from behind the desk. After ringing for him, she'd secreted herself out of sight and done a good job of it. I'd stopped noticing her once Gunner came in. She stood, appearing confused as to what to do next. "I'm going to have my wife call the cops and have you both arrested for shoplifting."

"Except that neither of us shoplifted," I said. "You know that, and saying otherwise is a crime for which *you* could be arrested."

Gunner snorted, his face filled with contempt.

"What do you get out of the bad publicity?" I asked, hoping to talk him out of involving the cops. "I'm sure we can expedite a reasonable agreement—take your bracelet back and be done with it."

"Do you have a check?"

"Blackmail is definitely a crime." I matched his narrow-eyed glare. "In case you were unaware, all of Mr. Mane's phone calls are recorded, and he has proof of your extortion attempt." Good bluff, I hoped.

"You think I can let every rich, bored woman come in and steal and get away with it?" Anger poured out of him. "Word of that gets around, and I won't be in business long."

"The Manes aren't about to tell anyone, and if you don't, then it remains a secret," I said.

"I still think it's best to involve the cops and let them decide who's committing a crime."

"That's a great idea," Mother practically spit. "Have my daughter arrested for a crime she didn't commit, and I will personally see to it that your name is dragged through the mud, and no one will set foot in here except to take pictures to show their friends. Bet the swanky hotel you're attached to will love the publicity."

Gunner sputtered but didn't respond. If glares could kill, Mother's edged his out, as far as I was concerned.

"Gunner," Naomi whispered and motioned him over.

He crossed to Naomi, and they exchanged words in a muted tone. Then he stamped back into his office, shutting the door with a bang.

"Thank you for the return." Naomi smiled benignly and opened the front door. "One more thing. In case it's not clear, no one in the Mane family is welcome here again. If one of them does show up, I'll be forced to call the police as a precaution."

"Understood." I set the jewelry box on the counter.

Once Mother and I had cleared the threshold and the door snicked closed, I hooked my arm in hers as we walked back to the car. As predicted, the valet had let Fab park in the front, off to one side.

"Well done," I said, and opened the car doors. "Mother was the star; she can give you the details."

Chapter Five

As Fab sped back to the Cove, she called Mr. Mane, reported that the bracelet had been returned, and warned him that, in the future, his wife should shop somewhere else. The conversation was short and terse. She hung up, annoyed, and turned on the radio.

"Why are you turning here?" Mother demanded as Fab turned off the main highway onto a side street once we hit Tarpon Cove.

"I need to stop by The Cottages and make sure they're still standing," I said. I'd told Fab ahead of time to swing by my property. "I need to make sure the inhabitants are behaving themselves."

"Take me home," Mother hissed.

"You don't get to pick and choose your fun," I told her in a lecturing tone. "You're going to have to suck it up and unleash a bit of your own weirdo-ness; you'll fit right in."

Fab laughed. "The alternative is hiding out in the office. There's snacks and cold drinks."

"No, she can't," I said. "I'm going to trot her around and show her off to those that don't know she's my hot, Jack-whiskey-drinking, cigar-smoking mother, which will blow my pretense of coming from normal beginnings."

Mother laughed.

"Why are we here?" Fab asked, turning the corner. "Do you need us to gun up and flank you?"

"I can't believe I'm going to tell you two not to shoot anyone. But don't." I pulled a pair of flip-flops out of my bag and traded them for my heels. "I'm here to make sure everyone's kicking and breathing. And that no felons have snuck in without me being told."

Fab pulled into the driveway and parked in front of the office of the ten-unit, u-shaped property I'd inherited from my Aunt Elizabeth. Each cottage was painted in an art deco color, with no two the same in case a guest stumbled back drunk. An abundance of tropical plants and colorful annuals in flowerbeds dotted the property.

My aunt would have been proud that I didn't cash out and instead continued to tend to the crazies that she left me and the new ones I'd acquired. Two of the originals were still in residence, and we currently had more guests than regulars, as I discouraged the latter.

Fifty pounds of black and grey jumped on the hood.

"Is that the cat from the motel?" Mother asked.

"Furrball is his name, and he moved here with his family." I waved, which the Maine Coon ignored. He stretched out and sniffed the windshield. "So be nice."

Fab, Didier, Creole, and I had partnered on a motel venture that was short-lived, as we were offered a good deal and sold the motel to participate in an expanded family venture. Much to the relief of the rest of the members of the family, as it had been one problem after another from day one. The new owners had made it clear that they weren't keeping the management team, so the obvious solution, since I knew that the couple I'd hired didn't have any place to go, was to invite them to move in here.

Cootie Shine had turned out to have legitimate fix-it skills; he showed up with actual tools and didn't just rely on a roll of tape and some spit, then hope for the best. He'd also been hired on as a maintenance man for our family-run real estate company and was on call for anyone in the neighborhood. His partner—Rude Banner, short for Gertrude—hadn't come up with a gig for herself yet but was working on it.

The three of us piled out of the SUV and stood in the middle of the driveway. "It's not like you're a first-timer," I said to Mother. "Since it's been a while, I'll give you a little refresher. The first thing you do is check out the porches and take a head count of how many guests are passed out; all will be from drunkenness. No drug use allowed or the offender gets kicked to the curb by one of your husband's burly employees. Then, after a visual inspection, you'll need to decide if they need help getting inside." Today's count: zero. "Next up, you check the blinds, and if they're moving, then you know there's excitement afoot."

"You have liquor in the office?" Mother asked in exasperation.

"This is a respectable joint," I said in faux indignation.

The sound of a child crying rent the air. And again. And again.

"It's coming from the pool." Fab led the way down the driveway and turned between two of the cottages.

The pool area was in the far corner on the opposite end of the property, which overlooked the beach. It surprised me to see it filled with oldsters — men and women in bathing suits, some of which should have been outlawed due to their briefness and the possibility of a body part breaking free. Most were lying on their sides on rubber rafts covered with beach towels, one leg in the air. Two men sat at the tiki bar nursing beers. The gate was closed, for a change, and I used my code to get in.

The "child" turned out to be a goat, and not one but two. One of the goats waited until the man nearest him rolled onto his stomach, then hopped on the man's back and lay down, making himself comfortable. The other sniffed the concrete.

Mac rushed over in a one-piece bathing suit

that accentuated her curviness. "Isn't it exciting?" she gushed, re-positioning her headband around her bouffant to keep it out of her face. "Rude's teaching goat yoga."

Macklin Lane was the manager and had been since shortly after I took over. She'd sold me on why she'd be perfect for the job, and as it turned out, she hadn't just been full of herself — very little ruffled her feathers, and she handled the diverse personalities at The Cottages with efficiency.

The short, grey-haired woman in question waved from the front of her class, an infectious smile on her face as she shouted encouragement to the participants.

Mother and Fab overcame their shock and laughed, following me into the pool area and stepping back to await my reaction.

"I know that look," Mac whispered in exasperation and crossed her arms. "Aren't you always telling me to keep the guests entertained? Most are in attendance, and they're loving every minute of it."

"Those are real live goats," I said, and took cover behind a chaise. Not knowing anything about the animals, I didn't want to make the wrong move and get bitten.

Mac didn't roll her eyes but close. "Their owner is right over there, sitting in that chair." She motioned to an older man, half-asleep with his feet up. "He's got this under control."

Sure he did. "Who cleans up after what that one is doing?"

Mac's eyes followed my pointing finger to the goat who had wandered over to the fence.

"You mean the one who's peeing," Mac said in a patronizing tone.

"Don't forget who's the boss here."

"Cleanup is Crum's job." Mac cut off my response with an arm wave and a humph. "Before you pitch a hissy fit, he's already agreed."

Crum was our resident retired professor from a swanky college—high IQ and acted like he was ten. The one Cruz's grandmother had got it on with.

"Over here." Crum waved his arms wildly over his head. "I know what you're thinking, and I've got it handled." He tapped the side of his head, indicating he was a mind reader. If that were true, he wouldn't do half the stuff he did.

"Goat yoga is the latest rage," Mother said with a sly smile.

"That's nice," I said, but my tone said otherwise. "I'm afraid to ask, but I'll brave it. Anything else going on I should know about?"

Mac shook her head. "No one died or got arrested or anything."

The one goat finished peeing, the other jumped up and did the same, and both started making the rounds of the guests, expecting to be petted and doling out some licks.

"Sorry to cut this visit short, but I've got to get my mother home for her nap," I said, and stepped closer, hooking my arm around her and patting her head.

Mother shook me off. "You're not funny."

"I thought it was a good one and would've been better if you'd gone along." Mac grinned at her, then turned back to me. "I've got some ideas I want to run past you, so I was thinking about scheduling a meeting. You bring food."

"This is a first. You usually call last-minute and tell me to get over here," I said.

"New leaf and all."

My phone rang, and I pulled it out of my pocket and waved to Mac. "What do you have for me?" I asked Xander, practically running out the gate. I skidded to a stop, realizing I'd left Mother and Fab behind. I turned and got glaring dirty looks as they caught up.

"I found basically nothing on Aurora Bissett." Xander let out an exasperated breath. "Not for lack of searching. Ran a credit report and hit a dead end, which means she had to have been paying cash or someone else was footing the bills. Her social media profile was scant and shows that she loved all things French, which makes sense, since it says she's from France. Her last post was a few months ago. And her handful of friends all had meager profiles."

"Anything that links to Fab?"

Fab heard the question and knocked me in the arm.

"I'll keep checking. If I get anything, I'll get hot on the phone."

"Wait... Did you happen to get the address where Aurora was murdered? Do you know if she lived there?" The three of us climbed in the SUV. "You're on speaker," I told Xander.

"Yes and yes," he said, sounding happy he had an answer I'd want to hear. "Do you want me to text the address?"

"Please," I said. "Try running a social media check on Fab and see if you get a hit on an Aurora connection that way."

"I'll keep you updated." We hung up.

I repeated the entire conversation to Mother and Fab, not remembering where they came in.

"Why run a check on me?" Fab asked. "Good idea, maybe, except that I don't have any kind of profile."

"It's a long shot, but I hoped that something would turn up that would link you and Aurora and we could check it out. Someone went to a lot of work to frame you for murder and make it so the cops would find it believable enough to take you in for questioning. Logically, you'd think there'd be a link somewhere." My phone pinged, and I looked at the screen. "Oh great. Aurora's address is in Miami. I'm tired of that drive."

"That's why you have a driver," Fab said smugly.

"Not today. Tomorrow. That will give me time to come up with something that's not illegal and that you have no involvement in."

"Whatever you come up with," Mother said in a lecturing tone, "it needs to keep you both out of trouble."

"I hate being in the backseat." Fab grumped.

"You're not. Look in your rearview mirror; I'm back here."

"You know what I mean."

Chapter Six

Another day, another drive to Miami. I could make this trip in my sleep.

"How did you get out of the house?" Fab blew up the highway, her gaze intent on two cars attempting to cut each other off.

I didn't care if they ran each other off the road; I just didn't want to go with them and felt certain the drivers around us felt the same.

I'd put in a demand for a large coffee, and Fab had it sitting in the cup holder; she'd even remembered to order extra everything. I'd quickly sucked down the delicious brew, making sure to get every last drop of whipped cream off the lid. "Being the good wife that I am, I didn't wait until the last minute and instead ordered Creole's favorite pizza last night and ran my idea by him while he was mid-bite. He gave me the stink eye as I launched into my spiel for buying off the apartment manager for a look around and had lightened up by the time I finished. It's his suggestion that I not lowball the guy and make an offer too tempting to refuse. So I've got plenty of cash on me."

"After demanding that I swear in my own

blood, Didier made me repeat my promise not to get involved several times, as though I'd forget, then finally let me out of the house."

"Sounds messy."

Fab wrinkled her nose. "I think the only reason Didier didn't make good on his threat to secure me to his side is that you made me stay in the car yesterday."

"Guess what?" I said with so much cheer that it garnered a glare. "New plan for today. Another idea of Creole's. He thinks you shouldn't even be seen in the neighborhood, that it could come back to haunt you, even though it's long after the murder. Sooo..." Da-da-da in my tone. "You'll drop yourself off at a trendy coffee shop, and when I'm finished, I'll come fetch you. Don't make it too far away; I don't want to get lost."

"No fair." Fab pouted. "You get to have all the fun."

"Not so fast, sweetheart. You're going to be the mastermind and do what you love best—tell me what to do. I'm wearing my Bluetooth." I brushed my hair away from my face to show her, then covered it back up. "You're going to direct me as I prowl through the apartment. I get that you won't have the benefit of seeing the exact layout, but they all have the same fundamentals and you'll direct me here and there."

"I like that idea."

"Thought you would. Don't get too creative," I cautioned, "as in air vents, unless I get free run of the place. My thought is I'll probably be chaperoned."

"Your cover story?"

"Reporter. A nice little profile on that poor, unfortunate Aurora Bissett would make my career," I mewled. "My boss would take notice, and I wouldn't have to cover cat and dog funerals anymore. Throw in a few eyelash flutters."

"Your shameless use of cats is shocking." Fab laughed. "Your story will sell better to an older man; a younger one will roll his eyes, but money is money."

"I'm so awful." I sobbed and covered my eyes.

"Stop that racket."

"Okay." I winked.

Fab pulled into the parking lot of a coffee house on busy Washington Boulevard in South Beach. "Nice area. Love the shops and restaurants."

I got out, walked around to the driver's side, and put Aurora's address in the GPS. Then I called Fab, who stood on the patio of the restaurant. "Testing," I said when she answered.

"Since we've done this before and know it works, we'll just maintain the connection; no need for constant chatter. I'm going to get a coffee and come back outside."

Aurora lived about five minutes away in an

older residential neighborhood. The fifteen-unit apartment building was well-kept and had cute curb appeal, with a row of flowers that flanked the walkway. I circled the block, came back, and parked. I pocketed my phone and cash and got out. "I'm here and walking up the walkway. Fingers crossed this works."

"Go unleash your charm."

The manager's apartment was clearly marked with a small placard in the middle of the door. I listened and heard the television, so I knocked and waited.

An older man opened the door. "We don't have any vacancies."

"I'm a reporter chasing a story and would like to look around Aurora Bissett's apartment. I promise not to touch anything, just take a few pictures." I pulled five one-hundred-dollar bills out of my pocket and held them out.

He eyed the cash with interest. "No mention of me in the story."

I shook my head. "I promise."

He took the money, grabbed a set of keys off the wall, and stepped out. "Follow me. You can't take all day. I can't have anyone seeing you; I'd lose my job."

"I'll hurry. And if someone sees me, tell them I said I was a cop."

"Good one."

He tromped three units down from his and unlocked the door, which opened into the living room and kitchen. There were only a few pieces of furniture and that telltale smell that someone had died.

"Haven't got the okay to clean the place out, and when that happens, got to do it myself." The man grimaced.

"The smell is a difficult one," I commiserated. "You might want to call a crime scene cleanup company that specializes in that kind of odor elimination."

"The owner will like that idea. Some things, he doesn't go all cheap on." He pointed to the only door. "She was murdered in there." He leaned against the doorframe, clearly unwilling to either come in any farther or go away.

I headed straight for the bedroom, phone out, and as soon as I was out of sight of the manager, pulled a plastic glove out of my pocket.

"Walk around and take pictures of everything from all angles," Fab directed. "We can go over them later."

I did that and got down on my knees, looking under the bed, then pushed open the closet door. "Not a lot of clothes and shoes," I mumbled so only Fab could hear. The framed pictures on the desk grabbed my attention, and I gasped, recognizing one of the men. "This place looks pretty well tossed, and judging by what's left, there's not much to find. Or the good stuff was already hauled away."

"Don't forget the bathroom."

"Going there now." I took pictures and came back out, shooting a video of the bedroom and bathroom. Before going back into the living room, I took off the glove and shoved it in my pocket. The manager was leaning against the door frame looking bored. "The cops empty the place out?"

"Pretty much. They were here for hours and hauled out several bags."

"How long did Aurora live here?"

"Almost two years."

"Did she actually live here or just use it as a closet?" I asked as I walked around the living room, continuing to shoot video, and went into the kitchen. There was nothing of interest.

"I will say she wasn't around much, but you know youngsters these days."

"Appreciate your cooperation," I told the man, as I finished up.

He locked up behind me.

I waved to the man and walked back to the SUV. Before pulling away, I scanned the building once again and all was quiet, as was the rest of the neighborhood. The manager had gone back inside his apartment. I drove the couple of blocks to the coffee shop, pulled into a parking space, and got out to change places.

"Boring," I declared. "Nothing of interest, except for one thing." I flicked through my phone, found the picture, and handed it to Fab.

"Gabriel!" Fab said in a shocked tone. "She knew Gabriel?" She continued to stare at the screen.

"Your ex-husband would be my number one suspect if I didn't know that he's dead. Ironically, law enforcement wanted to hang *that* murder on you too."

Fab leaned back against the seat and slowly scrolled through the pictures, then watched the video. "There are a couple of photos where they have their arms around one another. At the very least, they were friends." She flicked through everything again.

"It's an odd link. Dead man and now dead woman and both murdered. Logic would suggest that it's someone that both of them knew. Since you're the chief suspect, one would think you'd also know the parties involved... except that you didn't know Aurora." I felt like I was piecing together a puzzle, and it was clear that I didn't have all the pieces, probably not even close.

"Are you forgetting that Gabriel's murderer confessed and was carted off to jail?"

"Is it possible that Aurora still held you responsible?" I mused. "But then how did she end up dead?"

"When we get back home, I'll download all of this, go over it frame by frame, and see if I can pick up any clues."

"Let's do lunch and then go to your house and work."

Fab hit the gas, and we sped towards home.

Chapter Seven

It had been a quiet couple of days. Fab's father, Caspian, was in town and livid over the latest events. When Fab called with an invitation to come for dinner, she'd been so vague, I wasn't sure why she wanted me to show up. Creole had groaned at the invite and informed me that he had other plans in mind, so I called back and begged off, blaming Creole. The two of us headed down to Marathon, where he'd planned an overnight trip, and I left my phone behind, knowing that if it was an emergency, everyone knew they could blow up Creole's phone with calls.

It was addictive, sitting under an umbrella, watching the waves crash on shore, embracing a do-nothing attitude. We got home late, but it was as though some kind of radar went off, signaling my return; it didn't take long for my phone to start ringing. I glanced at the screen, then lay down on the bed and stared up at the ceiling. "Yes?" I said upon answering.

"I need your help," Fab said in a low tone.

"I figured, since you're usually fooling around with your husband at this hour."

Creole smirked as he rolled over top of me and lay by my side. He made an attempt to hog the pillow, but I held on tight.

"While you were off gallivanting around," Fab huffed, "Susie called to say Cruz wanted a sit-down. Caspian overheard me tell Didier and he invited himself along."

I inwardly groaned, having a good idea where this was going.

"It was a mess." Fab's voice was rising. "The meeting went bad so fast that Didier and I were speechless. When does that happen? Never," she answered. "Unbeknownst to us, Caspian had hired a high-priced criminal attorney from New York, Mr. Terry, to show up for the meeting. Once the introductions were made, it was downhill from there. Cruz put an end to Mr. Terry ordering him around like he was his personal lackey and shot questions at him. Guess what? The man hasn't even been admitted to the bar here in Florida; he still has to apply. A formality, he said."

I attempted to swallow my laugh. "And…"

"Cruz ordered us out. In a tone suggesting that we were dirtying the furniture. That wasn't bad enough; he called security. They showed up, one with his hand under his jacket, and escorted us out." Fab was close to full-blown hysteria. "On the way out the door, Cruz gave me a tight smile and wished me luck. My hand itched to slap the smile off Susie's face as we were led out, flanked by guards."

"Calm down," I said, certain it didn't register. Creole had rolled practically on top of me, listening; he shook his head. "We're not on Susie's favorites list, so I imagine that made her day; the only thing better would've been if it had been me being shown the door. As for Mr. Terry, I think it's a fairly easy process to get approved, so there's need to worry on that score."

"I don't like that Terry lawyer," Fab hissed. "He's stiff. Pompous. He had the nerve to look down his long snotty nose at me then shoot Didier a look of pity. I wanted to wipe his superior attitude off his face with my Walther and then rearrange his body parts."

I choked on a laugh. "You haven't murdered anyone yet, and some overpriced lawyer in a suit isn't a good way to start."

"I feel bad, sort of, not dealing with my own problems and instead shoveling them off on you." Fab sighed loud enough to wake the dead. "I don't know how to tell Caspian to let me chose my own lawyer, and I thought you could do it. I was ecstatic to get Cruz to represent me and wanted to keep him. We get along and agree on most things."

"The problem is that you haven't had your whole life to annoy Caspian like I have Mother, so it's not easy to tell him to butt out. Your relationship is still in the new stage, since you discovered one another as adults. Caspian hasn't been properly broken in about how irritating offspring can be."

Fab discovered on her own that the man she thought was her father had actually adopted her. Snooping through her mother's paperwork, she'd discovered the identity of her bio dad, and it had taken a while to arrange a meeting. They were still in the stage where they didn't want to disappoint each other.

"I knew you'd understand." Fab sounded relieved.

Her change of tone had me on alert. "What do you expect me to do?"

"Get Cruz to change his mind and take me back as a client. You're the only one who can do it. You've got keeping his family happy to hang over his head."

I cringed at the thought of facing off with Cruz again and asking for another favor. "Who's giving Mr. Terry the boot? He's not going to listen to me, especially since we haven't even met yet. I doubt he would listen even if we were acquainted." I didn't see any way to say no to Fab, and that gave me a stomachache. "And then you expect me to go one on one with your intimidating father to inform him of the change of plans. After the fact, I assume?"

"You do get it."

I could imagine the huge smile on her face. "There's a flaw in your plan." There were several, but now wasn't the time to point that out. "I don't know where and when to ambush Cruz. His office is a wild card, since he doesn't keep regular hours, and getting past Susie would be a trick."

Creole chuckled. I elbowed him.

"I overheard Cruz telling someone on the phone that he's going to be in his office early tomorrow morning to catch up with some paperwork before court." Eavesdropping! Of course, she would. I don't know how she interpreted the silence, but she continued, "I got us a connection in case we ever need to know a good time to drop in on Cruz, so as not to make a wasted trip."

I groaned.

"I chatted up the receptionist after Susie sniped at her. She understood my stress over the ongoing case, and on the way out, under the pretense of needing a Kleenex, cash exchanged hands."

"Let's hope she never gets caught. It's probably a good job."

"So you'll go talk to Cruz?" Fab asked.

"I'm certain I can sneak past Creole." I rolled over to face him and smirked. "Men are lame. He won't notice that I'm leaving the house in a dress and heels." I grinned at him.

"I have every confidence that you'll think of something. Someone's coming," she said in a frantic whisper and hung up.

I tossed the phone on the bedside table. "I'll

think of something. Just great. One of these days, I'm going to run out of good ideas, and then what?"

"I have some advice for you," Creole said.

"Who are you again?" I squinted.

He tickled me until I squealed. "Come clean with your husband about whatever wild hair idea you've come up with; it's not like he'll be shocked."

"Probably not. He's such a patient man." I rolled over and put my head on his chest.

"I warned Didier that once Caspian got wind of his daughter's troubles, he'd arrive in town with a big gun." Creole wrapped his arms around me. "Didier blew me off, insisting the man was quite reasonable. I can't wait to remind him of the conversation."

"That's mean."

"I'm going to ask and try not to be surprised at your answer. Your plan?"

"Barge into Cruz's office bright and early, and ad lib from there."

"You better go to sleep; you're going to need to be wide-eyed and on your game tomorrow."

Chapter Eight

I'm not sure how I got so lucky, but without me having to ask, Creole got up at the same time I did and dressed in black suit pants and a button-down shirt. Watching him get dressed was the highlight of my morning. He whistled at my choice of a curve-hugging black knit dress.

Since neither of us took the time to have a cup of coffee, at my suggestion, he hit the coffee drive-thru. On the way up Highway One, I programmed the address into the GPS.

Creole turned toward me. "What are you going to do if Cruz sics security on you?"

I'd thought about that. "I'm going to throw a fit of epic proportions."

"I'd appreciate it if I don't have to watch as my wife is led away in cuffs."

"Me too. I'm hoping to appeal to his better nature, saving blackmail as a last resort. It'll lose its effectiveness if I attempt it at every visit."

Creole squeezed my hand. "Just be your charming self."

I laughed. "You're the only one that falls for that."

He easily found a parking space not far from

the entrance. We rode up in the elevator, the doors opening into Cruz's office, which took up the whole floor. Creole and I walked up to the reception desk and pushed money at the woman. "If anyone asks, I barged right by you." She nodded.

After we walked away, Creole said, "I can't believe you paid her off. Not sure why I'm surprised." He laughed.

I led him down the hallway to Cruz's corner office.

The door to the office was open, and you had to walk right past Susie's desk to get to Cruz's inner sanctum. His door was closed.

Susie looked up and gave me a once-over. "He's not in today," she said smugly. "Any message that you'd like to leave, I'll forward to the trash." She peered around me. "Who are you?"

"Her husband," Creole answered.

"My condolences."

"I was about to feel a scintilla of sympathy for dumping all things Carmine into your lap, but it just vanished."

"Just so you know, go right ahead and ban Cruz's sainted relatives; they're perfectly capable of going elsewhere — there are nicer places to stay than that rundown property of yours. Now…" She pasted on a big smile. "This hasn't been fun. Have a day." She flung her arm toward the door.

"It's so sad I left my bullhorn at home. Note to

self: put it in the car." I turned and yelled, "Cruz," at the top of my lungs. I hoped I wouldn't lose my voice.

Creole chuckled.

The door flew open. "What the devil?" Cruz boomed.

"I see you're back," I said.

Cruz and Creole exchanged a once-over. "Who are you?" Cruz asked.

"My. Husband."

"Condolences, dude."

"You two think you're so funny, ha, ha, ha," I said.

"I'll take my twenty now." Cruz marched over to Susie's desk and held out his hand. "I gave Susie a chance to back out from betting against me about whether or not you'd be showing up. She figured there was a limit to your nerve, but I knew better."

I looked up at Creole and mouthed, *I'm sorry.*

He winked.

Susie opened her desk drawer and slapped the cash into his hand.

"Won't you come into my inner domain?" Cruz said with mock-graciousness and strode into his office, sitting behind his desk. We followed, as did Susie, who stopped at the open door. Cruz didn't seem to notice as he waved to the chairs. "As charming as your threats are, you're in luck... I need a favor." He leaned back in his chair. "I knew you'd be back. The father chose a good mouthpiece, but let's face it; he's not me."

Creole laughed.

"I recognize you. One of my old criminal clients?" Cruz asked Creole.

"Hardly."

"I'm done reveling in our civilized moment. What do you need?" I asked, then realized that it came out harsher than I planned and took a breath to calm down.

"Maricruz is hitting town." Cruz paused to let that one sink in. "She's been hot on my tail to get her a reservation to stay at that hovel you own. I offered up five-star beachfront accommodations, but no. She sulked until I told her I would ask. I've been putting her off as long as I can, and she shows no sign of relenting."

"Are you at least going to acknowledge that Granny is a handful and hard to control?" I asked.

Cruz shot up in his chair. "Stop calling her *that*."

"I'm assuming that you're insisting on the same rules as before." I wanted to remind him that he'd only issued them *after* all hell brook loose but stayed silent on that score. "I presume that you don't want her to get laid, so are you sending a guard?"

"You can go back to your desk," Cruz said to Susie, who was camped in the doorway, punctuating it by pointing. It surprised me when she shook her head and crossed her arms, taking a militant stance, her dark eyes glaring through him.

I decided to ignore her and turn back to Cruz. "How long is your grandmother going to be a guest? We'll do our best to keep her out of trouble, but we can't be held responsible if she breaks off her leash and runs wild." I'd started out so nicely and derailed quickly.

"Keep her away from the professor," Cruz gritted out. "I can't stomach hearing any more of his praises sung."

"Is it possible to foist her off on Carmela, since she's still in residence?" I asked. "Suggest some girl activities? Shopping? Something?"

Cruz shuddered. "Not a good idea. I don't want either of them getting hurt."

Great. Was he implying an old lady fistfight? I'd warn Mac. "So I can give Fab the good news that you're back on board?"

"Have her call for an appointment." Cruz stared me down. It was all I could do not to squirm. "One more thing before you go — you're going to owe me something extra for not throwing you out as soon as you got here."

"You're swell." I thought of several retorts and swallowed them all. "Of course, anything for you." I flashed the insincerest of smiles.

Creole and I stood and headed to the door. Cruz said, "One last thing. Tell Fab that her father isn't invited to any more meetings. You can keep it between us that I'm billing old money bags double."

I nodded and kept my phony smile in place. No way I'd be the bearer of that news. I left his office, restraining myself from running.

"I'm impressed. You held your own." Creole hooked his arm around me as we walked back to the SUV.

Once we were back on the highway headed home, I called Fab with the news that Cruz was back on board. She confessed to telling Caspian that she wanted Cruz as her attorney. He'd taken the news that I was pleading her case with a raised eyebrow. She left unsaid that he had no confidence I'd get the job done, but I heard it in her tone. Then I sent a text to Mac, telling her to accept the reservation for Maricruz.

I turned to Creole. "Lunch is on me. Anywhere you want to go."

Chapter Nine

Fab was once again busy entertaining her father, so I hadn't seen her for a couple of days, which was fine with me, as I hadn't heard what he thought of Cruz being back on board. I'd see them later at the family dinner Mother had organized, demanding that everyone show up.

I pulled into the parking lot of the short block that I owned in the center of town and slowed to check out the lighthouse that belonged to Fab, which she rented out as office space. I'd set up an area outside it for tourists who wanted a quick picture-taking opportunity. Junker's, on the opposite side of the property, was an old gas station that had been converted into an antique garden store. Finally, Jake's—a tropical-themed dive bar—was set back from the road. Its laid-back feel attracted locals to come in for a cheap cold one and the best Mexican food at the top of the Keys, and we had the contest ribbons tacked on the wall to prove it. Once we added musical entertainment, we attracted a new crowd of boisterous drinkers. We'd started booking local groups, and they'd become an instant hit. At the moment, all was quiet, and that was good. Fingers crossed it stayed that way.

I drove around the back and parked at the kitchen door. As I went through, I waved to Cook, who was arguing with a supplier. The kitchen was his domain, and he ran it without interference from me or anyone else. I cut down the hallway to the bar, where our pink-haired bartender and customer favorite, Kelpie, was stocking inventory.

"Hey, Bossaroo," she shouted, giving me a two-handed wave.

I walked around the interior and flipped on the ceiling fans, opening the doors to the deck and doing the same outside, plus flipping on the string lights that hung from the overhead rafters. I came back inside and slid onto a stool, then banged my hand on the counter. "Soda, please." I stabbed several cherries on a pick.

Doodad—AKA Charles Wingate III, who talked himself into the bar manager job and turned out to be a good hire—came out of the office, coffee mug in hand and notepad under his arm. He grunted, which was the best he could muster for a morning greeting. "Got a favor to ask you. Don't be bashful about saying no."

"As long as it's legal, it's a maybe."

"Got it—no guarantees." He downed his coffee and refilled the mug. "I've got a quasi-friend who's looking to unload a piece of property and needs a buyer. Pronto."

"Where? How much? Will it pass a title search?"

"Those are good questions that you'll need to ask *him*. I'll call and tell him to giddy up on over if you've got the time."

"Be clear with your friend that I'm not promising anything." I smiled at the glass Kelpie set in front of me and tossed in a pick full of cherries. "Does this friend have a name?"

"Hank Michaels," Kelpie answered for him. "The property is down by the docks, around the corner from The Boardwalk project your family owns." She grabbed a napkin and the pen out of Doodad's fingers and drew a crude map. "It's in that block of warehouse buildings that are all crappy and rundown."

Doodad snorted.

Kelpie jumped around, hands on her hips, sending her light-up tennis shoes into a frenzy. "If you were friendlier, you'd know a thing or two about other people's business. Act interested once in a while and not like you're mystified that the other person has the nerve to suck air."

I admired Kelpie's outfit. She was mostly covered today, except for her moneymakers, as she called them. She'd donned a low-cut bathing suit top and a flirty whiff of a skirt over workout pants. It occasionally occurred to me that I should suggest a dress code.

I'd sent Mac a text to hustle her backside over to Jake's. She had some new idea to pitch to keep the guests entertained at The Cottages, and if she was asking instead of implementing, it must be a doozy. She burst in through the kitchen and danced down the hallway, Rude in tow, fumbling along and doing her best to keep up.

"Introductions in order?" I waved my arm back and forth.

Kelpie rolled her eyes. "You act like we don't get around." She waved to the women and served sodas without asking. So they'd been in before. "How's goat yoga going?" She set the drinks on the bar. "I've been putting out the word. You could use a flyer."

"Do you think you could come up with something less cutting edge?" I eyed the two women.

"I wanted nude yoga, but Macster said you'd flip your frizz, so I went with the goats." Hands on her hips, Rude thrust her meager chest forward.

I didn't have the heart to tell her that it lacked the impact of the other two women. "How about, instead of all the bits hanging out, you compromise with skimpy attire?" I flinched, knowing how that would turn out—people would have to do a doubletake to ascertain if they were clothed or not.

Doodad grinned, having conjured up scantily clad women, I was certain. He held up his notepad and tapped it, his way of letting us know that he had important issues to bring up.

"Cootie would like to supply Jake's with moonshine for a small fee."

When Fab and I met the man out where he was living amongst the mangroves, he'd been cooking up the rot gut.

"*Felony*," I said. "Knowing that this subject was certain to come up, I did some research and found out that it's illegal. So. N. O. I'm not losing my liquor license over a brew that customers are certain to barf up, probably on my floor."

Kelpie accentuated that with the appropriate noise.

"Pass that along to Cootie." Doodad stabbed his finger at Rude. "If he's got a complaint, call her." He circled his finger in the air around to me.

"So, we're agreed that moonshine is ixnayed." I didn't wait for an answer. "Next on the list."

"Do you want to be here for band auditions?" Doodad asked.

The man was looking down, refusing to look my way; I knew he was grinning at his ridiculous question. "Yeah sure. You're on your own after ignoring my suggestion to go jukebox all the time," I said with faux snootiness. "With our clientele, the weirder the band, the better."

"That's a no." Doodad scribbled on his notepad.

"Next on the list?" I asked.

"Just my usual managerial *stuff*." Doodad ran his finger down the page.

"Don't bug me later with some annoying tidbit that slipped your mind." I turned my attention to Mac and Rude. "Would you like to go out on the deck?"

"Here's good." Mac straightened her top. She was dressed in business attire (for her)—a short ruffled skirt, halter top, and combat boots. "I'm pitching that we hire Rude here." She slapped the older woman on the back. "As our activity organizer, she'll keep the guests busy and happy. I can't do it all by myself. Another good idea…" She tapped her forehead. "We assign her to dog Maricruz when she shows up. She has a way of saying 'shut up and sit down' that folks respond to."

"I've got old-folks rapport." Rude beamed, dressed almost in carbon copy to Mac.

Doodad eyed her up and down, then looked down; his shoulders shook.

Before I could come with something inane to say, Mac slurped her soda so loud that all eyes turned to her. "If you're going to open the floodgates and let all Cruz's relatives romp back in, then I'm going to need to help." She blew out an exaggerated sigh. "They're demanding, and that's putting it nicely."

"I might commiserate with how over-stressed you are, except you've been sneaking Cruz's relatives in without a word to me. The boss," I wasn't complaining, as I knew it was one of the reasons Cruz was back on board. I turned to

Rude. "I want to hear your ideas ahead of time. Don't wait until the cops show up, and they will if you're doing anything naked."

A pounding on the front door brought the conversation to a halt. Doodad hustled over, unlocked it, and pushed it open, and an older man entered.

"Hank?" I whispered to Kelpie, and she nodded.

Doodad motioned me over, and the three of us walked out on the deck and sat at my reserved table. He made the introductions.

Hank Michaels—easily six foot and flirting with his late sixties, with a full head of bushy white hair—was dressed shabbily in worn shorts, tropical shirt, and dirty tennis shoes. At first glance, one would suspect that he was selling the building because he needed the money.

Kelpie came out, tray in hand, and set down a glass of beer in front of Hank and sodas for me and Doodad.

"I'll jump to the point," Hank said gruffly. "I've got a piece of property, a warehouse down in an older section of the docks. Not going to run a con and tell you that it doesn't need work because it does. It's structurally sound, but in need of prettying up, inside and out; the amount of work depends on your plans."

"Why not a real estate agent that can get you top dollar?" I studied him over the rim of my glass.

"I'm down on my luck." Hank smiled sadly. "I need start-over money. I want a quick sale and priced it accordingly."

Code for cash. "I'll need the address for starters, so I can check it out and forward the information to a couple of investors I know who might be interested."

Hank pulled out a crumpled piece of paper and handed it to me.

I smoothed it out and eyed the address, knowing the general area. "Any title issues?" He shook his head. "Just to let you know, any investor that I'd tell about the deal would only be interested in a straight-up transaction with no shortcuts."

"That suits me. I want everything done legally." Hank was looking me in the eye but fidgeting around.

"I'll need a couple of days, but one way or the other, I'll get back to you." I picked up my phone. "Can I get your number?"

He pulled a phone out of his shirt pocket that I knew at a glance was disposable and checked the screen. Apparently, he didn't know his own number or how to send a text, as he wrote it on a piece of paper for me.

I left Doodad to talk to his friend and went back inside. Mac and Rude had left, which left only a couple of regulars. I nodded to them. "What do you think of Hank?" Not sure why I asked Kelpie, but I did.

"Doesn't appear to have two nickels to rub together, so it surprised me when I heard he had property for sale. He's been in a few times. One-beer drinker. Never started any trouble."

"And he's Doodad's friend."

"That word is tossed around casually these days. I'd say it's more a case of they know of one another."

Three more regulars pushed their way through the door, waving and shouting to Kelpie.

"If there are any problems, I don't want to be the last to know." I waved and cut back through the kitchen.

Chapter Ten

Originally, Mother had planned for the family to try out a new restaurant in Marathon. But they couldn't or wouldn't guarantee a table where we could all sit together, and the dinner was moved to Fab's. Brad brought fresh fish off his boat, which had just docked, reminiscent of the days he captained his own rig and kept our refrigerators stocked. Didier and Creole volunteered to barbecue the fish and vegetables. Under Mother's tutelage, Liam had signed up to choose the desserts when he first joined the family, and this time was no different; he stopped at the bakery on his drive to the Cove. It was a warm, balmy evening, and Fab and I set the table outside overlooking the pool area and the beach beyond. We set the platter of food in the center of the tables, and everyone ate heartily.

Chief Harder, Creole's old boss and a family friend, sat across from me and shook his finger at me. He didn't appear all that annoyed that I'd sicced Mother on him. I'd known she'd issue an invitation that would be hard for him to turn down, which was why I'd had her make the call.

I leaned across the table toward Harder. "You haven't been around in a while. Buckle up, the fun is about to start."

He flashed me a "behave" look. Little did he know.

The dishes were cleared away, and we continued to sit outside and finish off the wine that Caspian had brought. A whole case, in fact, so we could drink all night. All controversial topics had been banned over dinner. All bets were off now.

"When is Emerson coming back?" Mother asked Brad.

Emerson had been Brad's family law attorney and helped him get custody of his daughter, Mila, when she was discovered in a foster home. The whole family fell in love with the little girl in a hot second. Once the case was over, the two began dating.

Liam stood and lifted Mila out of her chair, where she was about to fall asleep, and nestled her in a lounger. Earlier, Fab and Mila had chosen the blanket, pillows, and books that were arranged on the cushion.

"As you know..." Brad flashed Mother a look of annoyance but continued, "Emerson's grandmother said her final bon voyage and named Emerson executor and sole heir of her estate, which in addition to buckets of money also includes a considerable amount of property." He picked up his wine glass and took a healthy swallow. "Emerson wants me to relocate to the Hamptons."

"You and Mila?" Mother squeaked.

"N. O.," I said, loudly enough to catch everyone's attention. "I mean, is she the one?" I managed to lower my voice. "New York? That's far."

Brad smiled at me. "I told her no in my hemming-and-hawing way. I didn't want to hurt her feelings. It was an uncomfortable conversation that ended with, 'We can still be friends.' She was understanding, saying she knows how close I am to my family and how hard it would be for Mila and me to pack up and move north."

"On the bright side, Mother can put back on her matchmaking bonnet," I teased. "It's been a while, and it would be terrible if she got out of practice."

"So sad if Spoon suddenly found himself a widower." Brad glared at him. "Control your wife."

Spoon hooked his arm around Mother and kissed the top of her head. "Wifey is going to behave, isn't she?" he whispered in her ear.

"Yes," Mother squeaked out, turning beet red.

Fab tapped her wineglass and announced, "For those of you that might not know, Cruz has signed back on to be my lawyer."

"Now that that's been settled," Caspian said gruffly, "maybe the two of you can stay out of trouble and not engage in any risky behavior that could come back to haunt Fab." I tried my best not to be annoyed that he made it sound like I was the instigator of any unfolding drama.

"How about keeping a low profile, and I'm only suggesting until the cops have the murderer in custody," Didier said. "Farm out your clients' problems for others to solve."

Asking Fab to sit around and do nothing wasn't going to work.

"I forgot to tell you that, on our last trip to Cruz's office, he pulled out a video of an altercation between me and the dead woman that happened a couple of years ago in a restaurant in Miami." Fab huffed out her annoyance. "A copy had been sent anonymously to the district attorney."

"You and Aurora?" Creole asked.

Fab nodded. "After watching it, I recalled the incident. Aurora was drunk and annoying and attempting to crawl into Didier's lap. He, being a gentleman, was trying to unhook her arms from around his neck and get her to sit in a chair. I was out of patience and dumped her on the floor. Management came over, asked a few questions, and then escorted her out."

"The video only shows a short snippet of the altercation and nothing else," Didier said.

"I wonder who had access to a years-old video?" I asked. "And sending it anonymously...

Someone has it in for you. It would be nice to know who."

"The real murderer, perhaps," Brad said. "That person knows you're the primary person of interest. I imagine that they'd like it to stay that way."

"You need to be careful," Mother said.

"I'm happy to contact the investigating officer and see what I can find out," Harder offered.

"Madison told me that you're no longer with the Miami police department," Mother said.

"Mother's too nice to ask what happened, but I'm not. What happened?" I smiled at Harder.

Mother sighed.

Creole pinched my thigh. I turned a narrow-eyed glare on him.

"I got offered a great opportunity that I'm not at liberty to talk about quite yet," Harder said with a grin. "I opted to retire early and take two months before my start date for activities such as fishing and golf."

"We'll have to have a party for you when you start your new gig," I said.

"Probably not." Harder half-laughed.

Time to hijack the conversation in a different direction. "I heard an interesting proposition today." I told everyone about the conversation with Hank Michaels. "I drove by the property, and it's a three-story warehouse right around the corner from The Boardwalk. After cruising the couple of rundown blocks there, I thought it was ripe for a facelift. Right now, it's a magnet for trouble."

"And do what with them?" Caspian didn't sound impressed.

"He only owns the one," I answered. "I thought if we got them all, they'd make interesting office buildings and only add to the value of the area."

"Hank Michaels... the name rings a bell," Spoon said, and was silent for a minute. "As I recall, he's got a family feud going with his brother, who owns the other three buildings. The grapevine has it that the brother was approached a few times regarding selling. Turned every offer down flat. He's rich, and money isn't an issue. Whatever his reason for letting them deteriorate this long is, he's kept it to himself."

"It would be great if we could pick them all up," Brad said. "Doesn't sound like that option's on the table."

The guys bandied about the pros and mostly cons of buying one building and maybe never having an opportunity to purchase the others. They came to the conclusion that it wasn't cost-effective to buy a single property.

Creole looped his arm around me and pulled me close, whispering, "Your idea is a good one."

Not to the rest it wasn't.

The conversation segued into an update on The Boardwalk. It was well-run, and the commercial space all rented. The whole project was garnering favorable publicity and reviews and fast becoming a tourist destination for family fun.

Fab leaned toward me and asked, "Can you come into the office tomorrow? I'll have lunch delivered."

Creole's attention snapped to her. "Why?"

"I thought we'd go over my client list," Fab said casually. "Figure out ahead of time who to assign them to should something come up."

That sounded great, but she was up to something. "If you order pizza," I laughed it off.

I wanted to kiss Brad when he stood and said, "I'm taking my daughter home."

"I want to go home too," I whispered to Creole.

Chapter Eleven

The next morning, Creole got up ahead of me and fixed us both coffee. He handed me a mug, and I slid onto a stool next to him at the island.

"I think your real estate idea is a good one," he said. "Ideally, buying up all the buildings at one time would be best. Getting those couple of blocks renovated would be good for our Boardwalk project and the rest of the neighborhood."

"That's supportive of you." I blew him a kiss over the rim of my cup. "But the unofficial vote last night was a resounding no."

"Why not buy it yourself?"

That surprised me. I hadn't expected for him to suggest that I add to my portfolio. "Some think I own enough real estate."

"My motive's not all that pristine." He gave me a sneaky smile. "The busier you are with your own projects, the less time you have to run around town and get arrested."

"If this is about Fab, she really has tried to delegate and stay out of any more trouble. Today's meeting probably has to do with Gunz, as he's her only regular client right now and she's loath to bring up his name since he's misunderstood."

Creole snorted. "Misunderstood. That's a good one."

"On the scale of her crappy clients, he's not at the bottom." I smiled cheekily and stuck out my finger, which he attempted to nibble on. "No eyerolling."

"I've got a silent partner in mind. He's easily approachable. Bat your beautiful brown eyes and pitch your idea."

I made a face. "That's not professional."

"Just this one time. And only with him. Anyone else, and I'll break their face."

"Hmm…" I shot him a coy look. "Who could it be?"

"I have every confidence that you'll make the property a success. You have with everything else you own. Your track record speaks for itself."

"You really are the best husband."

"I'll have him call you." He slid my phone across the island, picked up his own, and made a call.

My phone rang, and I glanced down at the screen. "I knew it was you."

"Get dressed. Sweatpants and tennis shoes."

"We're going to go shoot someone?" I said with excitement. "Run for our lives?"

"You're not funny."

"I'm an acquired taste." I laughed at his

frown, then went and changed into one of my favorite outfits—cropped sweats and a t-shirt. I was back in the kitchen in a quick five minutes. I jumped in the air, arms out. "How did I do?"

Creole slide off the stool, picked me up, and heaved me over his shoulder. "We're off." He hauled me out the door and into his testosterone truck.

He drove across town and slowed at the property in question. "It doesn't appear to be a crumbling mess. That's a good sign." He continued past and cruised to the end of the street. "If these two blocks were renovated, it would clean out the remaining riff-raff and the criminal element looking for a place to hide." He u-turned and once again drove slowly. "See that truck?" He pointed over the steering wheel to where it was parked opposite the building. "It hasn't moved since we drove by the first time. And in a no-parking zone." He pulled up behind the older model pickup—which had tinted windows, so it was hard to make out who was driving—and it shot away from the curb. "Something to hide, maybe?"

"No license plate. You'd think the driver would be pulled over in a hot second."

Creole turned into the driveway and pulled in far enough that his bumper didn't stick out in the road. He helped me out. Ready with my camera, I took a couple of pictures as we walked up to the front of the three-story warehouse-style building, checking out the exterior. We rounded the side but didn't get far, finding it fenced. We backtracked.

"How many offices per floor?" he asked.

"One." At his raised brow, I said, "There's a parking space requirement, and the only lot is in the back. I'm also thinking about the traffic it would generate if there were hundreds of employees per floor."

"Is there going to be enough profit?"

"I'll meet with my CPA and talk to him. Whit's always harping on real estate; let's see if he green-lights this idea."

As we passed the front door, I paused and turned the knob on the off chance that it might be unlocked. It wasn't. We continued our trek over to the driveway and around to the back.

Surprisingly, one of the back doors was unlocked, so we went inside. The open space smelled of dust and dirt that had been there longer than the dead bugs scattered around the floor. In the far corner, a pile of belongings was spread out on the ground and a bedroll was laid out. It was evident that someone was living there, however roughly.

Creole grabbed my hand and tugged me backward.

"What?" I dug in my feet. And then I saw the blood—smeared on the walls and a trail across the floor, as though something or someone had been dragged to the front door.

"I'd say this is a crime scene." Creole had me out the door and over to his truck before I could get a second look. He pulled his phone out of his pocket, called 911 and identified himself, and reported what he'd seen.

"That was a lot of blood," I said when he was done. "And no body. At least not in sight. Do you think it's still inside?"

"From the little I saw, I suspect the body was dragged out the front door." Creole folded me into a hug. "It's a job for the crime scene unit, and they won't appreciate us tramping around in the evidence."

"I wasn't going to suggest that we go back in and look around." I couldn't stop thinking that I should've snapped a couple of pictures. That would make Fab proud.

"Do you have contact information for the owner?"

I nodded and took out my phone.

"The cops are going want it. So much for the quick sale he wanted."

Two cop cars blew up. Kevin got out of one and walked over. Creole stepped forward and told him what we'd walked in on. He led Kevin and the other officer around the back, and I stayed out of the way.

They weren't gone long.

Kevin walked over to me. "What do you know?"

I told him what happened from when we

pulled up in front of the building. "I have the contact information of the owner, Hank Michaels, if you need it."

"I was surprised to hear he was selling; he and the brother, Ted, have owned these buildings for thirty years," Kevin said. "Gossip has it that they've hated each other for just as many years. The feud started when Ted bested Hank on the deal for the other buildings, and he didn't find out until it was a done deal. Brotherly love and all."

"Hank didn't mention the brother when we talked," I told him. "He just stressed the need for a quick sale and didn't offer up any details. I haven't had time to check the title, but Hank did assure me that there wouldn't be any issues."

"Hank owned the building, alright," Kevin assured me.

"I'm surprised that these buildings haven't received a cleanup notice." They were all eyesores.

"Ted Michaels has connections all over town, so a blind eye has been turned on this area. It wasn't so noticeable when the whole area was run down, but now that it's been revitalized, the dilapidated buildings stick out."

"You're a fount of information." I smiled at Kevin. "There's one other thing..." I told him about the pickup.

"Creole mentioned it and said it didn't have tags; that should make it easy to spot. I'll put out an APB, and the cops in the area will be on the lookout. I'd like to talk to that person."

"I'm hoping for a happy ending and that the bleeder ended up at the hospital."

"Probably not." Kevin shook his head. "Hospitals are required to report things like that, and I'd have heard. I know where to find you if I've got more questions." He waved and went to meet the driver of a nondescript white van that had just pulled up.

Creole, who'd been talking to the other officer, broke off and walked over. "You ready?" I nodded. He scooped me off my feet and slid me onto the seat of his truck. He walked slowly around to the driver's side, checking out the street, and slid in. "Don't come back here by yourself."

"All that blood was a deal-killer. The building will sit here and rot some more before everything gets straightened out and it gets sold."

"Be interesting to have my dozen or so questions answered. Starting with: if someone is dead, which is likely, who is it?"

I shuddered. "Can you drop me at the office?" Creole eyed my sweats, and I chuckled. "Luckily, I have a change of clothing, or you-know-who would flip."

"Maybe not, if you play up the blood and gore that we stumbled upon."

Chapter Twelve

"This has been an eventful morning," I said as Creole, who'd brushed off my security card, and instead punched the button several times. The gate opened, probably so he'd stop.

He pulled up to the warehouse building that housed Fab and Didier's offices and where I claimed desk space, got out, and walked around, helping me out, then leaning down and kissing me. "You need a note?"

"I texted Fab. I notice she didn't answer; she needs to be reminded that stuff happens. I may let her find out about our morning on her own so she can be annoyed with me even more."

He felt up my back. "I can't believe that you strapped on a gun."

"Habit. I can't believe I'm with a man that leaves the house only partially dressed."

Creole laughed. "The last time I was shot at was when I was a cop. Can't say that I miss keeping one eye peeled over my shoulder, although I'm not completely out of the habit."

"I think it's not a habit that you should drop completely." I kissed him again, knowing that if I detailed all the times I'd needed a weapon, we'd be here all day and, by the end, he wouldn't be happy. "Have a good day. Stay out of trouble."

"Follow your own advice and call if you need anything."

"Will do." I smiled cheekily, waved, and entered the building through the garage. I was halfway up the stairs when the door opened and Gunz filled the threshold.

"You're late." He gave me a once-over and sniffed. "You just roll out of bed and reach for the clothes lying on the floor?"

"Ha, ha, ha." I held my stomach and gave him a dirty look as I scooted past him. "I've got an excellent excuse," I announced to Fab as I entered and went to drop my bag on my desk, then returned and grabbed a bottled water.

"Can't wait to hear this." Gunz shut the door and threw his bulk in his favorite chair.

"I suppose one of your relatives slipped their tether and is on the loose," I said, leaning against the corner of Fab's desk.

"You first." He smirked.

I sat next to him and turned to Fab. So much for dragging out the drama. I gave a colorful rendition of the morning, but avoided disclosing why we were at the building and neither of them asked.

"If someone went to all the trouble to drag the body off, it's possible it'll never be found." Gunz appeared thoughtful. "Though an identification can be made from the blood."

"If you hear anything, let me know," Fab said to Gunz.

"Before you hokey pokey on out of here, why don't you tell *me* what brings you by and I'll give the job my stamp of approval... or *not*." I stared down Gunz, who wasn't about to be outdone and glared back. "Since Fab is being eyed for murder in the first, she has to be careful about the jobs she takes, and with your long friendship, she might forget to tell you hell no."

"I need an envelope delivered to my relatives." Gunz pointed to Fab's desk, where a bulky manila envelope sat. "They live out in the weeds, and you can't expect me to drive out there."

If we're going to get shot at, then yes. You do it.

"I know what's coming next." He held up his hand. "It's cash for moving expenses."

I squinted at him as though that might make him retract anything that wasn't true. He didn't, which didn't mean he was telling the whole truth. I'd worm anything he'd failed to mention out of Fab. I stood up. "If you'll excuse me, I'll go pretty up so we can hit the road. Heads up: I'm going to need coffee," I told Fab, then headed to the bathroom for a quick shower and change.

I came back out in a full skirt and top, with low heels, and spun around, happy that Gunz had left.

"You look better than you did."

I made a face at her, noticing she'd eyed me

up and down, and felt inclined to remind her that she'd helped me shop for the clothes I kept at the office. I'd been slow to replace my wardrobe and flip-flop collection after my house burned. I knew Fab was ecstatic about the latter.

"All the details you left out of your story, you can tell me in the car." Fab stood and picked up her purse and keys.

"You first. I'm hoping this Gunz job is exactly how he portrayed it."

"Coffee first." She headed out the door with me right behind her.

In the car, Fab handed me the address, and I entered it into the GPS.

"It's on the outskirts of town. So what's the deal? Drop and go?"

Fab ignored my questions or didn't hear me. She unleashed a long sigh. "I had a delivery this morning. Dead flowers."

"At the office?" At her nod, I said. "That's creepy. I don't suppose there was a card."

"Good thing Gunz was there. I flipped, and I'm not sure what I would've done if I'd been by myself. He carried them out to the trash but came back with the card; said I should keep it. I opened it, and nothing, an empty envelope. I thought we'd stop by the florist on the way back."

"You wouldn't think a flower shop would put their name on a dead arrangement," I said. "I'll be the one to go in and ask questions."

"I hate not being in the middle of investigating my own case." Fab hit the gas in a fit of annoyance.

"Low profile, remember? I'm going to keep repeating it."

"I've overthought every angle of this case, sure that I'm missing something just out of my reach and I just need to worry every angle." Fab turned off the highway onto a residential street, a mixture of single-family houses and mobile homes. It looked like they'd all been storm damaged to one degree or another in the past. She slowed, as most didn't have easily discernible addresses.

"It was the lime-green house you just passed." I twisted in my seat and looked over my shoulder. "What the hell's going on? The dirt yard is empty, and I'm pretty sure the front door's standing open."

Fab used someone's driveway to turn around on the narrow street. "I'll run up to the door and be right back."

"What you're going to do," I told her in a no-nonsense tone, "is drive by again, this time slowly, and scope out the property. Then I dare you to tell me it's not creepy. Before you say, 'It's not so bad,' how about a good answer as to why someone would go away and leave their door standing open."

Fab drove by, and we both noticed that a window on the far end had been broken and shards of glass lay on the ground.

"If you plan on stopping, take me to the highway first, and I'll take my chances hitchhiking."

"I'm sure it's not that big a deal."

"You're ridiculous," I fumed, pulling my phone out of my pocket and calling Gunz. When he answered, I asked, "Are these relatives of yours expecting us?"

"Yeah, why?" he barked.

"Because there are no cars parked in the driveway or in the front of the property, the door is standing open, and there's not a human or animal in sight."

"Go ahead and leave. I'll call a cop friend to do a welfare check."

For a reformed criminal, he had a lot of cop friends ready to do him a favor. I relayed the conversation to Fab, and she drove off, eyeing each house as she passed.

I tugged her sleeve. She stopped and I rolled down my window, hung my head out, and asked a woman walking her dog, "Do you know if they moved?" I pointed to the house. "The lime-green one."

"Who are you?" she asked suspiciously.

I put on a friendly face. "My dad asked me to stop by and check on a friend of his. He tried calling several times and didn't get an answer."

"The yellow and white house." She pointed to the neighboring property. "They were dealing drugs. Your dad's friend called the cops. The cops raided the place. A bunch of people were hauled out in cuffs. It made the news, and it was reported that the cops were tipped off by someone in the neighborhood. We all knew who it was, as they'd complained the loudest and made several threats to call."

"When did you last see them?" I asked.

"Early this morning when I was walking Bayou. They loaded their pickups with boxes and hightailed it out of here. They weren't gone five minutes when two guys on motorcycles rode up and didn't stay long. I sure hope they're okay."

"Me too. Thank you." I rolled up the window. "I suppose you knew the whole story?" No answer. "And you came anyway."

Fab got to the end of the block, pulled into an empty lot, and idled the engine. "Gunz had gotten a tip that payback might be coming but thought he had more time to get his family relocated. The money was for the family to get out of town and not come back."

"Let's hope they're still alive," I said.

"The motorcycle riders wouldn't have shown up if they were dead."

"The cops want people to report illegal activity, and then the news outs them. Why?" I shook my head.

"Enough details were shared that a couple of men came snooping around, asking questions, offering money for information. You of all people know how the neighbors love to talk. It's likely that Gunz's family was outed by someone that they barbequed with on the weekends."

A cop car pulled around the corner and slowed as he drove by, continuing on to park in front of the house. He got out, gun drawn, and disappeared inside. A few minutes later, he was back. He leaned against his car door and made a call, then got in and drove away.

"He must not have found anything," Fab said, and pulled back onto the highway.

"I quit," I said in a huff. "No more backup for me. You knew this could be dangerous and didn't say anything." I turned and looked out the window.

"Gunz just got the tip this morning. You should be proud that I didn't get out of the car."

"Oh, brother. You would have if I hadn't been here to grouch at you."

Fab's phone rang, and she showed me the screen. Gunz. She answered and put it on speaker.

"My family called." Gunz sounded stressed, which was new for him. "They're fine. They got scared and got out at first light."

"What do you want me to do with the envelope?" Fab asked.

"Take it to Publix. They're parked at the back of the parking lot in two white work trucks. I got them a place to go out of town, and they're going to need the cash."

"I'll call when the job's finished." Fab hung up.

"What is this?" I asked in exasperation. "A lesson in minding your own business and not getting involved? If these people didn't have Gunz, they'd be totally screwed."

It was a short trip back to town. Fab pulled up alongside one of the trucks, rolled down her window, and handed over the envelope. "Call Gunz if you have any problems," she told the driver and backed out.

"Thankfully, that was uneventful. Anyone watching would be sure they just witnessed an illegal transaction go down."

"The florist is two blocks north."

I'd forgotten about the dead flowers. "Where was the envelope on the arrangement?"

"Gunz said it was on a flower pick stuck prominently in the middle of the dead roses." Fab pulled in and parked, then reached down and grabbed her purse, pulling out the envelope.

I jerked it out of her fingers and called her from my phone. "You can listen in." I got out, and before I shut the door, I said, "Don't you dare get out of this car." I marched inside.

There was a girl who appeared to be high school age behind the counter. "Is the owner or your manager in?"

"Just me." She smiled.

"I got a delivery of roses this morning, and they were dead."

"We would never..." She appeared flustered. "What's your name and address?"

I gave her Fab's name.

She got on the computer and, after a couple of minutes, said, "I don't have a record of an order or delivery. Maybe it was another store."

"This envelope was stuffed down inside the arrangement." I held it out.

She took it and glanced at it, then grabbed an envelope out of a card holder at the front of the register and handed them both back. "The one you have is old; they were replaced two months ago. These are the new ones."

"Maybe it was meant to be a joke of some sort," I said lamely.

"We would never agree to such a stunt." She looked upset, and it wasn't contrived.

"I believe you," I reassured her. "I get all my flowers here, and they've always been beautiful." I didn't, but she didn't know that. I waved and left, going back to the SUV and telling Fab what the girl had told me. "She came across as truthful."

"Which means we still don't have answers," Fab muttered, frustrated.

Chapter Thirteen

It had been a quiet couple of days.

Gunz had gotten his relatives out of town in the nick of time. Their lime-green hovel burned down during the night. It was declared arson. No suspects.

There was nothing new on the warehouse crime scene. Attempts to track down Hank Michaels had proved fruitless. Cops went to his residence, and the neighbors hadn't seen him. He lived in a one-room apartment in a rundown building. I'd guess that the rumors of him having money and a lot of it were false. They paid a visit to his brother, Ted, since it was well known that they hated one another. He slammed the door in their faces after telling them to contact his lawyer. The cops got a warrant and took him in for questioning. It was unclear how long he was detained, but it made headlines when he was released.

Creole was banging around the kitchen, grouching. "A good wife would cook me breakfast."

I slid off the stool, pushed by him, and reached into the cupboard for a bowl. I looked up at him. "What kind of cereal would you like?"

Before he could answer my smirk, there was a loud banging on the back door. "Why have a security pad on the fence when you give the code out?" He strode over and threw open the door.

Fab stuck two pink boxes in his face, which he took with a huge grin and put on the countertop.

"You saved me from cereal," he said with a humph.

Didier laughed and closed the door.

"Yum. You saved me from having to tie on an apron." I laughed. "I smell a bribe, and I can only promise that we'll listen while we eat." I got out plates and silverware and set the island while the guys made coffee. Fab and I unloaded the boxes and arranged everything on a platter.

"We should hold off on the reason for the visit until after we eat," Didier suggested as he filled the mugs with coffee.

I thought Fab would burst, but she managed to hold off until we were done. "I need you to come along on a meeting with a prospective client," Fab finally said.

"I'm not allowed to leave the house without my husband's permission," I said, flashing her a sweet smile.

Creole did a double take. "Yeah, what she said. I'll be needing details."

I winked at him.

"I got a referral from an old client," Fab started.

I groaned. "Your rich old men clients come with more problems than my tenants at The Cottages."

Creole and Didier laughed.

"The meeting is at a trendy restaurant in Miami. How much trouble can we get into with a large audience?" Fab stood and grabbed the coffee pot, refilling everyone's mug but mine, as I put my hand over the top.

"I don't know how you can ask that question with a straight face," I said. "What's the job?"

"My client, Mr. Berger, was involved in an indiscretion, and he's being blackmailed. He'd like us to negotiate a settlement for the pictures and ensure the utmost discretion going forward."

"So... Mr. Berger is married?" I raised my eyebrows. Fab nodded. "He allowed his goods to be photographed and couldn't figure out upfront how that could go wrong? And now he's going to pay a blackmailer with no assurances that she won't be back. If the woman is willing to stoop this low, her word is worthless. Does that sum it up?"

Fab nodded again.

"To Madison's point," Creole said, "how will you know that you're getting any and all files?"

"This Berger fellow is lucky the woman didn't sell the incriminating photos... or maybe there's not a market unless he has a household name," Didier said. "I've never heard of him."

"Berger thinks Jane, the other woman, will go

away with a hefty payoff."

"Let me guess, Jane Doe?" I laughed in the face of Fab's disgust.

"Poor Jane wasn't happy when she found out Berger wasn't leaving the wife." Fab wiped away a non-existent tear.

"That's a sad story, all right. I hope you're not giving any money-back guarantees. A trendy restaurant, huh?" I looked down at Creole's t-shirt, which hung to my knees, and over at Fab's black dress. "Give me a few. I'll disappear inside the closet and come out all cute."

"I can help you pick something out." Creole smirked.

"We don't have all day," Fab said drily.

I leaned forward and gave Creole a quick kiss, then slid off the stool.

It didn't take me long to grab the fastest shower in history, pick out a sleeveless pink dress and heels, and accessorize with silver jewelry. I twirled in front of the mirror and gave myself a mental thumbs-up for lunch in Miami. Fingers crossed it was waterfront.

I came out of the bathroom, and Creole wolf-whistled.

My cheeks warmed, and I winked at him. "I strapped on my Glock." I lifted my hem and flashed Creole. "You never know."

"You're going to call if anything goes south?" Creole poked his finger at me.

"I'll call on the way back," Fab told Didier and

leaned over to kiss him.

"Me too, babes." I kissed Creole.

The guys walked us out to the car.

Fab drove out of the compound, for once not like the road was going to burn up before she could get out.

"Miami, here we come. Again." I adjusted the seat and leaned back.

The drive north was uneventful. Fab flew up the highway and got us there in one piece.

The appointment had been made for the start of the lunch crowd. Fab circled the block, scoping out the exterior of the restaurant, and parked around the corner. Using the valet would hinder a quick getaway.

We got out, and I straightened my dress. "I imagine I'm going to be my usual charming self? Sit there and say nothing. Unless the subject of you committing a felony comes up. Such as Jane wanting to hire you to blow her lover away, but probably not before she gets paid."

"Negotiations aren't really my forte. I'd rather sneak up on her, say in her apartment, and threaten her to get her to hand over the damning evidence."

"Your real talent lies in tossing a house and finding every hiding space, then leaving it looking as if no one's been there." Now there was something I needed to put on my list of skills I had yet to learn and should. "Did loverboy give you a budget?"

"Mr. Berger will go up to 25K, but wants me to start low."

"Let's hope Jane is money-hungry and takes the first offer you throw at her so we can get out of here and hit the mall for lunch and shopping."

We entered the open-air restaurant and approached the front desk. Under other circumstances, I'd have loved to eat here. It was clearly a local favorite, as half the tables were filled and people were filing in behind us.

"We're meeting Jane Charles," Fab said to the hostess.

The young woman smiled, grabbed menus, and led us to a table in the middle of the room. Definitely not my favorite location. I knew Fab felt the same, as we traded raised brows.

I knew that blackmailers didn't have a look, but this woman—a thirty-something girl next door with blond hair pulled into a ponytail— wouldn't even begin to make my list.

Fab introduced us, and we sat. A bottle of wine had already been opened and sat in the middle of the table, and Jane's glass was full. The server came over and filled ours.

"Thank you for being on time." Jane fingered her diamond watch and picked up her glass. "To business." In one swift movement, she drew the glass back and sent the contents flying; the wine hit Fab square in the face, ran down, and dripped off her chin. Some splattered on the front of her dress. Jane slammed the glass down, shoved her chair back, and jumped to her feet, yelling, "Thief." She planted her hands on the table and leaned across it at Fab. "You stole all my money and left me and my child penniless," she yelled, even louder.

Fab wasn't often speechless, but this was one of those rare times.

Jane had caught us both off guard.

What the heck was she talking about?

Fab scooted her chair back.

Jane continued to rant at the top of her lungs. "You talked about keeping my money safe. You knew it was all I had. Penniless—do you know what that's like?"

The other patrons stayed glued to their seats, shifting somewhat for a better view of the unfolding drama. More than a few phones came out and were pointed in our direction.

I jumped up in front of Fab. "Keep your voice down. You've got the wrong person."

"You won't shut me up," Jane roared to the room at large, turning in a circle. "You crooked bitch. You stole every last cent. Did you give a thought to the fact that my daughter and I would be homeless? You just wanted the money."

"If you could calm down for a second..." I tried, taking note that all eyes were riveted on the unfolding scene and the restaurant had gone quiet despite being full.

"More lies—that's all you're going to spew," Jane spit.

A well-dressed man came running over. "I don't know what's going on and don't care, but you need to take it outside, or I'll be forced to call the cops."

Fab stood, and her dress rode up.

Jane spotted her weapon and screamed, "Gun. She's got a gun." She turned and ran towards the front of the restaurant.

"I called 911," a patron yelled.

I turned to what I presumed was the manager. "We're private investigators." One of us anyway. "We both have carry permits."

"Listen to me, just go. This isn't the kind of attention we need." He held out his hands in a placating motion. "I'll tell the police that the argument broke up and everyone left."

I reached in my purse and slapped money on the table. "Hope that covers the wine the other woman didn't pay for. So sorry." I grabbed Fab's arm, and we took the same path as Jane.

"What the hell just happened?" Fab shrieked when we got outside. "I've never... I don't even know her."

"Pick up your heels, and let's get out of here. The cops just arrived." I nodded to the cruiser that had just pulled to the curb.

Fab grabbed my hand and cut down an alley.

I don't know why I was surprised when we came out on the side street where we were parked. "Do you know every shortcut everywhere?"

"It was a gamble." Fab blew out a frustrated breath. "I didn't want someone from the restaurant seeing us and pointing us out to the cops. We might not get arrested, but we'd be detained for questioning."

"You know that neither of us did anything wrong."

"There's not a single person who had a ringside seat for that rant who'd believe you. Not even me, if I'd been there as a guest. I might have jumped up and held us for the cops, thinking about the child involved."

We got in the SUV and turned on Ocean Drive in the opposite direction of the restaurant. Neither of us wanted to risk being seen by someone who'd recognize us and turn in the license tag.

"That was Jane." I pointed to the blue convertible Mustang, top down, that just blew by us. "Get close enough that I can get the license number but don't follow her." At Fab's incredulous glare, I said, "You need answers for what the heck just happened, and how else are you going to get them? I'd love to hear what your client has to say."

Fab gripped the steering wheel and caught up to Jane at the next signal, which had turned red. I snapped a couple of pictures.

"Once we get the address, we'll arrange a meet and greet, and we'll have the element of surprise," I said. "Make sure Jane doesn't catch sight of you in the rearview mirror and call the cops."

"I know what I'm doing," Fab snapped.

I texted Xander the information. "Address. Pronto."

"What the heck is going on?" Fab asked in shock. She didn't wait for an answer but careened over to the curb, snatching up her phone and making a call. "Disconnected," she shrieked.

I caught the phone before it ended up in a pile of pieces. "Mr. Berger?" Fab nodded. "Is he local?" She nodded again. I did some quick research and found a listing — he was a real estate broker and owned several offices in the South Miami area. By process of location elimination, I called the South Beach office and asked for Mr. Berger.

"Mr. Berger is out of the office for the month," a friendly female voice said.

"I'm returning his call from two days ago."

"It must have been his assistant. Mr. Berger has been in Greece, vacationing with the family. I can transfer your call."

"I'll wait for his return." I thanked her and hurriedly hung up. "It wasn't Mr. Berger who called." I told her what the woman said.

"I don't understand." Fab growled out her frustration. She eased away from the curb and headed back towards home.

Chapter Fourteen

Fab blew over to the Interstate and pushed the speed limit all the way to the Cove. We rode in silence for most of the trip.

"There's a little something that I forgot to tell you that might make sense of what happened." Fab shot me a quick glance.

My first inclination was to make her feel bad about keeping secrets, but the day had been bad enough already.

"There have been several police reports filed against me for fraud."

"What?"

"I've got to go into police headquarters for a lineup. Cruz reassured me that it's a formality to eliminate me in the outstanding legal cases, since all the people defrauded claim to be able to identify me. I'm happy you talked him into representing me again; anyone else and I'd be freaked out and probably in jail."

"If there's ever a time that Didier, for whatever reason, can't accompany you to an appointment, count me in."

"I didn't... I never... A single woman with a child! Not even in the old days would I stoop so low. Old, rich men, now that's a different story," she said. "Another thing I forgot about or didn't want to think about—my credit report. I need to hire someone to remove all the fraudulent information. Someone had a good time creating accounts and failing to pay. Anyone looking would think I was a crook."

"Make a list of everything that needs to be done, and if need be, I'll get a referral from Tank for someone good." Tank was our lawyer for everything except murder one. I took out my phone and texted Xander again: "Do a thorough background check on Fab." Now would be a good time to unearth any surprises so they didn't come back to haunt her.

The ride was quiet and thankfully uneventful. "I texted the guys that we were on our way home, promising pizza at your house. If you don't have vodka and tequila, then we need to make a liquor store run."

"The staples of life. Our liquor cabinet is always stocked." She half-laughed, which was good to hear.

I got on the phone and called in the pizza order, trying not to forget any of the favorite toppings, ordered a salad, then texted the guys to pick up the order.

Fab pulled up to her front door and parked. Inside, I threw my purse on the bench and kicked off my shoes. We headed straight to the kitchen. I pulled down the pitchers, and Fab got the liquor from the bar and the rest of the necessary ingredients.

"If there was ever a day to drink…" Fab blew out a long sigh as she began to fill the pitchers.

I found a large jar of olives in the refrigerator, overloaded a couple of picks, and put them in a glass.

"How about the couch?"

"Works for me." I carried one tray into the living room, Fab the other. We each lay down on our own couch, which faced each other across the coffee table.

Fab poured me a margarita and handed me the glass. "You're not going to throw this on me, are you?"

"I don't waste tequila."

Fab tipped her glass. "Friends."

"I'm sorry I didn't move faster; that whole drama caught me off guard. Never would I have thought the day would turn out like this."

Fab kicked her heels over the end of the sofa. "When will we have Jane's address?"

"We'll be able to pay her a visit tomorrow. Since we have no clue what her schedule is, I suggest that we leave early and forget about any middle-of-the-night visits. The last thing you need is to get arrested for breaking and entering. They'd probably hit you with a worse charge, for which you wouldn't make bail. We also don't want Jane reporting the incident to the cops."

The doorbell rang multiple times. "It's the

guys," Fab declared and didn't move off the couch. "They're the only ones that play on the bell. Neither will cop to which one is the instigator."

The door opened, and Caspian bellowed, "Fabiana, where are you?" He strode across the entry, followed by a burly fellow with muscles for days, who I guessed to be a bodyguard. Creole and Didier were behind him, carrying in the pizza boxes.

"What the hell happened today?" Caspian yelled.

"Could you use your quiet voice?" I said, and got a searing glare in return. I put the back of my hand to my forehead in a bid for sympathy. Didn't work.

"Caspian said there was some kind of altercation," Didier said over his father-in-law's shoulder. "We didn't get the whole story."

Creole came in, and I sat up so he could sit next to me. "What happened today?" he asked.

"Better question," I said, "is how would you know?" I eyed Caspian and hurriedly sucked down my second margarita, thinking I'd need the liquid courage to keep up with him.

Caspian's eyes flitted to the bodyguard.

"So… you sent fat-ass here," I said, ignoring Fab's gasp, "to bodyguard your daughter—without her knowledge, I might add—and when the woman she's meeting flips her hinges, he what? Blends into the wallpaper?"

"How dare you to speak to me like that? I should tell your mother," Caspian threatened.

"I'm a grown-ass adult who's had a bad day, and I'll talk how I want." I almost laughed at the thought of sticking my tongue out at him. "As for your threat to tell my mommy." I pulled my phone out of my pocket and called her in spite of the shocked looks on everyone's faces. "*Mother*, Caspian wants to complain about my bad attitude. Hang on." I stood and shoved my phone at him.

Caspian took the phone and spoke in French, then laughed, sort of. "Sorry. Your daughter's been drinking, and it's been a stressful day all around." Whatever she said, he calmed down and looked chagrined. "We'll have dinner soon." He handed me back my phone.

I pocketed it and stomped to the front door, throwing over my shoulder, "I'm taking my drunken self home." I closed the door forcibly, then realized I'd forgotten my shoes. Damn. If I'd gone out the back door, I could've hit the beach. I stepped gingerly on the asphalt and headed home, groaning. "I didn't handle that well," I mumbled to myself.

My SUV pulled up alongside me, the window rolled down, and Creole stuck his head out. "Hey babes, want a ride?"

"I would love it and you. My feet hurt," I whined.

He jumped out and scooped me up, carrying

me around to the passenger side.

When he got back in for the nanosecond drive home, I asked, "Are you divorcing me?"

"Hardly. I would've asked the guard the same question as you, except I'd have refrained from calling him a fat-ass cuz then he'd kick mine."

I giggled. "Can I get another ride into the house?"

Chapter Fifteen

There was a knock at the door the next morning, and I was a little surprised that Fab hadn't sat out in the street and laid on the horn. And more surprised when I opened the door and Mother and Fab were standing there.

I motioned them in and kissed Mother. "I'm surprised you didn't honk or yell out the window... save you a trip inside."

"It's not ladylike," Fab said with attitude, taking a seat at the island.

Mother flashed Fab a "behave" look. "Did you get the woman's address?"

"How do you know about that? I suppose that's the reason for the tennis shoes you seldom wear." I glanced down at her feet.

Fab adopted an innocent look.

"Since you were sauced last night—" The only things missing were Mother's "oh no you didn't" tone and some finger-pointing. "—I waited and called Caspian back to hit him up for more details. He doesn't have experience with how your mind works—either of you, actually—but I figured there'd be an early-morning trip to question that woman to find out what in the heck motivated her to stage such a scene."

"Well deduced." I crossed to the couch, slid into my tennis shoes, and grabbed my bag. "Coffee's on me."

We filed out the door and got into the SUV. I got in the back and leaned between the seats to program the GPS. "Jane Charles lives in an old apartment building in South Beach."

"This is such a long shot. We're going all this way in the hopes that she's going to answer the door," Fab sulked.

"If not, we'll play our ace." I patted Mother's shoulder. "If Mother reps herself as Jane's granny, hopefully the neighbors will tell all." I glanced over her linen pants and top; she definitely looked younger than her sixty years. "We need to get you an ugly housedress and some equally ugly shoes and keep them in the car for our next adventure."

Mother groaned. "How many older women do you see trotting around in muumuus and slippers? Very darn few. Maybe if they're ninety."

"Good thing you're not one of them. I'd have burned your clothes and taken you shopping," Fab said.

"It's been too long since we shopped," Mother said wistfully. "I did get a lead on a location for designer shoes on the cheap. Spoon looked up the address and set the paper on fire. Damn internet."

I laughed. "That's a good one. You need to share it at the next family dinner."

Fab ran through the coffee drive-thru and sped out to the highway.

"I'm warning you," Mother scolded. "You drive too fast, and I may throw up."

"Good one," I said. "Except I feel compelled to tell you that I've issued that same warning and it didn't work."

While we drove, Mother questioned Fab about her legal woes. I'd heard it all, so I leaned back against the seat and texted Creole: *The girls times three are on the loose. Will call if bail moola is needed.*

I got back a heart.

It was an uneventful ride.

I scooted forward before we reached our location. "I thought all night about what happened. There's plenty weird going on. If this woman supposedly had business dealings with you and ever met with you in person, then she knew you weren't the same woman the second you walked up to the table and introduced yourself."

"You're sure you never met this Jane woman?" Mother asked Fab.

"It's possible that I could've crossed paths with her at a social event, but I've never had a conversation with her," Fab insisted. "Madison wasn't the only one going over every second from yesterday." She turned and made her way over to the beach.

"You're not going to like this," I said to Fab. "I think you should wait in the car."

"When do I get my life back?" Fab thumped her hand on the steering wheel.

"What if Jane calls the cops? What are you going to tell them? 'I came to harass her over yesterday's events?' The cops will want details, and when you say, 'She accused me of fraud'…"

Mother patted Fab's arm. "I was thinking I should be the one to knock on the door. Jane might recognize Madison." She looked at me. "Once the door is open, then you can take it from there."

"If she doesn't answer," I said, "I'll send Mother to door-knock around the building, looking for a gossipy neighbor who wants to be the first to meet Granny, who's come for a surprise visit." Mother made a face at me, and I laughed. "It's highly likely Jane has a job, and if you're on your game, you'll weasel the company's name out of said neighbor."

"It's surprising how people love to talk, no matter how many warnings not to come up on the news," Fab said.

"Showing up at her job might be awkward," Mother said.

"Or work in our favor." I smiled at Mother, who was excited about her new role. "Jane's not going to want her coworkers to know that she created a scene and accused an innocent woman. Even if she gets them to believe her lies, she'll be hot gossip."

"Most people don't want their coworkers knowing their personal business," Mother agreed.

"I want to listen in," Fab said.

"How are you going to do that?" Mother demanded.

"We worked out this new system, tried and tested. I call her on my phone and wear my Bluetooth, which can pick up a pin dropping, so she can eavesdrop."

"I've got to get one of those ear things," Mother said.

"You better be careful; your husband will send you to your room." I laughed.

"I love it when we play that game." Mother giggled.

Fab laid on the horn.

"What?" I scanned the street.

"It was something," Fab said lamely and shot me a glare in the rearview mirror. That was one way to end the possibility of sex talk.

"Just know, if you subject me to any sexcapade chitchat, I'm going to repeat it word for word to Brad," I said to Mother, whose cheeks flushed.

"Here we are," Fab announced and backed into a parking space in front of a pale pink shotgun style two-story apartment building.

I eyed the security door. "Good thing I pocketed my lockpick."

"I want to do it." Mother held out her hand, which I ignored. "I haven't had the opportunity to practice in a long time."

"Next time. We need to get in and out quickly." I opened the door and got out before she challenged me to arm-wrestle or some such thing. I stood on the sidewalk and called Fab. "Call if the cops pull up, in no way do you gallop to the rescue."

Mother got out and waved to Fab. "How are we going to know which apartment?"

"Let's hope the mailboxes are marked." I looped my arm through hers. "It's a crapshoot. Depending on the setup, sometimes the name is scribbled inside the box and only visible to the post people." I turned her to face me. "No guns. And not because I'm being mean. We don't want to spend any time in jail."

"There would be no way to spin that as funny to my husband." Mother grimaced.

"Mine either." We got to the double set of security doors. I peered inside, took one last glance over my shoulder, and picked the lock.

"That was fast," Mother said in awe.

I held the door open and pointed to where rows of mailboxes were visible. Most had names on them. Jane Charles lived on the first floor. Going back to the entry, we bypassed the stairwell. The only other door was locked. It had a small window, which I peered in. On the other side was a long hallway with doors off each side.

I got out my lockpick.

"Wait." Mother grabbed my arm. "I knock and you'll be where?"

"Off to one side or the other, just out of sight."

"If she asks 'Who's there?' I'll tell her it's her grandmother." Mother made a face. "She'll know it's not true, but it sounds friendly, so she'll probably open up?"

"I'm impressed." I kissed her cheek. "Under no circumstances do you do anything that could get you hurt." I shook my finger, which she smacked away. We came to a stop in front of Jane's door, located midway down the hall. "Keep an eye out for any movement behind the peephole," I coached Mother.

"If she does that and doesn't answer, I'll knock until she does."

I laughed. "You've just morphed into Fab."

Mother knocked, and we waited, both on alert. She knocked again. "No one's home." She put her ear to the door. "Nothing." She moved down the hall and knocked on the next door—also nothing—then turned to the unit on the other side and got lucky. A young twenty-something answered, and Mother went into her spiel.

"Oh cool, she'll be happy to see you," I heard him say. "Jane works at Rican's Gems and Jewels on Washington."

"Thank you, young man. Now I'll still be able to surprise her." Mother flashed him a big smile and headed for the exit.

I waited until the man closed his door, then ran to catch up to her. "Good job."

"I got the address," Fab said in my ear.

Mother and I walked out to the car.

The drive took less than five minutes. Jane could easily walk to work if she chose.

Rican's was located in a strip mall, along with a check cashing place and a liquor store. The sign read "jewelry," all right, but the larger green neon sign underneath advertised that it was also a pawn shop.

"Maybe they specialize in cash for jewels, as opposed to the other personal items that most places take," I said.

"Since there's a glass display case in the window, I'm thinking they're not interested in your kid's bike." Fab parked off to the side.

"Behave yourself." I hopped out, shutting the door and said 'testing,' then blew into the phone.

"Too much caffeine for you," Fab grouched.

"I'm ready for lunch, although it's a tad early. I'd like to sauce it up but don't want to become a drunk. I need my wits about me."

Mother joined me. "I've never been in a pawn shop."

"Just remember that they're not in business to give anyone a great deal. They want back the money they already advanced... and charged an exorbitant interest rate on." I rang the bell.

"That's Jane," I whispered to Mother, nodding at the woman behind the counter, who'd just buzzed us in.

"Remember, no guns," Mother said parroting my warning back at me.

I grinned at Mother, then turned to the woman behind the counter. "Hi Jane." I waved, holding the door for my mother and checking out the store. We were the only people there, except for whoever might be behind the security door.

Jane was doing her best to remember me, but it appeared that she'd forgotten my presence at yesterday's drama.

"Since there seems to be a lull in a business, I'll get to the point," I said with an edge, but managed not to lose my cool. "I was at the restaurant yesterday when you created a huge scene and accused my friend of theft and defrauding you. I'd like to know why you would do such a thing, especially since we both know it was a lie."

"I, uh…" Jane looked down at the floor and then towards the security door. "Can this wait until I'm off work?"

"You annihilated my friend's reputation in public, in my estimation, you're getting off easy, since I'm managing to be civilized. You want me gone? Answer my questions."

Jane's cheeks burned, and she stared at my nose. "It was a job. A joke." She grimaced. "At the mention of cops, I freaked out, and then saw the gun and ran. I didn't know what to do."

It took a minute for what she'd said to sink in.

"You're telling me that someone hired you to make a scene in a restaurant?"

Jane nodded, still not able to make eye contact.

I reached in my purse, and she gasped. I pulled out cash and put it on the counter, not removing my hand. "Start at the beginning, the more detailed the better. If you give me enough, I may add to this." I picked up the money and held it in my hand.

"I answered an ad on one of those internet job boards hiring workers to play jokes on people," Jane choked out nervously. "When I called the number, a woman answered. She said her company was Party Surprise and her name was Lisa Dean. She assured me that it was all in good fun. The woman sounded nice and professional, and it seemed above board."

"Had you worked for this company before?" I asked.

"This was my first job. It seemed easy enough and paid five hundred dollars. Never got paid and probably won't now. Yesterday, when I got back to my car, I called to report what happened, and the number was disconnected."

"How did you know what to say?"

"A script was texted to my phone, and the message stressed that I say it exactly as written."

"Ask to see her phone," Fab said in my ear.

"I was so excited." Jane flashed a hint of a smile. "I did some acting in high school and thought it would be fun. Instead, it just blew up.

I wasn't expecting the response I got; I thought your friend would see through the hoax, and when she didn't, I was happy to hightail it out of there."

"Do you still have the text on your phone?" I asked. Jane nodded. "Can I see?"

She turned and picked her phone up from the back counter, flicked through it, and handed it to me.

I read the text and number out loud. "You did a good job. You nailed it word for word."

"I'm sorry you were used that way," Mother said sympathetically.

"I take it this was all done on the phone?" I asked. Jane nodded, close to tears. "How were you supposed to get paid?"

"I requested that the money be direct deposited. I never thought it was a hoax. Tell your friend I'm sorry."

I reached in my purse, pulled out more cash, and handed it to her, even though I'd rather pull her hair out than pay her anything after the stunt she pulled. With sixty seconds of thought, she should've known it was a bad idea. But she'd upheld her end of the bargain. "I appreciate you answering my questions. One more thing — the name of the website where you found the job listing?"

Jane reached for a business card, wrote on the back, and handed it to me.

On the way out, I stood in the open door,

waiting for Mother, who'd paused to say something—obviously something nice, since Jane was smiling at her. I couldn't come up with anyone who hated Fab enough to go to all the work of arranging this... practical joke? Which downplayed the situation.

"You're nicer than me," I said to Mother as we walked to the SUV.

"You did fine. It was awkward, and I felt compelled to say something nice. I felt bad for how she was used, then stiffed."

"Who would go to all this trouble?" Fab threw out as we got back in the SUV.

"Anyone at all from your past that you can think of? Disgruntled client?" I sat back in my seat and pulled out my phone.

"Wouldn't it have to be a pretty big grudge?" Mother asked. "One that you'd easily remember?"

Fab refrained from squealing out of the parking lot as she headed back to the Interstate for the trek home.

I called Xander. "I got another job for you. I've got to warn you—no wild animals are involved."

Xander laughed. "Save those until I graduate."

I told him about the visit with Jane and gave him the website information and phone number, asking him to check out both.

"Who takes a job where you humiliate someone in public and thinks that won't go wrong?" Xander asked. "Old Jane was lucky she didn't get the you-know-what beaten out of her. Most people wouldn't have let her walk."

We hung up. "I'm going to miss him when he deserts us for a real job."

"Xander's even grown on *me*," Fab said. "He never turns down a job and has a quick turnaround time. Where to?

"Quick stop, and then we can go to lunch."

"Where?" Mother asked, and when I didn't answer, she said, "When we get back to the Cove, drop me off on some street corner—Spoon will pick me up." She turned and glared at me.

"No way," I yelled.

Chapter Sixteen

I kept up the suspense about where I needed to go until we got back to town. If you could call it that, since Mother and Fab hadn't asked a single question and the two talked all the way back. I lay down on the seat and closed my eyes, attempting to listen in. It didn't work.

"The welcome sign," Fab said.

I sat up and leaned through the seats. "To The Cottages," I sang off-key.

Mother shook her head like she had something loose inside.

"Grandmother Campion has hit town," I announced. "Besides checking on her, I need to do a welfare check on my tenants and guests and make sure that nothing needs my immediate attention."

"I remember the stories from the last time Maricruz was here." Mother wrinkled her nose. "It was hard not to believe, with so much talk, that at least some of the stories were true."

"You can make up your own mind when you meet her. The last and only time she stayed at The Cottages, she hit town like a spring-breaker in heat and stirred up all kinds of trouble, for which Cruz blamed me. The only reason I got to set foot in his office again is because she's been hounding him for a re-visit."

"Get Crum to keep an eye out. Didn't they hit it off last time?" Mother asked.

Fab snorted. "That's an understatement."

"It wouldn't have gone so badly if he weren't such a poor show," I said. "People don't believe that he's a retired college professor when he shows up in his underwear. His first introduction to Cruz pretty much sealed the fact that he'd never be welcome at any family get-togethers."

"I'll hang out with Fab," Mother said, "while you douse the fires or whatever you do."

"Mother, you might think you're taking the easy way out, but you need to rethink that plan. Last time, Maricruz took a shine to Fab and wanted to be besties. If you want to join the group, I'm sure they'll let you in." I smirked, and she scowled.

Fab pulled into a parking space in front of the office. "We'll do what we do best and make it up as we go."

I got out and opened the door for Mother. "I need you to be a good influence on this old broad."

"How would you like it if someone spoke about me like that?" Mother grouched. Her eyes were another story — they showed amusement.

"I'd punch them in the nose."

"Be sure you step back; I've heard if you break

someone's nose, blood flies everywhere," Mother warned.

Fab came around and joined us as the office door opened.

Mac rolled out in a pair of white cowboy boot roller skates with flowers embroidered up the sides. "We're in here." She waved frantically, as though she didn't already have our attention. Unfortunately, she almost lost her balance, and only the side of the building saved her from landing in the bushes.

"What's that on her feet?" Mother whispered.

"Wherever she shops for shoes, you're not allowed to go," I whispered back.

Fab laughed and led the way into the office, stopping just inside the door. Mac skated back to her desk and threw herself in her chair. Maricruz Campion was stretched out on the couch, her tanned legs draped over the back, dressed all in white, as if for a game of tennis... if we had courts or there were any close by.

"I heard you were stopping by to welcome me back." Maricruz princess-waved, a smug look on her face. "Did you bring a gift? If not, I like whiskey."

"You'll need to sit up so there's room for everyone." To my surprise, she did it without grumbling, giving a tug to her blond pixie-cut wig and crossing one boney leg over the other. I made the introductions.

Fab sat next to her, still obviously Maricruz's

favorite. Judging by the once-over I got, after which her nose went straight in the air, I'd fallen short, pretty much like last time.

"We want you to have a good time during your stay," Fab said.

What we want is for you to stay out of trouble.

"Yeah." Mac grinned.

Fab held up her hand. "Keeping Cruz's blood pressure in mind, it would be helpful if you could keep your antics to a minimum."

Mother sniffed. "Your grandson didn't speak to my daughter for a long time after your last stay, blaming her until he needed another favor."

Maricruz gave Mother a snooty once-over, and Mother returned it in spades. "Cruz needs to have more fun, and he needs to understand the importance of having all of it you can while you're still breathing. I'm sure you'd agree."

"I have plenty of fun. My much-younger husband keeps me quite busy."

Fab interrupted the stare-down. "Back to the discussion at hand. Anything we can do, within reason, to make sure that your stay is a fun one and that we stay in Cruz's good graces, we'll make happen."

"Heard you were dragged in on a murder one charge. What's it like to shoot someone dead?" Maricruz made a choking noise.

"It's true I was questioned, and because I didn't murder the woman, I was released." Fab made the same noise. "To be clear, I've never *murdered* anyone."

Maricruz grinned at her. "This is the 'behave' pep talk, and I get it, so... I'll try. How's that?" She stood. "Gotta go hunt Crum down. I have him penciled in for tonight and need to let him know it's a go for bar-hopping." She gave a dismissive wave and banged the door closed.

"I know," Mac groaned. "It's my job to make sure that Crum... does what? Neither of them drives, so I'll offer to pay for the taxi so they don't get arrested for drunk walking. I'm not giving him the sex talk, as in don't do it with her, because if they're busy in the bedroom, she's not out creating havoc."

"I'm surprised he's her type," Mother said. "Crum's kind of... rough around the edges."

"He's rumored to be good in the sack," I said, trying not to laugh. "He's not into relationships, much to the dismay of several women in the neighborhood."

"I don't believe you," Mother said in disgust.

I stood and motioned to Mother. "Let's go make the rounds, and maybe we'll find a few more ways to gross you out."

"Hit the pool area first." Mac eyed the clock. "You can catch the last ten minutes of yoga."

"Goats?" I groaned, and Mac nodded. "I thought that was over." I opened the door, and we filed out.

Mac skated around the desk. "I had to sign up for four visits and no money back."

"Done the goat thing," Mother said. "I wasn't impressed the first time."

Fab linked her arm in Mother's. "Once again, you're going to have hot news to share."

We started down the drive, and I noticed Miss January on her front porch, slumped over the side of her chair. Her cat was standing on its head, propped against the frame and staring at an odd angle. I did a double take and asked Mac, "Is that the same cat?"

"That's the stuffed version," she answered, as if I was a stupe for forgetting.

Mac had had some woman make a stuffed cat to replace the taxidermied corpse of Kitty, who'd been retired to the top shelf of the bookcase in the office. "Some people have commented—well, Joseph has anyway—that Kitty Two creeps them out. It does me too, but I wouldn't admit that to him."

Furrball, the Maine Coon belonging to Rude, hopped up on the porch from the back, grabbed Kitty Two between his teeth, and disappeared.

I was about to run after them when Mac grabbed my arm. "Furrball will bring her back. He takes her over to his porch, and they nap in the sunshine."

"Has Furrball met the original Kitty?" I asked.

"He has and wanted to eat her, so no more alone time for those two," Mac said.

I caught Mother's horrified look. "Just know that when you're ready to downsize, we've got a cottage for you." If looks could kill...

Mac skated around me and over to Miss January's door and beat on it. When it opened, an older man stepped out. "Miss January needs to get out of the sun." Mac turned and pointed, as though he wouldn't know who she was talking about.

The boyfriend, Captain or something—he'd been around for a while and hadn't turned up dead or been carted off by the law—was anti-social. Even saying hello appeared to stress him out. He stepped out in a pair of baggy sweat shorts, scooped her up in his arms, and took her inside, kicking the door closed. It opened again immediately. "Thanks," he said, and closed it again.

Miss January was an original tenant with a myriad of health problems. The forty-year-old looked twice her age, flipped off the doctors' advice regarding her impending death, and drank, smoked, and collected men like she was a dude-magnet.

Fab led Mother over to the pool so she could get an eyeful of barely clad oldsters toning up with goat yoga.

"Aren't there code restrictions?" Mother asked.

"I'm sure there are and that Mac has checked them out and we're in full compliance." I turned and stared at Mac. Chances weren't nil that she'd done all that, but close.

Mac stomped on her skates and grouched to Mother, "You know how hard is to come up with activities that everyone hasn't done before? Your daughter ixnays everything. The latest was strip poker."

"She's no fun," Mother empathized. "Sneak behind her back."

"That doesn't always work." Mac made a sad face.

Crum's door opened, and Maricruz and he stood in the doorway. Clad in his usual tighty-whities, he laid a lusty kiss on the woman.

"See you later." Maricruz giggled, straightened her wig, and headed off without a glance at us.

He made eye contact with me and shut the door.

"Come on, Mother." I grabbed her arm. "That's enough craziness for you. Don't want you getting any ideas. You start misbehaving, and all fingers will point to me, although I'll blame Fab."

"Too late." Fab pointed. "More drama just pulled in the driveway."

"What the heck?" Mac sputtered. "I offered Joseph a ride to the doctor, and he told me that Homer was taking him. Now he shows back up in a taxi?" She skated over to the passenger side of the car.

"I can see where those skates come in handy in getting from one side of the property to the other in short order." Mother nodded her approval.

Joseph opened the door, shoved his girlfriend into Mac's arms, and climbed out. He hung his head back in the window and paid the driver. The old war veteran didn't look any worse than usual.

"Isn't Svetlana dressed rather skimpily for a doctor's visit?" Mother asked.

Fab walked over and stood next to Mother. "I imagine she's popular, and that she's rubber and full of hot air isn't a turn-off."

Svetlana, Joseph's leggy blond blow-up companion, had been willed to him, along with a suitcase of accessories, by a friend, and they'd been inseparable ever since.

"I like her because she's never any trouble. And Joseph hasn't called for a jail pickup since she came into his life." I waved and walked over. Mother and Fab hung back, and I shot them a look that said *be nice* if they changed their minds. Whatever Fab said to Mother, they laughed. "How was your doctor visit?" I asked. Joseph, the only other original tenant, who also had terminal health issues that he blew off.

"Not getting any better. But I'm not dead. So, win there." He cackled.

"I'm happy about the latter," I said, and meant it.

"Ladies." Joseph tipped an imaginary hat and winked at Mother.

I didn't dare turn around.

Mac looped one arm around him, Svetlana under her other arm, and managed to walk in her skates by Joseph's side and escort him back to his cottage.

"I need a drink," Mother muttered.

"Shall we fight about where to go to lunch?" Fab laughed as we got in the SUV and roared out of the driveway.

Chapter Seventeen

After we'd taken Mother back to her car and we were on the way home, Fab reminded me that she and Didier were expected in Miami first thing in the morning for her lineup.

"Dress normal," I told her. "You need to blend in, not stick out."

"Whatever that means."

"Jeans and tennis shoes. When you get back in the car, you can put on your heels. That's my un-fashion advice. Forget the housedress and slippers."

Fab wrinkled her nose.

With Fab in Miami, I had the day to myself and decided to treat myself to a coffee. I hopped in my SUV and headed to the bakery, deciding at the last minute against claiming a table and instead flying through the drive-thru. I grabbed my order and headed down to the beach. It had been too long since I'd just hung out and enjoyed the slapping of the waves onshore.

It surprised me to see my brother's SUV in the front row of the parking lot. I parked next to him and scanned the sand, easily picking him out where he was sitting on the sand, Mila and a woman I didn't recognize picked up shells not far away.

If this was a new woman in his life, she was about to meet his annoying sister. I hiked across the sand. If she showed the slightest sign of crazy, I'd pack her off to Alaska.

"Hey bro." I sat down, sharing his beach towel, and leaned over to kiss his cheek.

Brad took the coffee out of my hand, snapped off the lid, and downed half of it. "Thanks, I needed that." He handed back what was left.

Mila spotted me and came running. She launched herself into my arms and laid a big kiss on my cheek. "You here to play with us?"

"I'd love to." I gave her a big hug. She jumped up and ran to the woman, grasping her hand and attempting to pull her over while smiling up at her.

"And that is?"

Brad rolled his eyes. "Our new neighbor, Miss Allie."

"Neighbor? What happened to the uppity dude that lived there?" I asked in a low tone. My brother still didn't know that the man had sold Fab and I information until that went south in a big way.

"Alex informed me that he was moving and didn't offer a reason. Not being nosey like my sister, I didn't try to worm it out of him. I did give him a fair offer on his condo, and he accepted it without making a counteroffer."

"And you sold to Allie?"

"I rented to her. I bought the unit to control who lives there and make sure it's not some whack job. Like the people you rent to." He smirked at my glare.

"You didn't bother to run a background check?" I squinted at him. "If you'd done that, you'd have used your sister. Wouldn't you?"

"Not necessary," he said firmly, his tone telling me he didn't want an argument. "You remember Stanhope?"

"Your hot friend that you threatened to kill if he got within a foot of me? He could've punched my V-card, and you ruined that." I faux-pouted.

Brad rolled his eyes. "Just because he was my best friend didn't mean I was willing to overlook that he was a he-whore. No way was he doing my sister," he growled.

I laughed. "What's Stanhope the Third got to do with Allie?"

"She's a family friend, and he called when she was planning to relocate and I'd just closed on the unit. So far so good. You'd never know she was next door, and that's the way I like it."

I studied Brad like he was an unwanted bug in my house. "Not to be rude…"

"But…"

"Stanhope may be an upstanding DEA agent, but he's a weasel."

"This is where you should be giving me big thanks for putting an end to romance with said weasel instead of copping an attitude every time his name comes up."

"Yeah, thanks. If his parents recommended her, that's one thing; if it was only him, check her out."

"As a matter of fact, the glowing praise came from his mother." Brad turned his attention to Mila, who was squealing over her shell finds and tugging on Allie's hand to move her closer.

"My brother thinks I don't know him very well. What really happened was Stanhope called and Brad was all 'sure, buddy.' Let me guess... you'd like to explore her talents?" I asked in a simpering tone.

"Ssh, she might hear you," Brad admonished with a frown.

The woman allowed herself to be dragged closer, where she stopped and pasted a benign look on her face.

"This is my sister, Madison Westin. Allie," Brad introduced.

"Miss Allie helped me make Daddy's bowl," Mila said excitedly and beamed up at the woman.

I stared at her quizzically.

"I'm a sculptor and was invited to career day at Mila's pre-school. At their request, I came back and taught a pottery class."

"So you're married?" I eyed the tall, statuesque brunette in running shorts and a tank top.

Brad pinched my hip, and I somehow managed not to jump to my feet.

"Single." Allie returned the assessing stare. "And not looking."

"It was amazingly nice of you to teach a class to young kids. It probably wasn't easy to organize."

"It was worth it. The kids were great fun and inspired my creativity." Allie ruffled Mila's hair.

"We're picking up shells." Mila smiled up at her.

"Another nice thing," I said. The woman matched my stare-down and didn't flinch.

"His sister, huh?" Allie raised her brows.

"I'll admit, I'm a tad over-protective." I smiled innocently.

Allie hunched down and said to Mila, "I have to finish my run, and then I'm off to teach another class. Maybe we'll see each other again, either out here, since I'm here every day, or at home."

Mila hugged her.

Allie stood. "Nice running into the two of you." She turned with a wave and ran down to the shoreline.

"A few minutes of conversation with you, and she's on the run." Brad glared at me, then watched as she disappeared down the beach. "I'm surprised you didn't ask for ID so you could do a background check."

"I thought about it." I stood and grabbed

Mila's hand, and went to grab the half-full bucket.

Brad stood and followed us, holding his hand out. "Come on, favorite daughter, we're going to Gammi's house for lunch."

"I'd invite myself along, but I'm meeting Creole for lunch."

He picked up the bucket and handed it to me. "You take the shells, wash them, and return them all clean."

"That's kind of risky. You know my affection for shells."

"Must be some DNA quirk." Brad snorted, looking at his daughter.

"Would you happen to know Miss Allie's last name?" I asked Mila.

"Kent." She beamed.

I leaned forward, and we rubbed noses. "You have fun at Gammi's house. I know you will."

Brad glared. "You are not to—"

I threw my arms around him and gave him a big hug. "If Allie's not crazy, bring her to dinner. If you think I'm bad, wait until she meets Mother. She survives, then ask her on a date. Don't think I didn't notice you admiring her well-sculpted muscles."

He picked Mila up and set her on his shoulders. We walked back to the cars and waved, going in opposite directions.

I got to Jake's ahead of Creole and placed an order before walking into the bar. Loud voices filled the air—two men fighting over a traffic incident, one saying the other ran him off the road. It was unclear if his car had suffered any damage. Apparently, he'd had the bright idea to follow the other driver to the bar.

Several midday regulars had claimed stools at the bar and were turned sideways, one eye on any impending action, the other staring down Kelpie's top. Beer in hand, ready for the words to get physical, they each picked a man and slapped down a dollar.

"Shouldn't you be over there, dusting off your mediation skills?" I asked Kelpie, who was leaning over the bartop.

She straightened and shook her chest, the bells sewn into her bra top ringing. "You know it's good for business." She air-boxed.

"Heads up: Creole will be here any minute." I ignored that I'd just wiped the smile off her face. "I'll need a beer and a cherry-filled soda."

"Given the importance of your bottom line, how about you go out to the parking lot and stall Creole until, with any luck, the fight is over?" Kelpie grinned.

"I'm tired of hearing that hooliganism adds to the bottom line. Besides, too late." I pointed to the front door.

All six plus feet of sexy Creole walked in and came to an abrupt halt. More than a few heads turned his way. He sized up the situation, closed the distance, and barked, "Knock it off," at the top of his lungs.

The entire bar quieted. The rabble-rousers turned, wide-eyed, and took a step back. "Get out." Creole pointed. "Now. Or you're going to jail."

One of the men skirted to the door; the other beelined for Creole, fists up. I pulled my Glock and shot at the ceiling. "I've got another bullet just for you," I said to the man, who'd come to an abrupt halt and turned. His face drained of color, and he beat it out the door.

"Babes." Creole grinned. "You're so hot. You'd shoot his worthless ass to protect me?"

"You're mine. I'm about to make the same announcement to the women ogling you." I came around the bar and threw my arms around him.

"Lovey-dovey doesn't sell drinks." Kelpie humphed.

Doodad stormed out of the office at the sound of the gunshot and glared at the ceiling. "That kind of activity isn't allowed in here," he told me with a finger-shake. "Shooters are banned."

Kelpie grumbled under her breath.

Cook hightailed it out of his office and surveyed the damage, clearly not impressed. "Your goat burgers are almost ready." He turned and walked back to his domain.

"You're not funny," I yelled at Cook's back.

I grabbed the tray with our drinks off the bar. Creole reached out, and I brushed his hand away. "You first." I pointed to the deck doors, then followed him outside and closed the door. I set his beer down with a curtsy, sat next to him, and kissed him.

Doodad came through the door without knocking. "None of that out here either." He flipped on the string lights and ceiling fans. "I'll be back. Got some info."

"Bring yourself a drink," I called to him.

"Where were we?" Creole leaned forward and gave me a crushing kiss.

"Oh ick," Doodad said, coming through the door and sitting across from us. "This is a family joint."

"The family that boozes it up together..." I laughed.

"That's info on Hank." Doodad slid a sheet of paper across the table. "What little I could get."

I didn't recognize the address for him on it, and there was a different phone number from the one I had.

"Not having much luck getting information on him?" Creole asked.

"Nope." Doodad shook his head. "I put out the word—free meal and drink to anyone who had good information. So far, nothing. People know of him, but no one has stepped forward to say they're actually friends. Since you're asking, I assume no body's turned up."

"Not so far, but the blood was a match, and given the amount of it at the scene, he's presumed to be dead," Creole told him.

"It would take a little work, but you could dispose of a body and minimize the chances of it turning up again," I said, "the Gulf being a prime spot."

"I feel bad," Doodad said to me. "I introduced you to Hank. Who knew a straight-up business deal would result in you walking into a crime scene?"

"What about the brother?" Creole asked. "He ever come in here?"

"Ted hasn't been in that I recall. I showed his picture around, which I got from an online profile, and none of the regulars remember seeing him in here either." Doodad held his phone out, showing the picture he'd found. "Ted's not a popular fellow; he's got a rep for being an unfriendly dick. Keeps to himself and counts his money, which he's purported to have piles of."

"I appreciate you asking around," I said, and Creole nodded.

Cook came out, tray in hand, and served our food.

I looked at both plates. "That's what I ordered." I pointed to Creole's plate. "Not this one." I sniffed the one in front of me.

"I'm trying out a new recipe," Cook said with a grin.

"No freakin' thanks." I picked up my plate and attempted to trade with Creole, and he jerked his back. "Don't you owe me or something?" I asked him and pushed the plate away. "No way, Cookaroo."

"You've been hanging around Pink Hair too long." Cook stepped back inside the door and came back with a different plate. He set it in front of me and took the other one away. "You're no fun."

"This is more like it." I smiled at my chicken enchiladas.

Cook started back inside.

"What was that?" Creole asked, indicating the plate in his hand.

"Cat tacos." He disappeared back inside.

"You're fired," I yelled at the top of my lungs.

Doodad got up and went back inside, laughing.

Creole fed me a bite of his lunch. "I'm pretty sure he was kidding."

Chapter Eighteen

Fab called after she got back from doing the two lineups. Cruz had told her that the two women complainants weren't able to identify the woman who'd defrauded them. "There were five us in a line, staring straight ahead, and if you ask me, there was only a slight resemblance between us. Maybe they do it that way so there's no mistake who you're identifying as a criminal."

"Happy that went well," I said.

"Here's the interesting part—according to Cruz, once all of us lineup participants were dismissed, he showed the women a picture of Aurora. Both identified her as the one who defrauded them."

"Now you know who appropriated your identity and used it to commit crimes. If only she were still alive; I have a hundred questions I'd like to ask her," I said.

"Tell me about it," Fab groaned.

"Need your help," I said. "Doodad got me an address for Hank Michaels, and I'd like to do a drive-by." I'd promised Creole that I wouldn't pick the lock and go in and snoop around. I'd wanted to ask if it was okay to bug the neighbors but decided I didn't want to get cuffed to his wrist.

"I'll be there in ten," Fab said.

I grabbed my bag and went and stood out front with my thumb out as Fab rolled up in her Porsche and parked. Both of us got in my SUV.

"Care to make a guess what we're going to find at Hank's address?" Fab asked as she turned north on the Overseas Highway, curving onto Highway One.

I told her what Creole had said about not breaking into Hank's house.

"Didier told me not to have any fun today. Then laughed."

Several miles later, we turned off the highway, and several turns later, the address turned out to be an RV park that had room for boats, in and out of the water. There was even a section where one could pitch a tent. Fab turned into the entrance and swerved to avoid hitting a woman riding her cooler, which was decorated with Mardi Gras masks and beads, propelling it with her feet.

We wound around the park, figuring out quickly that the spaces weren't marked.

"I'm thinking that Creole won't mind if I inquire after Hank in the office?" I got up on my knees and leaned through the seats to grab a backpack off the floor. I extracted a hot-pink floppy hat that I'd found at a flea market some time back and plopped it on my head, then opened the glove box and pulled out a pair of face-covering sunglasses.

Fab shook her head. "I'd pretty much count on Creole being perturbed when he finds out, if I were you. I'm going to wait here and keep the engine running, since management appears to be sitting on the porch."

I got out and rounded the front of the SUV, surprised to see that Fab had the window down. She hadn't gone so far as to stick her head out.

"Hi." I gave the guy a friendly smile, trying to channel my old-man rapport. "I'm looking for Hank Michaels. I wanted to say hello, since I was driving through on my way south."

The white-haired man gave me a slow once-over from head to toe and nodded when he got back to my face.

Guess I passed inspection.

"Hank's been gone about a month," he said, his voice gravelly and loud. "Lit out in the middle of the night in his boat. He was paid up, so what do I care?"

"Any idea where he went?"

"None. Want to come inside for a beer?"

"My friend's waiting." I pointed over my shoulder, backing up. "Thank you, though."

Fab laid on the horn.

For once, I could hug her. I waved and ran back to the car. "Don't send gravel flying on the way out," I said, sliding back into the seat. "This was a useless trip." I told her what he'd said.

"Maybe not." Fab turned onto the highway heading back and hit the gas. "Now you know he has a boat. Wonder where it's parked?"

"I don't know if they're as easy to track as cars."

We'd traveled about a mile when we were hit from behind, hard enough to send the SUV into a spin. Luckily, Fab managed to regain control. I looked in the side mirror and caught a glimpse of a truck with huge steel bars across the grill.

"What the…" Fab sputtered, easing to the side of the road on a remote section of the highway.

"Not again," I groaned. "More body work for my baby."

The truck pulled up behind us, and a guy jumped out and inspected the back end.

"Let's hope the guy's got insurance," I said, getting out to scope out the damage.

"Sorry, I got distracted and was driving too fast." He held his hands up in a friendly gesture. "You know how it is."

No, I didn't know, but decided to keep it friendly. "How about we exchange insurance information?" I winced at the back-end damage—the rear door was caved in, the bumper mangled. It could've been worse; at least it was still drivable. Suddenly, the man grabbed me from behind, shoving the muzzle of a gun against my temple. The passenger door of the truck opened, and another guy slid out and walked over, gun in hand.

"We're going to walk over to the passenger side, your friend's going to get out, and the four of us are going for a ride." The one with his arm around me poked me hard in the side of the head with his gun. "You don't cooperate, and I'll shoot you both. The boss doesn't care whether you live or die."

"What are you talking about?" I refused to walk, and he dragged me along the shoulder of the highway, my tennis shoes scraping the concrete.

"You don't steal from boss man and live to talk about it," the thug gritted out in a menacing tone.

"We haven't stolen anything from anyone. You've got the wrong women."

"Take it up with the boss. One way or another, he'll get what he wants out of you." The man looked amused at the thought of what that process might entail. He reached for the passenger door handle. Locked. "Open up or your friend's dead," he yelled and hit the window with the butt of his gun so hard that it cracked.

"Damn you," I muttered.

He gave me an open-handed slap to the back of the head. "Shut up."

The other man went around to the driver's side. "Damn door's locked," he shouted. "Won't be for long."

Fab hit the unlock button. The guy

manhandling me jerked the door open.

Out of instinct, I went limp and slipped to the ground.

Fab's bullet hit the man center mass. He dropped, trapping my legs under his frame. Thank goodness he wasn't some hulk; I scrabbled out from underneath him and winced as I rolled away through dirt and gravel.

The other man didn't waste time; he darted back to the truck without a backward glance and jumped behind the wheel. He roared away from the side of the road and into traffic without looking. Lucky him, there was only one car close by, and it swerved into the other lane.

I jumped to my feet and was almost to the driver's side of the SUV when Fab leaned out the window and shot a hole through the truck tire's sidewall. The driver skidded from one side of the road to the other, then barreled off the road into the chain-link fence separating it from the water that bordered both sides of the highway. It took a couple of minutes, but he managed to climb out of the truck and, after a quick glance around, ran down the road, not having the sense to know that he stuck out like a flashing neon sign.

Fab pushed her phone into my hand.

I opened the back door, climbed in, and called 911 to report the accident, a shooting with possible dead guy (even though I knew he was dead), and a man on the run, then gave a description of our location.

"What was that, an attempted carjacking?" Fab asked in an incredulous tone, twisting around to look at me.

"It was far more personal than that." I moved to the center and reached over to lock the doors before leaning back. "Those two were looking for us. The dead guy rambled on about us stealing money from his boss. My attempt to tell him he had the wrong women fell on deaf ears; he didn't want to hear any protestations to the contrary. He was certain that the boss would deal with us, and then kill us, I assume."

"The boss?"

"No clue," I said. "I'll tell you one thing—he was absolutely convinced he had the right women." I reached between the seats and awkwardly hugged her. "You saved us."

"Let's hope the cops see it that way." Fab shuddered.

I rested my forehead on her shoulder. "They will."

"You've got the phone; you call the guys," Fab said.

I called Didier's number, and it went to voicemail. Same with Creole. They must be in a meeting.

Cars blew by us, but none stopped. A few slowed for a gander at the truck wrapped in fencing.

It took what seemed like forever, but finally, flashing lights sped down the highway, coming from the opposite direction. Three cop cars, followed by an ambulance. They made an illegal u-turn, cruised up, and parked before and behind us, blocking us in. For once, I wished that Kevin was in one of the cop cars, but no such luck.

I opened the door and got out before the officers did, putting my hands in the air and moving to the front of the SUV, where I leaned against the hood. Fab mimicked me and we stood together.

"The maybe-dead guy is over there." I pointed over my shoulder to the passenger side.

Two officers approached, one gesturing for me to move off the road and onto the grassy strip. The other officer gave Fab the same direction but separated us by several feet. The officer with me asked the who, what, and why. I answered directly, not leaving anything out. I also told him I had a gun holstered at my back and my permit in the car.

He ordered me to remove my Glock and lay it on the ground. The other cop appeared to be putting Fab through the same drill, and the third officer had drawn the short straw and was assigned the dead guy. Another cop car tore up the highway in our direction and took off in pursuit of the runner.

"I swear to you," I said to the officer, "I have no idea what that man was talking about, but he was after us and seemed certain that there'd been no mistake. He made it clear that he'd kill us if we didn't go with him and his boss would likely kill us if we did. When we got rammed, it never occurred to me that it was anything more than a traffic accident. If my friend had had any clue, she never would've pulled over."

"Your SUV will be impounded. You're welcome to sit in the back of the patrol car while we finish up the investigation."

That idea made me shudder. "Do you mind if we move farther down this incline and wait next to the water?"

"Just don't want you getting hit by a car." He smiled amiably. "You're going to need a ride home."

"We don't live far, so it won't be hard to arrange a ride."

He nodded and went to join his partner, who'd waved him over.

Fab was still being questioned, and now my cop had joined them. I had no clue how long we'd been detained, but I was tired and thirsty. Finally, one of the cops escorted Fab over, and she and I turned and stared out at the water.

"I told the cops it was him or us," Fab said in a low tone. "I told the whole truth, no weaseling."

"Why haven't the guys called back?" I huffed, then realized that I'd left my phone in the car, so how would I know?

"They did." Fab shook her head. "My phone blew up while I was being questioned—one call after another; it seemed like a continuous ring. I told the cop that if he was into a little wager, it was probably my husband. That made him laugh. It was. I handed my phone off to the officer, who talked to Didier, and I'm pretty sure Creole got on the line because the conversation turned to legalese."

"If the cops can't figure out who the 'boss' is and arrest him, as in pronto, then we need to figure it out," I said. "He'll be back. Nobody goes to all this trouble and gives up."

"I shared those same fears with the cop who questioned me. He raised his eyebrows but agreed."

I leaned my head against the fence, but the chain-link dug into my brain, so I straightened. Tiny annoying bugs buzzed in the grass. They were harmless but would bite you to death, so neither of us would be sitting down.

Fab's phone rang again. *Didier*, she mouthed.

Didier did all the talking, and they hung up.

"The guys are sitting down the street, waiting for us to be released. When that happens, we're to walk along the grass a hundred feet or so and we'll spot Creole's truck—it's parked that way." Fab pointed in the direction we'd come from. "I'll get our purses, and we'll be out of here as soon as we get the okay."

It seemed like forever, but we were finally released.

When we reached the guys, Creole checked

me over and lifted me into the truck. Didier did the same with Fab, and they got into the back seat.

"What the heck happened?" Creole demanded, barely able to contain his annoyance.

Fab went first and told her version of events. I went second, filling in the gaps and sharing the bits that she hadn't heard.

"How are the cops going to find this boss guy?" Didier asked, his voice ratcheted up beyond his normal calm and cool.

"They're going to have to squeeze the second guy hard and do it fast," Creole said. "In addition to assorted felony charges, he's looking at a murder charge. You commit a crime and someone dies, even if you didn't pull the trigger, you hang."

Chapter Nineteen

Fab and I didn't argue when Creole and Didier suggested that we lie low for a few days until whoever felt he was owed a debt and was willing to kidnap and probably kill us was caught.

Being the good daughter that I occasionally was, I called Mother, related the events, and asked that she let the family know.

"You know how to get on my good side." Mother laughed.

"I suggest that you start with Brad or risk an earful of whining about his being the last to know."

She'd done just that, and Brad had brought Mila and breakfast the next morning. It was a short visit, as he had to zip her off to nursery school — no time to question him about his love life, or lack thereof, or the new neighbor. It reminded me to send Xander a text, asking him to check out Allie Kent.

Finally, I got a call that the Hummer was being released from jail. Creole drove me to the impound lot to sign the paperwork to spring it. Spoon had called with the offer to have it picked up on a flatbed and hauled in for repair, which I happily accepted. The flatbed was waiting when I showed up, and I waved goodbye as it rolled back to the Cove. I'd turned down the offer of a loaner car, telling Spoon my beater truck needed exercise, so Creole dropped me at the office, where I picked it up and gunned down the highway, parking it in front of the house.

Two days later, Creole called and told me that he had an update on the case, and he and Didier were headed home. I suggested that he bring lunch and we'd eat at Fab and Didier's, which would be a nice surprise for Fab. He laughed. "Bathing suits," I said before hanging up.

I changed into my suit, tied a wrap skirt around my waist, slipped into flip-flops, and grabbed my bag. I packed light, since I knew that Fab's house stocked everything, including a couple of changes of clothing. I walked down the stairs to the beach, across the sand and down to the water's edge, then kicked my way down to Fab's manse.

I walked up the steps and dumped my bag on a chaise. As part of the surprise, I laughed to myself, I grabbed supplies from the outdoor kitchen and cleaned off the table. I opened the cupboard and sighed, missing entertaining family and friends and going overboard on setting the table, then took down silverware and plates for four.

"I shoot intruders," Fab shouted from the patio door.

"Napkins or paper towels? Your choice," I yelled back.

Fab joined me at the table and eyed the place settings. "Since it appears that you're entertaining in my house, I should at least know who you've invited and if it includes me."

"What *doesn't* include you?" I ignored her glare, which lacked heat. "The guys are on their way, and I asked that they bring lunch. I could've said my house, but you've got the water toys."

"We're going to need drinks." Fab disappeared back inside.

I grabbed a bucket out of the cabinet and followed. While she went and changed, I filled the container with ice and got out iced tea, water, and beer.

"Creole's got news," I said when she returned, dressed in a skimpy black two-piece, a gauze skirt tied around her waist.

Fab hung over the sink and looked out the window. "They just rolled up. You should've done the ordering; Didier just got out with three shopping bags."

"Leftovers. Make sure you graciously offer some for me to take home."

The guys came through the door, laughing. Creole banged it closed, which earned him a glare from Fab, and he winked. The bags went on the counter. "Oh no you don't." I waved them away. "Outside."

Fab peered inside, then opened several drawers and pulled out serving utensils, grabbing napkins and a roll of paper towels. Creole picked up the bucket and went outside. Didier took the bags to the outside table, and out came loaded cheeseburgers and french fries. Not Fab's favorite, but she didn't complain.

"The two guys in the truck from the other day were Mike and Don, Mike being the dead one," Creole said. "He expired on the side of the road before the ambulance made it to the scene. Don, the runner, was picked up not far down the highway. His only other option was diving into the water, and then, oh yeah, nowhere to go that way either, except to swim around in circles. Eventually, he'd get eaten."

"Stupid." Didier shook his head. "Don's story is that Mike accidentally rear-ended you and you went into a fit of road rage and started shooting."

"Except Don fingered you for the shooting." Creole pointed to me. "And your gun hadn't been fired, and only Fab's fingerprints were on hers." He took a long swig of his beer. "Another factor in your favor: Don and Mike had rap sheets a mile long. In addition, the truck the two were driving was stolen, they had unregistered guns in their possession, and—the part I hated hearing the most—pictures of the two of you and the Hummer. He had zero credibility."

"So it wasn't mistaken identity," I said. I'd been fairly certain that it hadn't been.

"Did the cops get him to give up the name of the boss?" Fab asked.

"Don knew how to play the game, having been arrested a time or dozen. He demanded a lawyer, wanting to broker a deal before he'd spill his guts. He stressed that time was of the essence or the big kahuna would relocate, which he was adept at doing." Creole stood and refilled the drinks, sitting back down. "You remember the briefcase debacle?" He glared at Fab. "Where you witnessed said case being pitched out of a moving vehicle and couldn't hold yourself back from investigating? That bit of nosiness could've cost you your lives."

"The one full of hundreds?" Fab said.

"It was related to that? I was sure it was more of the tricks by whoever's out to get Fab," I said.

"The geniuses on that job claimed ignorance, kept their mouths shut and, with the help of a lawyer they couldn't afford, got a minimal jail sentence. But their boss apparently didn't take kindly to your role in losing his money."

"I was thinking that, if it didn't get claimed, I'd be getting it back." Fab smiled. "Finders-keepers law."

Creole laughed. "Turned out to be a quarter of a mill. Wouldn't wait for that to happen."

"So this Don guy worked for the same man?"

Creole nodded. "The cops set it up for Don to call the boss and tell him they had the two of you and were headed back to the warehouse. The cops surrounded it and got the head guy, Rick Shaw, a nondescript man in his late twenties running a fairly extensive criminal enterprise. He didn't attract attention, keeping a low profile as he dabbled in whatever made him money. Judging by what they found, it was substantial."

"Apparently, Shaw wasn't big on banks." Didier grimaced. "They searched his house and found millions."

"Used to be a person could deposit their ill-gotten gains in the bank, but those days are long over," I said.

"Millions," Fab mused out loud. "What was Shaw into that yielded that kind of money?"

"You name it, and it was all illegal," Creole said. "Drugs, guns, money laundering, murder for hire. The cops had known about him for a while and had just embedded an undercover officer into the organization. Arresting him jumped the gun, but one agency didn't notify the other, and now they all want to finger-point," he said in disgust. "They're certain they have enough evidence to keep him behind bars for a long time. It's the murder charges that they'd most like to make stick — then it's a life sentence."

"In hindsight and all that," Fab said, "I shouldn't have pulled over and investigated the flying briefcase. But I did, and I'm happy that someone like him is off the streets."

"What I'm happy about is that we don't have to keep looking over our shoulders for another of

Shaw's associates. Do we?" I asked.

"Shaw's got the money to hire big guns... or not, if he can't show that he got any of it by legal means," Creole said. "He's also probably trying to figure out who outed him, and since you've never met, he knows it isn't either of you."

"We're back in business." Fab smiled.

Both Didier and Creole glared at her.

Chapter Twenty

Fab called the next morning with the bribe of coffee and told me to be ready to hit the road in ten minutes. She wanted to go by the office and didn't want to go by herself.

I walked outside as she roared up in her Porsche. "We're going all fancy in the sports car today?" I looked down at my top and full skirt, which hid a thigh holster.

"Heck no." Fab unlocked the door to the beater truck. "Hop in." She slid in and across the seat to unlock the door.

"You don't even like to drive that over-priced machine of yours. Trade it in for something fun." I got in and dropped my purse between my feet.

"Then I wouldn't get to drive your fun cars."

"What's on the agenda today?"

"Quick check on the office. In and out. I can't believe that I'm about to admit it, but I liked it when Xander showed up every day. He'd call if the building fell down or something."

"I miss him too. The nice part is that he still has time to work for us while finishing college."

Fab hit the drive-thru for coffee. "No cup

holder?" She turned up her nose.

"I believe people back in the dark ages, before cup holders and the convenience of coffee drive-thrus, held cups between their legs or drank their coffee before leaving the house." I almost laughed at her appalled expression. "Maybe the auto parts store carries holders that fit in the window."

"I know—they have something that fits over this hump." Fab pointed to the floor.

I laughed.

Fab took the direct route to the office for a change. She was about to hit the gate opener when she came to a sudden stop.

We both gasped at the same time. Police tape crisscrossed the front gate.

"What the heck?" Fab said, leaning over the steering wheel.

"Pull a little closer." I rolled down the window and hung my head out. "There's nothing posted. Does this mean we can't enter?"

"How would I know?" Fab snapped impatiently.

"If there had been some kind of crime committed on the property, wouldn't the cops have called? You, anyway."

Fab hung a u-turn, then slowed in the middle of the street opposite the property and snapped pictures. "I'm not going with my first inclination to drive through the tape and ask questions later."

I fished my phone out of my purse. "I'm calling Creole."

As soon as he answered, I described what we'd found.

"Do not enter the property. I'll make a call and find out what's going on. Didier and I are on our way." He hung up.

Fab parked one building down in the driveway of a seldom-used warehouse the owner used to store automobiles. The offices at The Boardwalk were only a couple of blocks away, and it didn't take the guys long to get there. They rolled up in Creole's truck and got out, their boots hitting the ground.

Seconds later, a cop car pulled up from the opposite direction, and Kevin got out. He walked over and inspected the fence, then crossed the street to us. "I checked with my boss, and he made a couple of calls. He has no clue what's going on. It's not official. Suggested a prank maybe. It's happened before."

"If this were The Cottages, I'd get a prank being played, but not Fab and Didier's offices," I said.

"Open the gates," Kevin said. "I'll go in and check the property."

Another cop car rolled up. The officer got out, and Kevin walked over.

"Please," Fab groaned, "no dead bodies."

Didier opened the truck door and helped Fab out, putting his arms around her. "We're going to stay back and let the cops do their job." He gave her a quick kiss, then walked across the street and entered the code on the security pad.

"I second that idea," Creole said, and waited with Fab and me.

Didier stood back as the two cops tore down the tape and entered the property.

"If Mac were here, she'd want that tape," I said. "She'd find some entertaining use for it."

It didn't take long before the cops were back. They stopped for a short chat with Didier; then the second cop waved, got in his car, and left. Didier and Kevin crossed the street to us.

"No signs of a break-in; everything is locked up," Kevin said. "The only thing is that your snake is on the loose, and since I think it's poisonous, it's illegal to own. In case you're unaware of that."

I yelped.

"What are you talking about?" Fab demanded.

"The snake curled up to one side at the bottom of the stairs," Kevin told us.

"Snake?" Didier shook his head. "We're not snake owners. I don't even have to ask if my wife is snake-sitting; I know the answer. No."

That got laughs.

"I'd have thought it wandered in on its own except for the cage, which was sitting on a table not far from where it was resting, sleeping. Didn't get close enough to check it out."

"Isn't snake-wrangling in your job

description?" I asked.

"Funny." Kevin's tone suggesting that I wasn't. "No. This is a job for animal control if it's not a pet. Or your other option is calling a snake wrangler and making sure that it's rehomed following legal guidelines. In case you didn't know, you can't shoot it unless it poses a reasonable threat to persons or property."

"So I guess I won't be making a new pair of shoes," I said.

"One snake probably isn't enough for two pairs, so we'd have to fight over him or her." Fab grinned.

I laughed. We both garnered glares we interpreted as *this isn't fooling-around time.*

"You got a wrangler on speed dial?" Creole asked.

"You're asking me?" Kevin shot him a 'you're crazy' look. "You should be asking your wife." At Creole's growl, he said, "No clue. My free advice, not knowing anything about snakes and not wanting to learn, is I'd get someone out here. Don't do it yourself."

"I know someone." Fab walked back to the truck to get her phone.

"Anyone want to place a small wager?" I eyed the guys. "I'm taking Toady."

"No thanks." Creole grinned. "I'm not in the mood to part with a dollar."

"You can owe me. Toady can lasso an alligator; a snake should be easy-peasy. If not, he'll for sure know someone. Before your nose stays permanently hiked in the air," I said to Kevin. "Toady's well-respected within the Miami police department. When he calls, they respond."

"Some people just rub you the wrong way. He pointed that out to me once," Kevin said.

I laughed. "One thing about Toady—you know where you stand, because he'll tell you in explicit terms."

"I'll show you where the snake is, and then you're on your own." Kevin started across the street, the guys following him.

"Take pictures," I called.

Chapter Twenty-One

The next morning, Creole was sitting at the island finishing his coffee when I hurriedly dropped a kiss on his cheek and attempted to skirt around him and out the door.

"Nice try." He grabbed the back of my shirt, and I skidded to a stop. "What are your plans for the day?" He eyed my outfit, lifting the hem of my full skirt and noting the Glock strapped to my thigh.

A horn blasted.

"Can't keep Fab waiting." I jerked to get out of his hold, coming up short. I couldn't tell him Fab's last words before hanging up: *Dress for a shootout.* I was sure she was kidding. "Fab was short on details. You know how she is."

Creole hooked his arm around me and opened the junk drawer, getting out the Beretta kept close for those just-in-case situations. "Don't think I won't shoot her tires out." He opened the gate, and to both our surprise, Fab was behind the wheel of Didier's Mercedes. My beater truck had apparently fallen out of favor. He led me over to the driver's side window. Fab waved but didn't roll it down.

I laughed.

"You laugh now," he whispered in my ear, "but later… I can outwait you," he yelled.

Fab cracked the window. "What?"

"You're grounded," he said to me.

I didn't dare laugh again.

Creole spun me around and dragged me back toward the house. We'd taken three steps when…

"Is this better?" Fab yelled.

He turned me back around, and Fab had her head stuck out the window.

"Where are you taking my wife?" Creole barked. "The truth."

"My client would like me to attempt to make contact with a man who's been named sole heir to an estate."

"Why not call him?" Creole's blue eyes narrowed.

"If my client had a number, he wouldn't need me," Fab said, her tone less-than-friendly, but managed to refrain from being outright hostile. "Quick job. We'll be back in a couple of hours."

"Was that so difficult?" He didn't wait for an answer, but walked me around to the passenger side, pushing me up against the door and giving me a big kiss. "Listen up." He lifted my chin and grinned down at me. "If your friend is full of it, call me, and I'll come pick you up." I nodded, and he kissed me again, then opened the door and I slid inside.

I rolled down the window and waved as Fab headed out of the compound.

"I thought you two were going to smooch all day," Fab grouched.

"If you didn't go out of your way to be so annoying, I could've skated out of the house by myself and you could be halfway to your appointment."

"No fun in that." Fab blew down the highway headed north.

"Creole's going to go over the video footage you sent him again, see if there's anything he missed. He was surprised that you didn't mention the security cameras outside the gate to Kevin yesterday."

"I wanted to look at the footage first. If I'd recognized the person who strung the tape, I'd have confronted him myself. Didier and I got into a disagreement over that plan of action, and I had to agree never to do that without talking to him first."

"The whole snake thing creeps me out." I shuddered. "I refuse to obsess over how fast things could've gone wrong if it was one of us who'd come face to face with it."

"It was a huge relief to shuffle the snake problem onto Toady and let him deal with it. He didn't even hesitate."

"He was probably excited to be called; his animal rapport goes way beyond dogs and cats. An added plus is that the guys like him and know he's not going to do some half-wit job."

"A uniformed cop hung that tape," Fab said. "Surprised me after Kevin told us law enforcement wasn't involved. Interestingly, whether purposefully or not, and I suspect it was the former, the man kept his face turned so the camera couldn't pick up a clear shot."

"Creole was surprised to see that he wore the uniform of a local sheriff's deputy. He sent Kevin a copy of the image in the hope that maybe he'd recognize the man. He reported back that there was no one in the sheriff's department with that coloring and build, said another deputy commented that the guy must have gotten his hands on a fake uniform."

"I asked Creole to find out if the wrong location was taped off. He was a step ahead of me and said that no police reports had been filed for the entire area."

I groaned when I looked up and realized we'd taken the curve north. "Miami? How much farther?"

"A mile or two."

"That's so vague. Knowing you, that could mean Georgia. Spill where we're going and the details of the case, and start by naming the client." Rule for myself: from now on, ask these questions ahead of time.

"Gunz—"

"I should've known."

"If you'd wait before cutting in, I'll give you

the details."

I made a motion to zip my lips.

"Gunz's got a cousin whose mother died and he's her sole heir. The thing is that years ago, Gunz heard that the son was dead. That wouldn't be a problem except that no death certificate can be found on file anywhere. Gunz had Xander do some checking, and he came up with an address, which would suggest that either the man is alive and well... or someone assumed his identity."

"Does he have a name?

"Are you going to be attitudinal all day?"

"Probably."

"Harris Olds. Happy now?" Fab wasn't interested in an answer. "Gunz has Xander checking death records around the state and researching old news items, as he remembers Harris dying in a bar fight over drugs or some such."

"Wouldn't Mrs. Olds know her son had been dead for years and thus named another heir?"

"They weren't close."

"That's an understatement," I said, ignoring Fab's glare. "If the Mr. Olds that we're planning on visiting isn't the real deal, then what? He shoots us to cover up that he appropriated someone else's identity? Alternately, I'm sure there's more than one Harris out there, so this one could be one of the other men."

"You're so dramatic."

"You want some drama?" Not waiting for an answer, I punched her in the arm.

"Oww."

"That was fun." I smiled at her. "Thanks for helping me relieve some tension."

Fab grumbled under her breath, but her mouth was turned up at the corners. "We're going to be folksy and friendly and not call into question his truthfulness or lack thereof. I've got an old photo, so I'll have a good idea if this Olds is the man we're looking for."

"Where exactly are we going? I'll put the address into the GPS for you."

"Everglades City."

"What?"

Fab rubbed her ear. "Could you lower your voice?"

"Maybe. This is the very last time I get in a car with you without knowing *all* the details." I'd already made a note of it for the future, which didn't do me dip today, but next time… I jabbed my finger at her. "Be prepared."

"I can play hardball too." Fab flashed her creepy smile. "I'll just drag you into the car." She flexed her muscles.

"I'm going to require perks unless you want me to whine the day away."

"Fine. Whatever."

"That was way too easy," I grumbled. "Snakes. Now alligators. Just another day. Is the report Gunz gave you in your tote bag?"

Fab nodded. I unhooked my seat belt and bent between the seats, pulled out the file folder sticking out of the top of her bag, settled back, and flipped it open. It didn't take long since Fab had already shared everything he'd told her. The picture was an old one, a teenager with a cheeky smile. No red flags stuck out.

The drive was just under two hours. Fab had been forced to stick to the speed limit, as traffic was light and the highway was heavily patrolled by law enforcement. Eventually, she pulled off the highway and turned to the south, passing a few airboat places and, surprisingly, an airport for small private planes. She veered onto a dead-end street that backed up to a small section of the Everglades on one side and ended at a murky strip of water. It wasn't hard to locate the address, even without an identifying number, as there was only one house within at least a mile — the rest were commercial properties. Fab turned into the long dirt driveway. At the back of the property sat a large manufactured home, a warehouse, and another oblong outbuilding with two cars and pickups parked in the front.

"I'm happy we didn't come out here at night. It would be creepy driving out here, the headlights the only thing illuminating the road."

"You could scream out here for years, and no one would hear you," I said.

"We're not going inside," Fab said adamantly and turned in front of the house, then turned again so we were headed back out.

"Harris Olds." I flicked the folder open and double-checked, knowing Fab's penchant for getting names wrong. "Do you want me to stand behind the car with my Glock, ready to shoot?"

A forty-something man came out on the porch in stained overalls with no shirt, bushes of chest hair sticking out both sides, and grubby rubber boots.

What had he been doing? I didn't want to know.

"He's not armed," I said. "Unless he's got a firearm stuffed in his pants."

"You're coming with me," Fab said, and got out. I followed. She waved to the man and called out, "Harris Olds?"

The man nodded and clumped down the steps. "We acquainted?"

"I'm here on behalf of your cousin, Gunz," Fab said.

"He in prison?"

I laughed. "He's shined up his image."

"Huh. What do you know? I'd invite you in, but the dogs aren't stranger-friendly. We can take a seat on the porch."

"This won't take long." Fab flashed him a friendly smile. "I don't know if you're aware, and if you're not, I'm sorry for your loss…"

Harris had a "what the heck are you talking about" look on his face.

"Your mother has passed on."

"So what?" he growled. "If you're here wanting anything for that woman, you're banging on the wrong door."

"She named you her sole heir."

"Good one." Harris belly-laughed. "There must be a catch."

Fab told him the truth without exaggerating or leaving out anything pertinent. "It was rumored that you'd died, but no death certificate could be located."

"You wanna know why folks thought I was dead?" Harris spit out.

Of course we did.

"There was a car accident fifteen years ago," Harris said. "My best friend, Robert, was driving, and he died on impact. I survived, but with memory issues, though eventually everything came back. The exact circumstances are unclear, but it appears that our identification got switched. The coroner called my loving mother and asked her to come identify me, and she never showed up. She was called several times and, after the first time, didn't even answer the phone. The mix-up was sorted out fairly quickly and Robert was correctly identified, but I never spoke to that woman again. And now, to hear she left me something, anything... She must've either forgotten she made a will or that she left everything to me. She must be spinning in her grave."

"We'll do whatever you like," I said.

"Don't go feeling bad for me; I can see it on your face. She hated me because I reminded her of my father, who was long dead. She told me that moving day was my eighteenth birthday; I moved out at seventeen. Never looked back. It forced me to make a life for myself; one that couldn't be taken away."

"I know a few things about wills. Everything can be handled in the mail," I said. "You can do what you want with the proceeds of the estate."

"I feel like I'm being pranked, but since you're the only two out here and neither of you has camera equipment, I suppose not."

Fab reached in her pocket and handed him her business card. "I wrote Gunz's number on the back so you can contact him directly."

He took the card. "I'll call him and then decide what I'm going to do."

"You can reach me at the number on the front anytime." She waved and got back in the car.

I waved, and with one last look around, I also got in. "This is a little too remote for me."

"Wonder what he does out here?"

"I'm surprised you didn't leave me to break the news while you snooped around the property."

"I thought about it… for a second, then factored in the dogs, which didn't sound friendly, and the remoteness and decided that, for once, I didn't need to know."

Chapter Twenty-Two

My phone rang as we were headed back into Tarpon Cove. Doodad's face popped up on the screen. "I'm afraid to ask why you're calling," I said upon answering and putting it on speaker. "If it was good news once in a while, I might feel differently."

"Maybe next time. Hank Michaels' brother is here. Again. Demanding to speak to you."

"I didn't know he'd stopped by before," I said.

"That's because he made the mistake of taking on Kelpie, who pointed a shotgun at him. Before you get 'tudy, it wasn't loaded, but he turned tail," Doodad relayed, sounding more harried than usual. "When he got to the parking lot, the pussy coward called the cops and wanted to press murder charges."

I bit my lip to keep from laughing.

"Kevin strolled in, his underwear in a bunch, and lit into him, saying, 'It would have to be attempted murder, since you're still alive.' I got the distinct impression that old Ted had been a burr in Kevin's backside before and he wouldn't miss him a bit should he expire on the spot."

"It might be nice if someone forwarded calls meant for me to me. Maybe I could've waved my magic wand, and the cops wouldn't have had to show up," I said. Fab and I traded a grin.

"Do you want to hear the rest of the story?" Doodad asked testily.

"You sound like you need a nap, but entertain me first."

"Some say sarcasm isn't attractive, but I wouldn't be one of those people." Doodad chuckled. "Where was I..." he said, drawing out the drama longer than necessary. "The cops swarmed the place."

"You just said that Kevin showed up and no mention of a partner."

"Just checking to see if you're listening." I waited him out in silence. "Okay then. Ted claimed Kelpie threatened his life and said he wanted her jailed for an eternity. Kelpie claimed she was scared for her life and protecting herself because Ted threatened her. The regulars at the bar—those that were left; as you know, the ones with warrants beat it out the back—backed up Kelpie. Based on the disgusted look on his face, Kevin believed about a scintilla of the various versions. Lucky Kelpie—Kev-o has a soft spot for her and enjoys staring at her double G's or whatever size they are."

"Do you think you could finish the story?"

Fab covered her mouth and laughed.

"Kev suggested that the next time Ted wanted

to speak to you, he should call and make an appointment."

"Free soda for Kevin."

"Please..." Doodad snorted. "We soda his ass up to keep on his good side, and that works some of the time, but only when nothing really illegal is going on."

"I'm sure you won't mind if I slide in a question. Why not call and tell me about annoying Ted before this?"

"Kelpie wanted to tell you in her own way, worried that you'd fire her."

I made a weird noise that surprised even me. Fab smacked my shoulder and gave me a finger-shake. I attempted to smack her hand away, but she was too quick.

"I didn't know that her way meant not telling you at all." Doodad let out a long exhale.

"We're going to be there in a couple of minutes." From the amused and interested look on Fab's face, I felt confident she wouldn't dump me off and make me go alone, which I was grateful for. "So give me the quick skinny on what Ted wants."

"He's got questions about his brother. Who is still missing, by the way. Turns out that Ted is person of interest number one on the cop radar. I'm assuming he's digging up any info he can to get off that list. I know I would."

"See you in a few." I hung up.

Fab pulled into the parking lot of Jake's and

around the back.

"Maybe Ted wants to hire you to track down his brother, or what's left of him." Fab smirked.

I got out and shoved the door closed, then trooped into the kitchen and down the hall to the bar. The barstools were filled with regulars, and a few of the tables in the open space were occupied. The doors to the deck were open, but I didn't see anyone outside.

Doodad, who was at the far end of the bar, saw me coming and waved, closing the space between us.

I turned to Fab. "You ditch me for a free drink or whatever, and I'll get even."

"He's over there." Doodad pointed to the only person in the place sitting by himself.

Ted noticed my approach and stood, coming towards me, pure unadulterated anger etched on his face. "You Madison Westin?" he barked, loud enough that a few heads turned.

"I understand you'd like to speak to me." I motioned back toward the table where he'd been sitting. "Shall we have a seat?"

"Right here is fine," Ted gritted out. "Not good for my health to be alone with you. This way, all your customers will know what a murdering whore you are."

All conversation in the bar stopped, and patrons shifted in their seats, their attention turning to the two of us.

"I don't know what you're talking about. If

you don't lower your voice, you can leave."

"There's not law one about how loud I can talk, and I'll be damned if I'll lower my voice. Everyone can hear. That way, if I disappear like my brother, the cops will know where to look and get it right this time. I couldn't care less what you did with my brother's body, but I'm not going to take the blame. You got that?"

Spit landed on my clothes. "I met your brother one time. We discussed a real estate deal. I went to check out said property, and it was evident that a struggle had taken place. So I called the cops. End of story."

"Lying bitch."

"It sucks to be a suspect in a crime you didn't commit. But you're the one exhibiting anger control issues. I'm telling you for the last time that I just met your brother and don't have a clue what happened to him. I suggest you hit the exit and don't come back. You're banned. You show up again, and the cops will be called. Force my hand, and I'll get a restraining order. That won't advance your 'I didn't do it' defense."

"You killed him over a real estate deal," Ted ranted.

"You've had a contentious relationship with your brother for… how long? Years, I heard. Now he's dead. Makes sense you're a suspect."

He lunged. Ready for him, I went sideways.

Fab pointed her Walther in his face. "Get out."

Sirens wailed outside. One of the patrons had

called 911. Because apparently a yelling match wasn't enough excitement.

Kevin rolled through the door first. "I volunteered." He waved.

Yeah, sure!

"Who wants to go first?" Kevin asked.

Ted angrily sputtered, "She's a murderer," and rambled on about this, that, and the other, ending with, "She needs to confess, and you need to lock her up."

Kevin listened patiently until Ted's spit hit his uniform the second time. Looking disgusted, he ordered, "Sit down."

Another cop strolled in and exchanged a few words with Kevin, who came over to Fab and me. "What happened?"

I told him what went down. "He thinks I offed his brother over that old warehouse."

"I'll tell him that you've been investigated and cleared." Kevin started to walk away.

"If I have to, I'll get a restraining order," I told him. "It's bad for business when I have to shoot customers."

"I don't like the extra paperwork either." Kevin smirked.

I turned and tugged on Fab's sleeve, pulling her over to the deck door. "Why me? Creole was there the day the two of us checked out the warehouse, but I didn't want Ted to know that and start haranguing him."

"Ted doesn't have the intestinal fortitude to

take on someone who's built like Creole and could take him out with one punch. My guess is that he's got no one else to blame, and somehow, you were one of the last people Hank talked to. It's stressful being accused of murder when you didn't do it. We've got that in common." Fab grimaced.

"The difference is that you're not going around confronting people, pointing the finger, making a scene. Thank goodness business isn't dependent on high-brow folks that couldn't risk having their image tarnished by showing up here. I'd be screwed."

"We both know that once word leaks about what went down, and it will, this place will be packed." Fab grinned.

Ted and the other cop went out the door. Once they cleared the door, conversation started up again.

Kevin came back over. "I told Mr. Michaels not to come back. If there's a next time, he'll leave in cuffs. I also told him you'd been investigated and weren't a suspect."

"Did that calm his shorts?" I asked.

"Not much."

"Do you have any clue what happened to Hank?" I asked.

"You know I can't discuss an open case."

"How about a headshake one way or the other?"

He glared at me and shook his head.

"I suppose it's been long enough that there won't be a happy ending, with Hank showing up alive." The thought of him turning up dead depressed me.

"I'm sure I'll see you soon." Kevin waved and walked over to the bar.

"You want my advice?" Fab clapped me on the shoulder.

"I suppose."

"We didn't know Hank, and my thought is if we did any investigating on our own, Ted would see it as evidence of our guilt if he got a whiff," Fab said.

I sighed. "You call the guys and I'll place a to-go order."

Chapter Twenty-Three

The guys weren't happy with Ted Michaels and didn't give him the free pass of assuming that he was acting out of grief since they both knew he couldn't stand his brother. I talked Creole down from beating the snot of him, impressing upon him all the trouble I'd get into if he were in jail and not around to keep an eye on me. I also told Creole that Kevin had given Ted the boot and told him to stay gone.

"There better not be a next time," Creole grouched like an angry bear.

"You're the best husband," I soothed.

"I might like where this is going." He grinned.

To build up more good-wife points to be redeemed when I really needed them, I informed him that Fab and I were taking the day off from fun and guns the next day and going out to lunch. I'd tried to sell Fab on a new dive that had opened recently, making it sound five-star, but she'd heard about it already and laughed at me.

I waited for her outside and waved like a crazy person when I saw her approaching in the Mercedes. I ignored her shaking her head and climbed into the passenger side.

"Whatever you're on, you need to cut back," she said, and stomped on the gas, then laughed and slowed.

We headed south and hadn't gotten very far out of town when Fab's phone rang.

"What?" Fab shrieked into the phone. "What the hell happened? Where is he?" She u-turned with barely a look, to a chorus of honks from the irate drivers behind her, and flew back to the Cove. "I'll be there in a few minutes." She threw the phone down and gulped air.

"You need to take a calming breath and slow down so we get to wherever we're going in one piece." I grabbed the cheater bar, which I hadn't done in a long time.

"That was Tarpon Cove Hospital." Fab had the steering wheel in a death grip. "The nurse administrator woman said she was sorry to inform me that Didier died in an accident and asked if I had a funeral home I wanted them to contact." She squealed through the tail end of a yellow light. "What will I do without Didier?"

Didier dead. I pushed down the sadness. I needed to be strong for Fab. "They could be wrong. We just talked to a guy declared dead by mistake."

"The woman said he had me as an emergency contact in his wallet."

For once, I was thankful that she knew every shortcut in town. I'd try not to complain in the future. Fab screeched into the parking lot, and the two of us jumped out and raced in through the entrance and up to the reception desk.

"I got a call that my husband died, and I want to see him."

"He'd be in the hospital morgue, and you'll need an escort." The woman, calm under the circumstances, asked a couple of questions and waved us to a chair while she got on the phone. "Someone will be right with you."

I grabbed Fab's arm and led her to a chair, then went back and inquired whether or not my husband had been admitted. She checked her computer, gave me a small smile, and told me no.

Creole wasn't there. Where was he? Why hadn't he called? Or my brother. They were all partners and always knew what each other was doing. Not a one of them would let Fab get an impersonal phone call.

Fab sat stone-still, her face devoid of expression, and stared straight ahead.

It seemed to take forever, but was probably more like ten minutes, before a middle-aged woman with a friendly demeanor approached and stood in front us.

"Fabiana Merceau?" The woman introduced herself as Luanne Field.

I grasped Fab's hand.

"I need to see my husband." Fab stood.

"Follow me." Ms. Field led the way down a

long hallway, opened the door to an office, and waved to a chair. "I need to tell you something and didn't think the lobby was the right place. I'm sorry... but whoever called you was mistaken. We don't have anyone here by the name of Didier, as a patient or otherwise."

I gasped. "How could a mistake like that be made?"

Ms. Field ignored me. "My assistant is checking the nearest hospitals. Maybe you got the name of the hospital wrong." Her tone suggested that she didn't believe that.

Fab put her hands over face and bent down.

I gently rubbed her back. "She didn't make the phone call up. I was sitting right there." Anger seeped into my tone.

"I wasn't suggesting... We've never had anything like this happen before." Ms. Field stood. "Let me check with my assistant." She practically ran out of her office.

"Where's your phone?" I snapped.

"The car," Fab mumbled.

I'd thought to call back the number and find out who did call. Instead, I pulled my phone out of my pocket and called our funeral friends. Raul answered, and I told him what had happened.

"I've never heard of that happening," Raul said. "It's quiet here right now. Dickie and I will call every hospital in the area and call you back. We'll help you figure out what happened."

I called Didier's phone, and it went straight to

voicemail. I left a terse, "Call me." I hung up and texted 911 to him. Did the same with Creole's phone. Then I called Brad.

"Where are the guys?" I demanded once he answered.

"They're in a meeting with the building department. Should be over soon. Why do you sound frantic?"

I told him what had happened.

"No way," Brad practically shouted. "Creole would've called unless he was hurt, and you say he's not in the hospital. I'll interrupt that meeting and call you back."

Ms. Field came back in. "We haven't been able to locate your husband in any of the local hospitals."

"That's good news." I stood and tugged Fab to her feet. She showed signs of having been run through a wringer and looked about to cave on her feet.

"I want to offer my sincerest apologies," Mrs. Field said.

I wanted answers from her but figured she wouldn't know what else to say since she didn't have any. "We'll be in touch." I pasted on a lame smile, led Fab out of the hospital, and helped her into the passenger side. She didn't even acknowledge getting in the car. And she didn't offer any argument about my driving. I scurried around the front of the Mercedes and got behind the wheel.

"Maybe he's not dead," Fab whispered, a bit of color returning to her cheeks. She leaned her head against the window.

My phone rang, and it was Brad. "Come to the office."

"You got good news?" I asked hopefully.

"I'll have something by the time you get here."

"We're on our way. I'm driving, so it may take a couple extra minutes."

I picked up Fab's phone and checked the incoming calls. I wanted to beat on the steering wheel when I saw that the last call was from 'Caller Unknown.' I started the engine and roared out of the parking lot.

"Now you're the one who needs to slow down and get us where we're going in one piece," Fab said drily.

"Brad wants us to come to the office. We're just a few blocks away. He's tracking the guys down now and will have some kind of update for us."

"I don't want an update," Fab said morosely. "I want my husband."

Fab wasn't the only one who knew a shortcut or two. I roared down a back road and breezed past her office and over to the Boardwalk. I parked in reserved parking and was about to jump out when my phone rang. It was Raul. I answered and put it on speaker.

"We called all the hospitals and morgues in a hundred-mile radius, and Didier isn't in any of them," Raul reported.

"That's great news. Owe you big. I'll call back with an update." I hung up.

"Didier's not dead," Fab said hopefully. "Where is he? I need to see him."

The pain on her face made my heart hurt. "Of course you do."

We ran upstairs to the office. Brad was waiting with the door open.

Fab walked in ahead of me. Didier was standing there with his arms open. She ran into them, and he picked her up and hugged her for the longest time.

I backed out of the office and into Creole, who hugged me. Brad followed, closing the door.

"What the hell happened?" Creole hissed.

We walked down the hallway and into the second entrance to the offices. Creole sat on the couch and pulled me down next to him.

Brad opened the connecting door and yelled, "When you're done smooching, we're in here."

I shook my head. "Ever the romantic, bro."

"A little levity is called for," Brad said. "I've had a crappy hour since you called. I can't imagine what Fab's been through… and you."

Fab and Didier opened the door and came in. Didier claimed a chair and pulled Fab into his lap. She curled into his chest.

"What the hell happened?" Didier demanded.

I gave him the details.

"I'm calling the hospital tomorrow and

demanding they investigate," Didier said in a terse tone. "That kind of mistake is unacceptable." He set Fab on her feet, stood, and scooped her into his arms. "We'll talk tomorrow."

When the door closed, Creole said in an angry tone, "Nobody makes that kind of mistake. Unless there are two bodies and IDs get mixed up, but that wasn't the case here. And then there's the number the call came from, which clearly wasn't the hospital's. This was done on purpose."

"It would have to be someone who knows Fab and Didier well," Brad said. "This was meant to inflict maximum emotional pain on Fab."

"Whoever did it hit their mark," I said. "Fab was devastated. She's the toughest woman I know and never caves under pressure. It was heart-breaking to watch her crack around the edges."

"Who hates her that much?" Creole asked. "I'd think the list would be short and she could point to a possible culprit."

"We've asked that same question a couple times of late," I answered in exasperation. "The dead flowers were weird enough. Then the police tape at the office, the snake, and now this."

Brad asked Creole a bunch of questions about the recent events. "One incident could be a fluke, but add them all up and you two need to be careful. I know that Fab is the target, but you hang out with her enough that you'll be in whoever's sights too."

"This all started after the murder of Aurora Bissett, which someone's tried to frame Fab for and thus far failed," I reminded him. "Shortly afterwards, these incidents started happening. A family member thinking she's guilty and wanting revenge? Except Xander ran a check and discovered that the only family is in France."

"Or the real murderer is frustrated that Fab's not sitting in a jail cell awaiting trial and is escalating the games," Creole said. "But to what end?"

"It's odd that one way or another, we've somehow gotten involved simultaneously in two cases without viable suspects," I said, thinking of Ted Michaels. Although he was an ass, I didn't think he killed his brother. "I find it interesting that the investigation into Fab's case hasn't turned up another person of interest. You can bet the cops are beating the bushes, checking out every lead. They either want to find the real culprit or make an ironclad case against Fab." I looked up at Creole and stuck my thumb out. "I need a ride home. Preferably one that will swing by the taco wagon and get us a couple orders of mini tacos."

"I have to pick Mila up." Brad stood. "I called Mother and had her pick her up from school. Told her something came up."

"No reason to keep secrets. Go ahead and tell her," I said.

"That will cement my favorite-son ranking."

Chapter Twenty-Four

After sending me a text that she and Didier needed alone time, Fab didn't answer her phone for a couple of days. Enough of that. I knew what it would take to force her back out of the house.

I rolled out of bed, showered, and put on a pink cotton swing dress, then wavered over my shoe choices before selecting wedge flip-flops.

Creole rolled onto his side, shoving a pillow under his head, and whistled. "Where are you going this early? Looking hot." He crooked his finger.

I grinned and walked over to sit on the edge of the bed. "I'm…" I blew out a breath. Instantly, his smile vanished, replaced by a look that said he was on high alert. "Ambush breakfast. It only works if one arrives at an early hour."

"Didier and Fab need more time."

"Nonsense. But it isn't for the lovebirds. I'm headed to Mother's."

"One might think that would switch off my trouble radar, but it doesn't." He scooted around me and got out of bed. "Give me five, and I'll be ready to go."

"That's not necessary."

"Yes, it is," he said flatly. "Whatever you're up to, why hear a vague second-hand version when I can get a ringside seat? The expression on Spoon's face when you get him up at the crack will be worth the trip." He disappeared into the bathroom.

"Don't dawdle," I yelled.

Five minutes turned out to be ten. He reappeared, still with his morning scruff, dressed in jeans and a button-down shirt, looking delicious.

He grabbed my hand and led me out the gate.

I squealed at the sight of my Hummer parked in front. I walked around and examined every inch, fingering the back and bumper where it'd been damaged, and admired the fact that I couldn't tell it had been in another accident. "Did you know?"

"Spoon called and said he was having it delivered as a surprise." Creole held up the keys.

I laughed, took the keys, and got behind the wheel, gunning the engine and heading out to the street.

"You went the wrong way," Creole said.

"Bakery first. Then Mother's."

The two of us went in together, and I practically cleaned out the bakery case, loading up Creole's arms with pink boxes.

"You sure you got enough food?" Creole asked with a raised eyebrow.

"I'm sure the leftovers will end up at Brad's."

There were very few cars on the road. I zipped over to Mother's and up to the security gate. I reached into the glovebox, pulled out a gate card, and stuck it into the slot in the panel. The gate opened immediately, and I pulled through and parked.

Before I could put the card away, Creole took it from me and gave it a once-over. "Where did this come from?"

"Friend of a friend of a... you know how that works."

"Let me guess—it opens every gate in town."

"Pretty much." I got out, closed the door on whatever he was asking, and went around to his side, where he had the back door open. "Can I help?"

He shook his head. "You'll need your hands free to pick the locks up to Madeline's. I hope you plan on knocking once you get to their front door."

"Of course." I'd bet on an eyeroll, but he bent his head down.

"Just a warning: you might see something that you can never scrub from your memory."

I walked ahead of him, just to show how efficiently I used my lockpick. Mother had given me a key, but there was no fun in using it. I punched the elevator button and held the doors open.

"I had no idea what your daughter was up to or that she wasn't invited," Creole practiced in a shocked tone on the ride up.

"Tossing me under the bus is going to come back to haunt you." The elevator arrived at Mother's floor. I flounced to the door and gave it my best cop-knock, loud enough to wake the dead. I wasn't sure what the neighbors' reaction would be and might have to suggest to Mother that she spread the leftovers around.

I heard rustling behind the door before it flew open. "What the devil?" Spoon demanded. He was dressed in jeans and a pullover sweatshirt, with bare feet.

"Aren't you going to invite us in?" I pointed to the boxes. "We bring food."

Mother came up behind him in a red mid-calf cotton dress. "You can come in with or without food. Would you like coffee?"

Creole and I trailed in after Spoon and down the hallway to the kitchen, where Creole set the boxes on the countertop.

"I smell a setup," Spoon grumbled.

"And it smells good." I shot him a cheeky smile.

Mother grabbed plates, napkins, and silverware and headed out to the patio. I reached in the refrigerator and pulled out one of the bottled ice teas that I'd rapidly become addicted to and followed. The guys put together a tray of coffee mugs, glasses, and a pitcher of orange juice, and Creole carried it outside while Spoon grabbed the bakery boxes.

Everyone filled their plates.

"I like being the one surprised with food." Mother smiled at me.

"Not so quick," Spoon warned with a slight smile. "There's a trap here, and it hasn't been sprung yet."

I sent Creole a glare to wipe the goofy grin off his face. It had no effect. "You men are so suspicious."

"With good reason," Spoon growled.

Mother smiled, enjoying every moment.

"I'm appalled that you would think I'd come over with a trap in my back pocket. I have a plan that I need help executing, and who better than Mother?" I smiled sweetly.

Spoon shook his head.

Creole held up his hands, conveying *I'm an innocent party*.

"I'm in," Mother said.

"Hold on." Spoon stared at Mother. "What happened to hearing the details before agreeing… or not?"

"Hold on, big guy," I said. "This is about Fab. She needs to shake off that cruel prank and jump back into being her bossy self. Especially before one of her clients calls me." I shuddered. "My big idea is to throw a party for those two — show them that we love them. I'd suggest Fab's house, since it's bigger than mine, but that won't work because Mother is the only one she won't say no to. So we'll have it here. Who does a party better than Mother? No one. An upside: Mother can boss me around and I'll see to the details."

"That's very sweet," Mother said. "I think it's a great idea. You came to the right place. I love a good party."

"What else?" Spoon tapped his finger impatiently on the island. "This family doesn't do get-togethers without a lot of drama."

I turned to Creole. "What do you think?"

"It's a great idea." He leaned forward and kissed me.

Spoon glared at him. Creole laughed.

"I'm thinking it should be soon, as in the next night or two. You strong arm Fab into a yes," I said to Mother. "I'll bring food that can be barbequed and foist the cooking off on the men. I'll grab dessert from the bakery and bring the wine."

Mother got up and went into the house, coming back with a notepad.

I leaned over and hugged Spoon. "Thank you for my surprise. The Hummer looks great. I already love having it back."

"It was a fairly easy job. It's amazing how many times that car has been put back together, and it's still running," Spoon said. "My guy wasn't out in the garage cussing up a storm, like he's done with some vehicles, so that's a good sign."

"Fab might dodge your call like she has mine," I told Mother. "If you don't get an

answer, phone Didier; he'd never duck the call."
I added, "Maybe don't tell them it's going to be
the whole family; let that part be a surprise."

"Is Caspian in town?" Creole asked.

"We can push that call off on Spoon, since
they're amigos of some sort." I squinted at him.
"You bonded over boat parts or some such?"

"Make it two nights from now." Spoon
scribbled with his finger for Mother to make a
note. "That gives Caspian time to fly in from
where-the-hell-ever he is at the moment. He's
told me he doesn't like to miss family dinners
and all the excitement they engender."

"Aren't you worried that you'll be minus a
friend when Fab's surprised with a family
dinner?" Creole asked me, smirk in place. "Fab
hates surprises as much as you do, if not more."

"I'm so charming; who can stay mad for
long?"

Everyone laughed.

Chapter Twenty-Five

The surprise went off as planned. Fab and Didier were shocked. Didier recovered first and was gracious, while Fab openly glared around the table, which everyone ignored. The rest of the family was present and accounted for. Caspian had jetted in and loved that Fab had been surprised, though he wasn't happy about recent events.

It was Mila who lightened Fab's mood, lifting her arms and wanting to be picked up. Fab twirled her around and turned away so they could engage in secret girl talk.

I'd come early and set the table on the patio. I'd stopped at the flower stand and got a long, low arrangement. Now everyone was seated, their wineglasses filled for the toast. Fab and Didier were at one end of the table, Creole and I at the other.

I stood up and raised my glass. "Dearly beloved... we're here tonight to honor and pay tribute to Didier." I took a sip.

"This isn't a funeral, Madison," Mother said in a stage whisper that everyone heard.

She sounded embarrassed, so I avoided

making eye contact. "Where was I?" I smiled at Didier, who winked at me. "We're here because Didier is family and our friend, and we want him to know he's loved. This beats a real funeral, where you don't know what kind of... stuff people are going to come up with to say. So..." I glanced around the table at the bemused stares. "Who would like to go first?"

Brad raised his glass. "To a good friend. Happy you didn't croak." He shot me a lifted brow, and I nodded.

I kicked Creole and sat down.

"Ouch."

All eyes turned to him. "Didier's a good guy," he said, and tipped his glass.

Fab laughed, which was good to hear. "It's very nice of you to arrange this party." She toasted Mother. "That day. That call. It's hard to put into words. I'm very happy this isn't some sort of real funeral thing." She glared at me, then leaned over and kissed Didier. "You can bet, though, that Madison would plan some splashy affair at the funeral home."

Everyone laughed.

"It's the damnedest prank I ever heard of. That's not a strong enough description, but there are ladies present." Caspian tipped his glass to Didier. "I too am glad this isn't a funeral. You're like a son to me."

"Be nice to hear that the responsible party was caught, so you'd get a few of your questions answered," Liam said. He held up his glass. "Happy you're still breathing." He and Didier laughed.

Liam had been adopted into the family when he was a pre-teenager and Brad dated his Mom.

"Whoever did it was clever; it took some careful planning to pull off without leaving a trail back to the culprit," I said. "And that someone deserves a bullet in their posterior."

"I agree," Mother said.

From the murmurs around the table, everyone agreed.

"I love asking this question," Caspian said. "Any exciting news?"

I raised my hand. "Almost got into a bar fight… but not quite. Girlfriend here pointed her Walther at him and he backed off. Then the cops showed up and escorted him out."

Fab filled everyone in on the details.

Before anyone could contribute their two cents and suggestions for me to sell Jake's, Liam's arm shot up. "Car theft is up on campus."

"That's big business and never seems to be on the downhill slide," Spoon said. "The university is an easy place to fill orders, as it has lots of choices and easy access."

"You have an alarm on your truck?" I asked Liam.

"Spoon had me bring it in, and his guy put one on." Liam tipped his glass to Spoon.

"Here's some news." I winked at Brad, and he

knew I was about to put him in the hot seat and shook his head. "Brad has a hot new neighbor. A slinky brunette."

Brad shot me a dirty look, emulating the noise a car makes skidding to a stop, which made Mila laugh. She was sitting on his lap, a book in front of her, along with a sippy cup of milk so she could join in the toasts. "I hadn't noticed."

"He's probably not interested because it's clear she could kick his behind," I teased.

"I went over and welcomed her to the building," Liam said. "Being all neighborly. Took sodas. If I were older, I'd hit on her, but she's probably looking for someone who's been out of high school a little longer than me." He laughed at himself.

"How about testing the waters?" Mother said with exuberance. "Bring her for a family dinner."

"Madison already had that awful idea," Brad said, an eyeroll in his tone. "Any sane woman would beat it out the door before dessert."

"If she can survive an entire meal with us, you'd know it's worth giving her a closer look," I said.

"She's not livestock." Brad snorted.

"No, she's not." I winked.

"Caspian," Mother said, catching his attention, "you should share something fun."

Caspian laughed and refilled his glass. "Nothing new here."

Chapter Twenty-Six

Creole had left to go to his office, and I was lying on the couch, updating some files on my laptop, when my phone rang, Mac's face popping up.

"Dead body," she whispered. "You've got to get over here."

I heard a scream in the background.

"Gotta go. Hurry." She hung up.

"Sorry, cats." I shifted my feet out from under my two felines, Jazz and Snow, and jumped up; true to form, they went right back to sleep. I changed into a jean skirt and t-shirt and slid into tennis shoes. Two minutes. I grabbed my bag and phone and, on the way out the door, called Fab. When she answered, I said, "Be ready to go in one minute."

I jumped in the Hummer and sped down the street to Fab's. I hung a u-turn, squealed to a stop at Fab's door, and laid on the horn.

Fab opened the door, arms crossed, and glared.

I rolled down the window and yelled, "Dead body. You coming or not?"

She disappeared back behind the door, which she left open, and I deciphered that she'd be coming. She came back out with her tennis shoes in hand. "I'll drive."

"Not today," I yelled back, gunning the engine.

I couldn't see through her dark sunglasses, but I suspected she was shooting me an annoyed look. She slid into the passenger seat with a huff. "This better not be a trick."

I roared out of the driveway and down the street, forced to slow for the opening of the security gate. "Frantic call from Mac. So... if the dead body isn't really dead, blame *her*." I blew out to the highway.

"I'd prefer that you go back to driving like an old woman so we get there in one piece. Plus, I'd think you'd be tired of having your car at Spoon's for body work."

"I'm channeling my inner race car driver."

Fab readjusted her seat belt and glared out the window.

I bit back a smirk and fairly flew to The Cottages, backing into Mac's driveway. If only I'd been a smidgen faster and arrived ahead of the cops; now there was no time to look around without a deputy breathing down our necks.

We got out, and Fab shoved her hand under my nose. "Give me those keys."

"You have your own set." I marched across the street and met Mac coming up the driveway.

She paused and waved to Kevin, who'd blocked the driveway and was getting out of his police cruiser.

"Dead body?" he asked. "Everyone was alive when I left for my shift this morning. What happened?"

Some time back, Kevin's previous place had blown up, thanks to a neighbor cooking an illegal substance, and my brother had moved him in, unbeknownst to me. I'd threatened eviction a time or two, but that had only resulted in threats being tossed back and forth. Now, enough time had gone by that we'd begun to tolerate one another.

"Maricruz," Mac said, as though that said it all.

I gasped. "She's dead?" I would be too, once Cruz found out.

"No, and that's the happy ending," Mac said.

"I wasn't able to finish my coffee, and you're giving me a headache." Kevin motioned for Mac to follow him. Fab and I weren't about to be left out and trailed along behind.

"Maricruz went bar-hopping late last night and brought home some kid, who died in her bed," Mac relayed. "She woke up this morning, noticed that he wasn't sucking air, and screamed. I was making my morning rounds and went running. Unfortunately — or not, depending on how you look at it — one of the guests called 911."

"This shouldn't come as a surprise to you, but calling the cops should have been your first inclination," Kevin said in a lecturing tone.

"Even Madison and her friend know enough not to muddy up a possible crime scene."

"Maricruz already told me that she didn't murder him. I believed her because she didn't want to call Cruz. You'd think if she thought she was going to need an attorney, she'd want him."

"Where is the pain in the... woman?" Kevin asked.

We'd arrived at her cottage. The door stood open, and it was eerily quiet inside.

"Maricruz grabbed a beer, mooched a cigarette off one of the guests, and went to sit by the pool," Mac said.

"You might suggest that she get her grandson on the phone, pronto," Kevin said as he walked inside. "He'll flip if this isn't done by the book."

"We had that conversation, and when I told her for the third time, she jumped ugly and told me to mind my own business," Mac said, turning to us without moving from her vantage point just outside the door.

I flipped my imaginary coin. "You get to call Cruz." I pointed to Mac.

She crossed her arms and stomped her bedroom slipper. "How am I supposed to maintain our copasetic relationship if I deliver news like that? We won't. So I'm not."

I hoped, given a few minutes, she'd come around. "The deceased? You said kid. Is he underage?"

"Oh heck no. Twenties. But she's eighty if

she's a day. He could be Cruz's kid."

I hadn't realized I'd been holding my breath waiting on the answer until it came out in a rush.

"Any clue how he died?" Fab asked.

"Maricruz didn't seem to know, insisting he was fine when they hooked up," Mac relayed. "I wanted to go inside and have a look but didn't think that was a great idea. Didn't want to leave my fingerprints or anything else pointing to me. I decided second-hand information was fine with me, even if I have to read about it online. Maybe she wore him out... you know, in the sack."

Fab made a choking noise. "I'm going to call Cruz. If it's left up to the two of you, my lawyer—who I happen to need right now, in case you've forgotten—might quit on me. I'd be stuck with ass-bite or whatever you called him." She shot me an amused glare.

"So sweet, sensitive Fab is going to deliver the bad news?" I questioned. "Don't go far because I'm listening in."

"I'm not going anywhere either," Mac said.

Two more cop cars showed up. We decided to get out of the way and made our way to the barbeque area, where we crowded around the cement table. It was the one place you could sit and have an unobstructed view of anything going on while still being enough out of the way that we might not be told to leave the property.

Fab pulled out her phone. "Susie, this is Fabiana Merceau, and I'd like to speak with Mr.

Campion," she said in an excessively saccharine tone.

I motioned for her to hit the speaker button, which to my surprise, she did.

"Mr. Campion can't take your call at the moment. I'll make sure he gets the message, and he'll get back to you, I'm sure," Susie said, although she didn't sound sincere.

"I'm standing here with a dead body and the cops."

"Hold on."

"This better not be a prank," Cruz said when he got on the line.

"I have some unsettling news that I thought you'd want to hear right away." Not getting an answer, she continued. "Last night, Maricruz brought a young man back to her cottage, and when she woke up this morning, he was dead."

Now would come the test of whether she could maintain her calming tone.

After a long pause, he barked, "What the hell are you talking about?"

I wondered if Susie had her ear to the door. Loud as he was, she could have heard from her desk.

"I thought I made it clear that someone was to keep an eye on her." There was the shuffling of papers in the background. "I won't be back," he snapped at someone, my guess Susie. "Fabiana, where's my grandmother?"

"She's sitting out by the pool. The cops are

here investigating."

"You tell Maricruz that I'm on my way and remind her that she speaks to no one until I get there and give the okay. Understood?"

"Anything I can do, you've got my number."

I clapped when Fab had hung up and put her phone back in her pocket. "I'm happy that you agreed to be her keeper and not me."

"This is a two-person job, and I'm nominating you." Fab grabbed my arm.

Mac's phone rang, and she looked at the screen. "It's Susie." She grimaced.

Just then, Crum whistled from behind a palm tree and motioned us over, so we cut across to where he was hiding. Mac followed us, lowering her voice as she talked to Susie, who appeared to be firing questions and expecting answers. Crum was dressed in a pair of ill-fitting cutoffs that were made for someone a few sizes larger than him, as evidenced by the jump rope he'd tied around his waist to hold them up, and a faded t-shirt that had once advertised someone's business but had since been doused in bleach.

"This isn't my fault," Crum said in an agitated whisper. "I was doing my part, keeping an eye on the missy. Took her out to dinner last night, and we came back to my place. She wears me out with all her game-playing. I fell asleep. Got me a good night's rest. I was surprised to find her gone this morning, but relieved. I'd just finished my coffee when I heard the screams. I knew right then that the day had gone to hell."

"You're telling me that Maricruz got out of your bed and went bar-hopping?" I asked, more than a little shocked. "Then brought another guy back with her?"

"She did what?" Crum huffed. "I didn't know all that. She could've woken me up, and I'd have taken a pill and you know…"

I covered my ears. "Cruz is going to flip. The last time she came here acting like a kid on spring break, he exploded and blamed everyone but her. But at least no one died."

"Happy ending." Fab smirked. At my *what the hell* look, she said, "I'm talking about her last visit."

I noticed Mac was standing close by, wincing, with the phone held away from her ear. "Is Susie on the line?" At Mac's nod, I wondered what she was yelling about and said, "Get some advice from her as to how to handle Cruz."

Whatever Susie said in response, Mac laughed, but stopped when she saw me glaring at her.

"Dead?" Crum shuddered. "You don't suppose she… I've got to go inside and lie down. Don't mention my name unless you have to." He disappeared, looping around the property back to his cottage.

"You better go and check on Maricruz, because if she sneaks off, Cruz will kill you," I said to Fab, who shot me a militant look.

Mac put her phone away. "Susie said not to get involved. Hang out and be available if Cruz has a question, but don't get in the middle."

The three of us took the same path as Crum, which took us to the pool area without having to cross paths with the cops as they did their job.

"What about our guests?" I lamented. "No worries about the regulars; they won't poke their heads outside until the cops leave. You'd think they were wanted."

"Don't you worry," Mac reassured me. "There's only one first-timer. Soon as the cops clear the place, the rest will be out on their porches, treating it like a show. This is the kind of activity that draws them in. The only problem is that when the next group checks in and there's no dead body, I have to field the complaints."

"You two better not bail on me," Fab said. "I might need you to cover the exits in case Grandma decides to make a run for it."

Fab and Mac trooped through the gate into the pool area. Maricruz was stretched out on a recliner, still in her bathrobe, a towel over her face.

Fab pulled up a chair and sat next to her.

I remained at the gate. Seeing Kevin coming across the driveway in my direction, I went to meet him. "Cruz is on his way and wants her to wait before answering any questions," I told him.

"I figured. Talked to the guests; no one knew anything, and they were a disappointed bunch."

He shook his head. "Where do you find these people?"

I laughed. "You're a cop; you deal with this every day."

"The coroner is on the way. We need him to sign off before we can haul the body away." Kevin cracked a smile. "I'm going to commandeer the barbeque area."

"I want to go home, but Cruz has named Fab Maricruz's keeper, so I'm stuck."

"Good luck with that. Fab's got her hands full." Kevin walked off with a wave.

I went back to the pool area and claimed a chaise under the tiki umbrella and out of the sun. The location in the far corner was ideal for a partial view of comings and goings without being noticed… at least right off.

Fab took Susie's advice, and when Cruz entered the pool area, she walked over and exchanged a few words before he went over and pulled up a chair next to his grandmother. Fab came over and sat next to me, and Mac hightailed it back to the office.

"Maricruz has no clue what happened," Fab told me. "She told me that when she woke up, he'd already expired. Her word—she couldn't bring herself to say dead. Freaked her out. Thought he was playing a prank, but it didn't take her long to figure out that he wasn't. That was when she ran outside."

"If you weren't a friend, I'd have snuck out of

here already," I said. "Now we can't; at least, not without being seen."

"Not so fast. I'm thinking you're about to get your wish." Fab nodded to Kevin, who was making his way back to the pool area. He paused inside the gate and motioned to Cruz, who helped his grandmother to her feet, and they moved to the barbeque area.

"I suggest that we exit through the side of the property; we can get back to the car without being seen," I said.

"Let's go." Fab stood, and I followed.

Chapter Twenty-Seven

Fab and I raced back to the SUV and jumped in, eager to get away from The Cottages.

"I've got to go by the office." Fab rounded the corner and headed back to the highway.

"I need something to drink," I gasped dramatically. "I should feel bad, leaving Mac to deal with Cruz, but who better? If I try to be helpful, he'll end up with another hate-on for me. I'll wait, and hopefully he'll have Susie call with his next set of demands and I'll know that all's forgiven."

"Mac confided that Susie swears she'll quit if she gets saddled dealing with Maricruz. The woman's demands are endless, and she's unappreciative."

"I hope this is the last time she visits." I grimaced. "Cruz's other relatives are nowhere near this high-maintenance."

Fab drove into the drive-thru. "Your usual?"

"Margarita to go." At her laugh, I said, "Okay then, iced tea, extra ice."

Fab placed the order times two and flew out of the drive-thru.

I settled back in my seat, tore the paper straw

wrapper open, and blew it at Fab. It fell short, hitting her on the shoulder. "You got a client waiting for you to show up?"

"Ignoring my phone for a couple of days wasn't my best idea; it garnered me a few nasty messages." Fab sighed. "Didier wants me to run a check on my clients, including ones I've done work for in the past, before accepting any jobs."

"Maybe not the ones where you're one hundred percent sure that the jobs are on the up and up, but for the rest... I think it's a great idea. Send the work Xander's way; that will keep him busy and happy."

"The whole drama that ensued after that horrible call about Didier brought us closer together." Fab smiled. "It strengthened our bond. I didn't think that was possible."

"I'm happy that something good came out of that dreadful episode." I reached out and squeezed her arm. "We're going to get this figured out. Find out who's doing these things to you."

Fab pulled up in front of the security gate and waited for it to open. "We shouldn't be here long; I just need to pick up some paperwork." A foot inside the gate, she hit the brakes. "What?" she shouted, pointing out the windshield.

A person lay face down in the parking lot, barefoot, in a blue hoodie and jeans. If I had to guess, I'd say male. The question was: dead or another prank? If this was some joke, whoever it was was committed to tormenting Fab. They hadn't moved, and you'd think they wouldn't want to run the risk of being run over.

"I don't think we should investigate." I double-checked to make sure the car doors were locked. The body still hadn't moved. How did it get there? The gate code had been changed after the snake incident.

Fab put the Hummer in reverse and flew backwards out into the street, waited for the gates to close, then crawled down the street, looking left and right. The street was empty.

I pulled my phone out and called Creole.

"You better be okay," he growled upon answering.

"How about 'Good to hear from you, babe'?" Total silence. "There's a dead body in the parking lot at Fab's office... or someone who's taking a joke way too far. I vote on the former."

Creole shouted for Didier. "Where are you now?"

"Fab backed out and parked catty-corner across the street." I heard a door slam in the background. "You'll be happy to know that we not only stayed in the car, we didn't even open the doors."

"Stay where you're at; we're minutes away." The guys must've run down the stairs, as I heard an engine turn over.

"It's nice to have an ex-cop in the family," I said to Fab after I hung up.

"There's a chance it's the real deal, and I don't have the stomach for a close-up of a dead body today."

"If it's a horrible joke, I'd think whoever that was would be climbing the fence or otherwise making his getaway... however he got inside. Which is a question we need an answer to, no matter how this plays out."

"You can bet I'll be all over the security tapes. I love these offices; I'm hoping I don't have to move because some crazy is on the loose." Fab rested her forehead on the steering wheel.

"Put a word in Caspian's ear, and he'll post a twenty-four-hour guard."

"I won't have to ask. Once he finds out, it will be a done deal." Fab pointed to the rearview mirror. "I guess Creole knows how to blow over the speed limit."

I flipped my visor down and watched as Creole's truck sped up and the security gate rolled back open. He parked off to the side.

Fab and I got out and shot a quick glance at the inside of the property. The body hadn't moved. We met them in the roadway, and Didier enveloped Fab in a hug while Creole laid a crushing kiss on me.

"I'm happy you two called and didn't investigate on your own," Creole said. "You coming?" He held out his hand.

I wrinkled my nose. "Gee, thanks. I'll wait here."

Didier spoke to Fab in French, and she responded with a small smile.

Creole and Didier walked across the street and entered the property. Didier locked the gate in the open position.

"You're not going?" I raised my brows at Fab.

"I told Didier to take pictures, and he laughed."

We watched as Creole nudged the body halfway up on its side with his foot and lowered it again. Didier, by his side, covered his nose. Creole stepped back and pulled out his phone.

"It's a real corpse," Fab groaned.

"Two bodies in one day." I walked over to the driver's side of the Hummer and hit the button for the liftgate, then walked back around and hopped up on the ledge, leaning against the side. Fab followed and stood at the bumper, continuously checking out the street. Creole and Didier walked off the property and joined us.

"Dude is dead all right," Creole announced. "It wasn't a recent event, as some deterioration is evident."

"The smell is…" Didier groaned.

"Be happy it's outside. You should probably still call my crime-scene-cleaner guy once you get the okay," I said.

Didier gave me a look of disbelief.

"He does a good job. There won't be a stain or any telltale sign."

A couple of police cruisers came around the

corner and parked across the street.

"I'm surprised Kevin didn't get the call," Creole said.

"He's probably still busy with the body at The Cottages," I said, then mentally kicked myself as I remembered I hadn't updated them.

The guys snapped their heads around and stared.

"Granny Campion went bar-hopping last night, got herself a boy toy, and he died in her bed." Why pretty it up?

Creole laughed. "Good one."

He and Didier went to meet the cops.

"Creole's not going to think it's funny when he finds out it's the truth," Fab admonished. "Nor is Didier, but I'm blaming you."

"I did my part; I told the truth. Creole will catch on quick when I ask him to follow up on the cause of death. It shouldn't take long to rule out murder."

Fab jumped up next to me and stretched out.

"Don't get comfortable." I watched as the deputy headed our way. "You're going to be happy that we didn't do any investigating. The questioning will be short, since we don't know anything."

Fab sat up.

"Who wants to go first?" the deputy asked.

I pointed to Fab, who didn't skip a beat and relayed the details. When she was finished, I said, "What she said. Thank goodness."

"It's a gruesome discovery," the officer said. "Any clue how the man got on the property?"

"No, and I'd like to know the answer to that," Fab said. "Guess we're going to have to tighten up security."

He thanked us and walked away.

Creole came over and told us that he and Didier would hang out until the police finished their investigation. "If you want to go home, it's your choice."

Fab and I exchanged a glance, silently agreed, and waved our good-byes.

Chapter Twenty-Eight

"Rise and shine," Creole growled in my ear.

I attempted to scoot away, but he was straddling my body. "Is the house on fire?" I whined, cracking one eye open. It was barely daylight.

"I've got an early meeting, and we're going to go out for breakfast."

"Not hungry." I rolled away and jerked the sheet over my head.

The sheet disappeared in a second. He scooped me into his arms and walked me into the shower.

After our shower, I chose a jean skirt and a top, slid into a pair of sandals, and threw tennis shoes in my bag. Then I asked Creole, "Do you have my whole day planned?"

Creole smirked. "I don't, but you might want to check with Fab."

He drove up to their door and parked, which surprised me, as I'd figured we were going to a restaurant. He came around and opened the door.

To be annoying, I attempted to slide out of his reach.

"No you don't." He grabbed my foot, slid me into his arms, and didn't let me down until we got to the door. "Try to behave yourself."

Who, me? I shot him a shocked expression. "Just know that if Didier serves kale, this marriage is on the rocks."

Creole made a barfing noise in my ear. I attempted to jerk away, but he held tight. "That's my way of commiserating if such an outrage were to occur."

Didier threw the door open. He had a chef's apron on over his jeans and t-shirt. He zeroed in on me, smiled and motioned us inside. "Did you leave your lockpick at home?"

"You have me mixed up with Fab. That's one of her tricks. You have to know by now that everything yours is hers."

The guys laughed.

Didier led us into the kitchen. Fab waved. She was filing glasses with orange juice. The island had been set for the four of us. Didier served us waffles hot off the iron, which he knew to be a favorite, while Creole filled the coffee mugs.

"Creole and I decided that we should have regular meetings, and what better time than over breakfast?" Didier said. "It gives you two the opportunity to update us on any issues that may have slipped your mind."

"You have to admit that we're getting much better at keeping you apprised of the body count," I said. "I shot off an email to our funeral friends and asked that they get us an update on Maricruz's lover."

"I wouldn't phrase it that way in front of Cruz." Fab winced.

"I asked one of the officers about a possible corpse at The Cottages, certain you were exaggerating," Creole said. "They both agreed there was one and were happy that they didn't get the call. One said, 'Everyone that lives there belongs in a mental hospital.'"

I sniffed. "I hope you set them straight; they're not all crazy."

Creole wrapped his arms around me and kissed the top of my head. "You only think that because you deal with them all the time."

"You hear back from our digger friends?" Fab asked.

"If they heard you say that, they'd think you were hilarious, and you're not. Me—they'd think I lost my mind."

"And…" Fab made a "go on" gesture.

"See what I have to put up with?" All eyes were on me. "I did hear back. Do I want to share?" I tapped my cheek, enjoying Fab's glare. "Okay. There were no outward signs of foul play—bullet hole, knife sticking out of his torso, bruises around his neck." I accented that with a choking noise, ignoring Creole's chuckle. "The coroner is running toxicology reports, and those take a while. Good news from Mac—Maricruz wasn't led off in handcuffs but packed her stuff and hit the road with her grandson." I held up crossed fingers. "Hopefully, never to return."

"You would think she'd want to keep a low profile until she's in the clear," Didier said.

"I wouldn't count on that," I said. "Although she's probably not going to like being under the spotlight the cops shine on her. She should behave, as Cruz can only protect her so much."

"Since you dropped the ball on Granny guard duty, let's hope he doesn't take his frustration out on me and dump me as a client," Fab said.

"I'm ignoring you." I scowled at Fab and stuck my nose in the air. "That woman needs a twenty-four-hour guard. The only thing that saved us from having mayhem committed on our persons by her outraged grandson was that there were a couple of other Campion relatives who were guests, and they gave him an earful. Got that tidbit from Mac and Joseph. The latter eavesdropped out his window."

"Mac must have done the same," Fab said.

"Please. Mac would be offended at any suggestion that she lurked out any window. She's got the guts-slash-nerve to stomp up in her latest creative shoe choice, park herself next to the renowned lawyer's side, and hang on like a persistent bug. Got that from another of my eavesdroppers extraordinaire—Crum. My favorite part: Cruz gushed his thank-yous to Mac, ponied up an IOU and cash, and told her she was to use both on herself and 'not on one of these people,' punctuating that with a wave around the property, as though she wouldn't know what he was talking about. He climbed into his bazillion-dollar sports car and was gone in a roar. Vroom…"

"So Cruz left The Cottages, not happy but not annoyed either?" Fab asked.

"A win for you." I shot my hand in the air.

"One murder discussed, now…" Creole looked at Fab. "You must have an update for us. I'm certain you went over the tapes as soon as you got back."

"You're not going to believe how it all went down," Didier said. "I wouldn't had I not seen it with my own eyes."

"The security camera caught a black Lexus pulling up on the other side of the street. A man got out, took aim with a pistol, and shattered the security camera that monitors the front," Fab said. "Lucky us, he wasn't very good at his job, in that he didn't check out the property very well and missed the two cameras on the sides."

"Then he jumped the fence?" Creole asked, looking askance at the idea that that was how it went down.

I couldn't imagine dragging a body over a ten-foot fence.

"Nope. He drove off. I rewound the tape several times, as his actions made no sense and still didn't answer the question of how John Doe got there. I decided that he must have come to check out the property and would be back. Minutes later, a helicopter hovered overhead and dropped the body."

"What the...?" Creole snapped.

Didier nodded, verifying that he'd seen what Fab described.

"Unfortunately, the angle of the other two cameras didn't capture any useful information," Fab said, disappointment on her face. "He was too far away to make an identification."

"You've got someone with a major hate-on for you and plenty of money to blow," Creole said. "Once again, I'm back to that list, which can't be very long. Do you know anyone with a helicopter at their disposal?"

"My father," Fab said. "But we can safely cross him off the list."

"It's unsettling that there's no easy answers," I said.

Didier stood and cleared the plates.

"I'll do the dishes. Fab can supervise, tell me what to do," I offered.

Didier winked. "They can wait." He refilled the coffees and sat back down.

"What are your plans for the day?" Didier asked, looking back and forth between Fab and me.

"One of my clients called and I've got a small job," Fab said. "Before you make up some hokey excuse that you'll have to take back, you're coming with," she said to me.

"That depends. Who's the client?" I asked.

The guys sat back, amused looks on their faces.

"Does it matter?"

"In light of recent events, yes. Some of your clients give me a headache before the job even gets started."

"Gunz."

"Hold off on the groans, guys," I said. "Thus far, Gunz has been upfront about his jobs, and he'd never knowingly put his soulmate in danger."

"Would you stop? Gunz and I are friends, business associates."

"I know you can't help that you're a man-magnet." I winked at her.

"You done?" Fab asked, out of patience with me. I nodded. "We're taking his cousin, Rena, to rehab."

"Does Rena want to go?" I looked down and bit back my first thought: *sucky idea.* "Let me guess, you're going to tie her up... cuffs, maybe? Gag her, so I don't have to listen to her whine all the way?"

"You done?"

"One more, and then I reserve the right to more after that. To where, by the way?"

"Homestead." Fab was clearly ready to strangle me. "There's some luxury treatment center up there. We'll make sure Rena's settled, wish her the best, and skate out the door." She turned to Didier. "See what I have to go through to get her in the car?"

"Not every time," I defended myself.

Creole stood. "I for one found this enlightening and think we should do it more often." He leaned down and kissed me, then motioned to Didier. "We've got a meeting."

Chapter Twenty-Nine

Fab pulled up in front of a nondescript two-story apartment building off a side street just south of the Cove and pulled into a parking space in front of one of the units.

"Put on your sympathetic face, and let's go get her," Fab said, and opened the door, turning to me. "When we get back to the car, I'll need you to sit in the backseat with her."

"No way. In. Hell," I spat. "This is why you needed me to come? Forget it. I'll drive. You sit in the back. So what if it takes five extra minutes to get there."

"When do I go on a job without you?" Fab asked in a placating tone. "Never. So calm down. I thought you were the better choice, since you tend to get along with all types of people."

"Good one." I looked out the window. "Is that Rena?" I gestured to a boney twenty-something woman who'd poked her head out the door.

"Let's get this over with." Fab got out and headed over to the woman.

I dragged my feet, coming up behind her.

"Fab?" Rena asked. "Gunz's friend?" The dark-haired, dark-eyed woman had a drawn look and a vacant cast to her eyes, her skin pale despite her tan.

"We're your ride to The Villas," Fab said with a big smile.

It was apparent from the way that Rena stood, door half-closed, that she wasn't going to invite us into the dark tomb behind her. In case she changed her mind, I took several steps back, ready to make up an off-the-cuff lame excuse why I needed to stay outside. She reached back with one arm, rolled her suitcase out, and slammed the door.

I reached for the suitcase, and she jerked it away. "I've got it."

Fab walked her to the car and held the door while Rena climbed in and put her suitcase next to her feet. I got back in the passenger seat and discreetly locked the door.

Fab circled around and got in the driver's seat, then surprisingly backed out sedately and drove to the highway. She waved to catch my attention and mouthed, *Talk to her*.

I made a face, about to blurt out something inane, when Rena started singing. Off-key. I turned in my seat. "Do you need us to make a stop anywhere?"

"Nope." She continued to sing.

Fab smacked my leg for more lip-reading. I turned and stared out the window. She'd taken the turn north, and I settled back for the short drive. I caught movement out of the corner of my eye and lowered the visor until I could see the backseat in the mirror. Rena was gyrating across the seat, one way and then the other, lost in the magic of her off-key singing. I stared as she shimmied out of her pants, then closed my eyes, giving my head a small shake, sure I was seeing things. Her top landed next to her pants, and she continued to sing in her bra and g-string.

I turned in my seat to face her and noticed that her vacant expression had been replaced by a manic one. "You're going to need to be dressed to check in," I said in a low, patient tone, the same one I used for Miss January.

Fab adjusted the rearview mirror.

"I'm in my happy place." Rena's voice had gone up several decibels, and she now belted out the unidentified tune.

"Step on it," I said to Fab. We needed to cut the twenty-minute drive in half.

Rena stuck her stiletto-clad foot between the seats. "Like my shoes?"

I did a double take. Where did those come from? Rena had worn a pair of tennis shoes out of the house. "They're pretty." I pasted on a smile.

Rena stretched out both legs and leaned back in the seat, and the short reprieve we'd gotten from her singing was over.

She suddenly sat up and leaned forward. "Are we getting closer?"

"Another few minutes," I said. "You should

get dressed."

"Nakedness releases your inner power," Rena sang out, her bra landing on her pile of clothes.

Fab stopped for a red light.

When it turned green, Fab hit the gas. At the same time, Rena threw open the back door, pitched out her suitcase, and jumped out after it. She tripped in her heels and landed in a heap, banging her head on the pavement. She managed to get to her feet, rubbing her knees, and was struck by a car. That driver hit the gas and raced off down the road. In fact, none of the cars stopped, although a few slowed. Maybe because she was naked except for a g-string. Thankfully she wasn't dead, as evidenced by her twitching on the ground.

Fab slammed on the brakes and jerked the car to the side of the road, to the irritation of the drivers behind us, who laid on their horns. Both of us jumped out and ran back to Rena, who'd landed partially in a lane and now rolled precariously from side to side, mumbling something unintelligible.

Fab and I each grabbed an arm, ignoring her high-pitch scream, and dragged her out of the way of oncoming traffic, not wanting her to get run over again.

I got out my phone and called 911, reporting the accident and giving the location. Fab crouched down, talking to Rena, who for lack of a better word was tripping out. Not being drug-savvy but having seen plenty of people on them, I put money on her deciding to take some hallucinogenic before leaving home.

"You need to call Gunz."

"You want to trade places?" Fab asked. I made a face in response. "You call him. He'll answer when he sees your name."

"Gunz will also know that it's not good if I'm the one calling." I took my phone back out and called him.

"What happened?" Gunz demanded when he picked up.

I told him. "The ambulance is here. My guess is they'll be taking her to the nearest hospital."

"Rena swore that she wanted to get clean," Gunz said in frustration.

I didn't know her, so I wasn't venturing a guess on anything. "I'll have Fab call you with an update as soon as she can." We hung up.

The paramedics got out and unloaded a stretcher. Rena had been somewhat calm while in la-la land, but when the paramedics attempted to transfer her to the stretcher, she went into fight mode. They managed to get her strapped down while she screamed nonsense at the top of her lungs.

The cops rolled up behind the ambulance and came over to question Fab and me. They wanted a description of the hit-and-run driver, but all I had was a dark sedan. Fab added a Toyota of some sort. They took down our information and directed us to the hospital.

"Since we're not family and will probably not be allowed to see Rena, why don't you call and make sure she arrived, then call Gunz and shove the problem in his lap," I said, ready to go home. It would be a long time before I could scrub seeing another person hit by a car from my mind. "Rena might be looking at some criminal charges. Whatever happens, they're not going to be releasing her until she sobers up."

Fab pulled off the road at the next exit and made the calls. For once, I was happy not to be listening in on Gunz's call. From the sound of it, he wasn't happy.

After Fab hung up, I said, "Even if I'd been sitting in the back with her, my only option would've been to handcuff her when she started taking her clothes off, which I'm sure she would've fought. I have no clue how I could've kept her from jumping out of the car. Grab her by the hair? Except I wouldn't have thought of that until after she hit the road."

"This is so surreal," Fab said. "Wonder why she changed her mind? She's lucky she's not dead."

"If you get another of these kinds of calls, suggest that your client call in a professional," I said. "They would've known as soon as Rena answered the door, or shortly thereafter, that she was high on something."

"Thank goodness she didn't die."

Chapter Thirty

Fab headed back to the Cove. "Lunch? Somewhere fun."

"My stomach just rolled at the thought of food. I'll take something cold to drink."

Fab easily found a drive-thru and ordered us iced teas, and then we were back on the road. I was about to offer a tip or two about how to handle Gunz when I noticed that she was distracted, shifting her focus from the rearview mirror to the outside side mirror and back again.

"You know I hate being in a car whose driver isn't paying attention to the road," I snapped.

"We're being followed."

"Are you sure?" I flipped my visor down. Stupid question, as Fab wouldn't make a mistake like that. She wasn't the paranoid type, although she had good reason of late.

"Black Lexus two cars behind us." Fab continued to stare at her rearview mirror. "I'm fairly certain I saw that same car on our way out of town, and now it's tailing us, hanging back, changing lanes. It's been behind us since we left the accident scene. You know what else? It looks suspiciously like the car from the other night, the one driven by the man who shot out the security camera."

"Maybe he's just going the same direction as us. There's nowhere to turn off, after all."

"You didn't notice, but I've kept to the speed limit, taking my foot off the gas to avoid hitting the brakes." Fab sniffed. "At least a dozen cars have blown by, but that car has slowed every time. You know everyone speeds on this highway."

"You're right. We'll have to lose them somehow." I watched in the side mirror, wondering what our tail was planning to do.

"You come up with a plan yet?"

"It's time to swap rides. The last thing we want is for whoever it is to follow us home. Retire the Hummer, at least temporarily."

"How do we do that?" Fab demanded. "The person dogging us will know."

"Stop at our favorite outdoor mall; we'll window-shop and buy some time." I picked up my phone and called Spoon. "Favor, please?" I asked when he answered. "You're on speaker."

"I got carte blanche from the wife to jump and then ask questions." Spoon chuckled.

"Fab and I will take Mother to lunch for that one. We're being followed." I told him about the tail. "I came up with a half-baked idea on the fly. You send out your flatbed to pick up the Hummer and take it to police impound, if you have an in; then I can arrange for a pickup."

"Don't have that connection." But it was clear from Spoon's tone that he liked the idea. "I'll have to work on one. How about I take it to a pay-by-the-week lot? Two reasons: I can make that happen, and if anyone shows up snooping around, you'll know. Later tonight, after hours, I'll send a truck over to pick it up and haul it back here. I can store it until you're ready to get it back."

Fab gave a thumbs up.

"Great plan. I thought we could come out of a store and put on a show of being shocked that it's being hauled away. Maybe stage having a few words with the driver as he leaves me standing there."

"If someone is following you, why would they break off to follow the Hummer instead of hanging around to see where you two go next?" Spoon asked. "Once the Hummer is hauled away, how do you intend to get away from this guy?"

"I'm thinking that the two of us can sneak out the back. I'd like to leave him cooling his heels and clear a path to my doorstep."

"I'll send Billy in his truck to pick the two of you up and drop you wherever you want. I'll have him keep an eye out to see if the flatbed picks up any interest. If the two of you pick up another tail, then I'd suggest calling Creole; he'll know how to corner them without their getting away."

"We'll find a parking spot close to the ice cream store."

"You're going to need a loaner," Spoon reminded me.

Fab shook her head.

"Fab's got that covered."

"I'll call you back when the flatbed arrives."

Fab picked up her phone, and from the tone of the conversation, she was talking to Gunz, who obviously wasn't holding a grudge about the mess with Rena. When she hung up, she said, "Gunz is going to leave a ride in front of the lighthouse. He'll have his guy deliver something that there's a million of on the road so we blend in. So now all we need to do is get there without being seen." She paused. "I'm thinking once we sneak out, hopefully we won't be spotted and tailed again."

"I don't think we should involve the guys at this point, if only because I don't want someone tailing them," I said.

"They won't like it, but I agree. This is going to reinforce their determination to have regular meetings."

"It creeps me out that the four us are on someone's radar and have to be constantly looking over our shoulders for a tail or worse."

"This is all my fault," Fab said angrily. "Who? Who has it in for me? None of these events can be written off as random."

"All of these weird things seem to be swirling

around the murder of Aurora. It's hard to believe that everything's not linked."

"You should probably keep your distance from me until this is figured out," Fab said, sadness in her tone.

"Nonsense. That's a terrible idea. That would mean you'd be traipsing around town without backup. Didier wouldn't let you out of the house unless you were shackled to him."

Fab wrinkled her nose. "I don't want anything bad to happen to anyone I care about."

"It just means that we're going to have to be on high alert. If it looks suspicious, then we call Creole, and if not him, then the cops."

Fab drove into the parking lot of the mall and easily found a space.

I picked up my phone. "We're here," I told Spoon.

"My guy's not far behind. Wait until he's got the Hummer loaded and then come running to confront him; he'll hop in the cab and take off. He's looking forward to being part of the drama, and he's also promised to be on alert. Billy should be there now and have already scoped out a spot to watch for anyone following the flatbed."

When I hung up, I said, "Ice cream's on me."

Before getting out, both of us changed our sandals for tennis shoes.

"The Lexus just pulled in and parked an aisle over," Fab said as she joined me and we walked into the store.

We both ordered a scoop of raspberry ice cream in a cup and sat in the window, with a clear view of the parking lot, leaving our sunglasses on so we could look around and not be noticed.

"I've kept one eye on the Lexus, and no one has gotten out," Fab said.

"Do you think he's following us or the car?"

"I'd follow us. I don't see where the car would hold any useful interest, unless you haven't made the payments or it was being jacked to fill an order. But then he'd have someone with him." Fab grinned at me.

We watched as the flatbed pulled up and loaded the Hummer. As soon as the driver was finished, we went running out and up to the man, who smirked openly at us. Everything went according to plan, and he drove out.

I turned to face Fab. "Now what?"

Fab pulled me close, shoving my head on her shoulder and patting my back. "I'm comforting you."

"Ouch."

She shoved me upright. "Let's see if the guy follows." She led me back across the parking lot, and we were just about to disappear inside the mall when Fab turned and jerked on my arm. Contrary to the plan, Billy got out of his truck, approached the Lexus, and rapped on the window. The car immediately pulled out of the space and left through the nearest exit.

"That was unfriendly," I said.

"The driver knows he was made," Fab said.

"Let's have Billy drop us off close to Jake's. We'll go down the walkway and loop around to the back. The gates aren't locked to give runners a head start."

"Isn't that aiding and abetting and punishable by a stint in jail?"

"Hardly." I snorted. "I don't direct them to run or allow them to hide out."

Fab smacked my arm. "Billy's leaving; you need to run after him."

"He'd never do that."

Billy jumped in his truck, drove over, and yelled out the passenger window, "Ride?" He laughed.

I told him where we wanted to go.

"Crouch down. Just in case. Although I plan on taking the scenic route to make sure we're not being followed." Billy waved us into the front seat. "I got a friend who lives at the trailer park; you can cut through there to Jake's and not be seen by anyone."

"Did you see who was driving?" Fab asked.

"A forty-something man. Difficult to get a good read on his features because the window tint was so dark. I did get the license number."

"I'm going to tell Doodad that your meals are comped. So don't be a stranger."

"You don't—"

I cut him off. "I want to."

"No one's following us. I'm certain the guy in the Lexus doesn't even know that you got a ride. Boss man's not happy with the latest turn of events."

"Reassure Spoon that we're on alert."

Billy came to a stop in the parking lot of the trailer court and cut the engine. "You know the way. Since I'm here, I'm going to say hello to my friend. No one will bother you on your way to Jake's because everyone minds their own business."

We got out and slunk around the corner unit and through an opening in the fence that dropped us into Jake's parking lot. A silver RAV4 with tinted windows sat in front of the lighthouse.

"Gunz did say he was sending over a popular model so we wouldn't stick out on the road," Fab reminded me.

"Where to?" I asked.

"We're going to drive around town, and once I'm sure we haven't attracted any attention, we're headed home."

I called Xander and asked him to get on IDing the Lexus.

It didn't take long for him to come back with a report that the Lexus had been stolen out of Miami Beach several nights ago. Another dead end.

Chapter Thirty-One

I'd warned Fab the previous day that if she planned to hang out with me, she'd need to accompany me to my businesses so I could make sure that no felonies had been committed on either property without my knowledge.

"What if I have a client appointment?" Fab demanded.

"You don't, or I'd have heard about it."

Fab picked me up, and we'd only gotten a couple of blocks up the highway when a car turned in front of us. Fab slammed on the brakes and made a disgusted noise. I craned around and slapped at Fab's arm. "Follow that Nissan. Hurry up."

I reached in my bag and pulled out my baseball hat and sunglasses.

"What's going on?" Fab demanded. "This guy appears to be headed out of town. How far do you expect me to follow him?"

"Roll up alongside him so I can get a good look. I think that's Hank Michaels. The dead guy," I added at her confused look. "I need a good look. Hank won't recognize you, but we had a face-to-face meeting."

It took several miles, some maneuvering, and a slowdown in traffic for a vehicle that had been disabled. Lookie-loos. But it worked in our favor. They made it possible for Fab to maneuver up alongside the Nissan.

"That's him." As Fab slowed down to let him get ahead again, I leaned back in my seat and stared out the window. "Hank Michaels is alive. Why wouldn't he step forward and put an end to the investigation into his murder?"

"What do you want me to do?"

"Follow him," I said without hesitation. "With any luck, he won't notice."

"What if he's headed to Georgia?"

I texted his license number to Xander with a rush request. "So far, every address that Xander has chased down for that man, he no longer lives at. Wherever he relocated to, he didn't leave a forwarding."

"Why do you care if he's dead or alive?" Fab asked.

"Because his dickhead brother, Ted, has started a whispering campaign all over town, telling anyone who will listen that I killed him and am getting away with it when he knows damn well that it isn't true." I blew out a frustrated breath mixed with anger. "Anything to turn the spotlight off him. I realize that no one I care about is paying attention to anything Ted says, but who knows what he might be able to stir up. You'd never let anyone get away with smearing your name."

"This Hank character must know that he's presumed dead and leaving his brother to hang for the crime." Fab glanced over at me. "Wonder what he's gaining by perpetuating this hoax?"

"Creole offered to take care of Ted. I could probably get a twofer, but then I'd have to visit him in jail."

"Neither of them is worth the effort." Fab got behind Ted and followed at a distance. "I'm good with going as far as Miami; after that, you need to be prepared with Plan B."

Fab dogged him down the highway. He exited at Coconut Grove and headed east, toward the water, eventually turning into a marina. According to the sign, they rented slips and storage. At first glance, it appeared to be several acres, filled with warehouse buildings storing boats. Hank drove past a large parking lot and continued down a narrow road, curving around to the side of the property, where it had limited parking and he got the last space. He got out and, without a glance around, headed down to the marina, where the slips appeared to be at full occupancy.

"You need to morph into sneaky-girl and get out and follow him," I said to Fab. "I'll circle the property, more than once if I have to, and pick you up." She parked and we both got out. I got behind the wheel, rolled down the window, and yelled, "Pictures."

Fab didn't break her stride and waved over her head.

I idled and watched as she followed Hank down the docks. He never turned around or seemed aware that anyone was behind him. That told me he was comfortable in his surroundings. I sat where I was until a pickup pulled around the corner. I looped back around and, this time, found a parking space, but it was a bad location for monitoring comings and goings, so I moved back to my old spot, getting over so hopefully, if another car appeared, it could go around. Still, it would be a tight fit. I needed to replace the old binoculars, which had been stolen out of the SUV months ago. They'd be helpful right now.

There were three rows of slips with a dozen or so boats in each row. Fab followed Hank to the last row and disappeared, reappearing in less than a minute. When she got to the end of the dock and was about to come out the gate, I got out and went around to climb in the passenger side.

"Got pictures of Hank's boat and the ones next to it, which clearly identifies the location." Fab handed me her phone. "Now what?"

"I'd like to confront him." Seeing the look of *no way* on Fab's face, I added. "This job requires muscle. It appears that Hank faked his death and set me up to discover the 'crime scene.'" I made air quotes. "And oh yeah, even if it wasn't his plan to set his brother up to take the rap, he's not stepping forward and putting an end to the man being investigated by police. So who knows how desperate he'd get at seeing me again."

"For a man with secrets, and big ones, he's not very aware of the people around him," Fab said. "You've got the upper hand in that you know where to find him and he has no clue that you know."

"Hopefully, he's not about to blow town."

"Why would he?" Fab shrugged, dismissing the idea. "He doesn't know anyone's onto him. When following him, I took stock of the other boats, and judging by how they're secured, I'd be surprised if any of the other owners are living aboard. Wonder if the people that run this place even know he's staying on his boat?" She tugged the end of my hair. "I volunteer Didier and myself to come back with you. I don't think you and Creole should confront him on your own."

"Creole's going to want me to call the cops, reminding me that it's their job to figure out what old Hank is up to." I gritted my teeth at the thought of not confronting him and getting a couple of questions answered. "Which I agree is a great idea… after Hank and I have a chat."

"Is it a crime to fake your own death?"

"That's an interesting question."

Chapter Thirty-Two

It took two days to coordinate a return trip to Coconut Grove. Creole had another meeting with the county that took precedence, in that it was about getting final permits for a project. I'd already begun to plan how Fab and I could sneak out in the early dawn hours and what it would take to confront the man, but the downside of being married to someone who knows you almost better than you know yourself is he caught onto the mental plotting immediately.

He tipped my chin up so I had to look him in the eye. "Promise me you'll wait for me to go with you. From what you told me, I doubt Hank's going anywhere."

"You're right."

"That wasn't a promise, sweetness." His glare missed the mark, as he almost laughed. "Don't think I won't play hardball."

"I promise. To wait."

"Hands out in front you and repeat that." He twirled his finger.

I did what he asked. "I wouldn't do something so sneaky as promise with my fingers crossed. Good idea, though. Maybe next time." I'd already discarded the idea of sneaking out at dawn, knowing I'd never get out the door without drugging him.

The next morning, Creole and I got into the SUV and drove the short distance to Fab's. Before I could suggest he lean on the horn, the door opened and the two came down the steps.

Creole got out, walked around the front, and handed Fab the keys. "Since you know where we're going..." He opened the passenger door and helped me out and into the back, sliding in next to me.

If Fab had been somewhere once, she didn't need directions to get there again.

Didier got in the front and looked over the seat. "Do you miss all the room your car has?"

"This is a great loaner, but it makes me appreciate the Hummer that much more," I said. "But I'm leaving it stored until the case with Fab is solved."

Fab cut through the coffee drive-thru without having to be asked and ordered for the four of us before hitting the highway.

"What's the plan?" Creole asked once we turned north.

Didier turned. "This Hank character probably won't be very cooperative if you shoot him first," he teased.

"I just want answers; no bloodshed." I scooted over next to Creole and laid my head on his shoulder.

"Once he gets over the shock of being discovered, he's not going to like having his secret discovered," Fab said. "Oh well."

"There's the off chance that Hank doesn't know he's been presumed dead and all the drama that's ensued," I said.

"Not likely," Creole grouched.

We drove the rest of the way in silence, retracing the same route as the other day. Fab cruised the parking lot and located Hank's car, parking next to it.

"Here's how this is going to go down," Creole said. "Didier and I are going to board first. You wait on the dock. As soon as we have a look around, we'll give you the signal."

The four of us got out, and Fab led the way down the dock. It was easy to spot his boat, as he was the only one sitting on the deck drinking coffee.

Creole and Didier boarded without an invitation, which had Hank's head spinning around. Creole did all the talking. After a minute, he turned and motioned to Fab and I, and we climbed the ladder.

Hank wasn't the least bit happy with the intrusion. He checked Fab and me out, settled on me, and said, "You. Madison Something."

"That would be me." I took a seat on the back bench.

The other three hung back.

"I'm certain you know the whole town thinks

you're dead, since you set it up that way and used me to do it." Although angry, I kept my tone even.

"Nothing personal."

"How could it be, since we hadn't even met before? But I'm entitled to some answers."

"Don't know what you're doing here and don't care." Hank pointed to the stairs down to the dock. "Leave before I call the cops."

It was an easy bluff to call. "Go ahead and call. I'll wait right here. You can tell them we boarded without permission, which will probably be a 'so what' after they find out about your phony death. Did you want to use my phone?" I held it out.

Hank waved my hand away. "No hard feelings. You were just a means to an end."

"What was your end game?"

He didn't say anything, just turned his head and stared out at the water.

"The cops think your brother murdered you," I told him. "He confronted me in the middle of Jake's, falling all over himself to blame me, even though there isn't a scintilla of evidence. I was never a suspect, but did that matter to him and his attempt to ruin my business? No." Of course, if I were named a suspect, the bar would be standing room only for weeks. But I certainly wasn't going to mention that to old Hank.

"I don't know why you're whining. You're not in jail, and neither is that bastard, Ted."

"So this was all about some family feud with your brother? Isn't setting him up to fry for your murder when you're not even dead going a little far? If he were executed and you were found to be alive, you'd spend the rest of your life in prison." I struggled to keep from losing my temper.

"My loving brother has screwed me one time too many," Hank shouted at the top of his lungs. "Always getting the *damn* upper hand. The one time I one-upped him was over that stupid building." His fist shot in the air. "I put out the word that it was for sale and at a bargain, knowing that Ted would, using a straw buyer, scheme a way to buy it for a song, then turn around and rub my nose in it."

"So you decided to sell me a 'poor me' story that you were practically destitute as part of the hoax?"

"You women are so sentimental." Hank sniffed, amused. "I'm not going broke anytime soon. My net worth equals my brother's," he boasted. "We've always been competitive."

"If that's the case, then you overplayed your hand, and I'm surprised that he didn't see through your ruse from the start. Maybe he did, hence the reason you involved me in your game." Getting even was quite the motivator for some people, and apparently, he was one.

"Ted's not the brightest." He didn't believe that or he wouldn't find his brother worthy of being taken down.

"Where did the blood inside the building come from?" I'd had a few thoughts about that since finding out he was alive and rehashing the events over and over.

"Mine," Hank declared, proud of himself. "That was easy enough. Had my blood drawn a couple of times and hired someone to create a crime scene."

"Some artist?" I said sarcastically.

"That's what I thought. Got my money's worth, now didn't I?"

I really wanted to knock the smug smile off his face. "Let me see if I got this. Brotherly feud. You set him up for your murder. Out of curiosity, would you've stood by while he got executed? Attend the execution maybe?" He didn't seem overly concerned about Ted's death as a possible outcome.

Hank smiled. "Moot point, as he hasn't even been arrested." Noticing my look of disgust, he said, "You don't know what it's like being the youngest, always trailing just behind."

I was the youngest and would never plan such an elaborate ruse. I wasn't about to disclose that fact, as the less he knew about me, the better. "Here's how this is going to go. You've got one day to come back to life. I don't give a rat's flip about your petty grievances with your brother. What I do care about is my reputation, and I won't have it whispered for years that I offed you. One thing I feel fairly certain about when it comes to Ted—he'd keep the whisper mill going."

"I'm not—"

I ran my finger across my throat. "Yes, you are. If you don't, I'll be the one to call the cops. Faking your death might not be a crime, but I bet they'd look long and hard for something to hang you with for wasting their time. You end this sham or I'll sue you... for emotional distress and loss of consortium." I looked at Creole, who grinned and winked. "Drain a few million from your crusty fingers."

"Maybe we could—"

I stood. "No, we couldn't." I started for the steps and turned. "You've got one day. I suggest you call your lawyer and get busy on a story. Run again and we'll find you again."

Didier and Fab had climbed down the steps and were standing on the dock. I followed Creole, who held out his hand and helped me down.

Hank leaned over the side. "The building is still for sale. But not at a bargain."

I turned. "You can take that building and shove it up your—"

"Clean up your mess," Creole cut in. "Stay out of the Cove. It would only take a phone call to make you disappear without a trace."

The four of us walked up the dock, not another person in sight.

"I thought he'd have a better story than petty revenge over one-upmanship," I said.

Creole hugged me to his side.

Once we were back in the car, I whispered to Creole, "Thank you for coming," and kissed him.

Chapter Thirty-Three

We were almost back to the Cove when Fab's phone rang. She didn't answer, which was a first. It rang again. Didier picked it up and looked at the screen. "It's your friend, Gunz." He put it back down.

"Wonder what he wants. You want me to answer?" I asked.

It rang a third time, and Fab answered.

"Fab never puts him on speaker," I told Creole.

After a few noncommittal responses, she hung up.

I waited for Didier to ask, and when he didn't, I did. "What did Gunz want?"

"Yeah," the guys echoed.

"He's got a job," Fab announced to a groan from the guys. "He wants me to meet with some shyster contractor that screwed one of his relatives, follow him, and get an address. He's left keys for some ramshackle house at the lighthouse."

"You'll need to call him back and get a guarantee that when we give him the info, said shyster won't end up dead," I said. "That happens, and we could end up in jail."

"Gunz doesn't operate like that anymore."

"Anymore." Creole snorted.

"Gunz is one hundred percent legit," Fab declared.

I'd heard Fab say Gunz was legit several times but never one hundred percent and wondered if that was true. I'd ask later.

"Gunz's going to use the info to get the money back, and then he's going to run the man out of the Keys so he can't prey on other homeowners."

"Have you met Gunz?" Creole clipped Didier on the shoulder.

Didier twisted in his seat. "Briefly. A couple of times back when we all lived together, so it's been a while. I do remember him being hot for my then-girlfriend. I've suggested recently, several times in fact, that she reintroduce us, and she's dodged that request."

I bit my lip to keep from laughing. One didn't easily forget Gunz. He'd honed his "don't mess with me" persona, and although he could be affable, he rarely displayed that side of himself unless he knew you well.

"Gunz this, Gunz that," Creole grumbled.

Didier nodded.

Creole searched me, running his hands down the sides of my body, and pulled my phone out of my pocket.

"Don't you need a search warrant?"

"Not if you give me permission to use it,

which I would suggest that you not agree to if asked by law enforcement... unless, of course, they have a warrant. But for your husband, I'm sure you won't mind."

"That's very slick of you."

He scrolled through the phone, found what he was looking for, and placed a call.

"Something wrong?" Gunz's voice reverberated out of the phone.

"I'm calling on behalf of Fab and Madison's husbands. If you want to continue your business relationship with the two women, then you'll meet with us. It's about time we reintroduce ourselves; I'm sure you'd agree." Creole's tone matched Gunz's surly one.

Gunz lowered his voice, so I couldn't hear his response.

"We should be at Jake's in about ten minutes. How about we meet there?" After a pause, he finished the conversation with, "See you there." Creole handed me back the phone and tugged Fab's hair. "I'm sure you know the way."

Fab hit the gas and sped down the road. Didier said something to her in French, which she ignored, pressing the gas harder. She squealed into Jake's and parked in the front, then got out and stomped across to the lighthouse. Didier leaned against the bumper and waited for her.

"I'm assuming us girls are invited to this little soiree?" At Creole's nod, I said, "Let's go inside, and I'll go run off anyone who dared to sit out on the deck. I'll tell any squatters that it's been red-tagged."

"Once that gets around, the bar will fill up, everyone will squeeze into the outside space, and it really *will* fall down."

"Kelpie would be over the moon at all the drama." I grabbed his hand and tugged him through the front door. I waved to the woman in question and pointed to the deck. "You order the drinks for the four of us. Gunz brings his own."

"Now that's some cheap. I'm surprised you let him in."

"He rarely comes inside; he wouldn't want to catch anything. You know, bugs or anything." I laughed. "Besides, I have no intention of stocking designer water on the off chance he might stop by. Regulars slurp it out of the fountain." I left Creole at the bar, to be flirted with and ogled by Kelpie and one of the regulars, and went out to the deck. It was empty. There'd been numerous complaints in the past that it was a suck place to sit, as all the action happened inside. I untied the closed sign and tied it on the doorknob, then cleaned off our regular table.

Creole opened the door, a tray in hand that held two bottles of beer and two glasses. "I ordered your usuals." He served the drinks.

Fab and Didier came in behind him, and she set an envelope on the table.

There was a knock on the door, and Gunz

poked his bald head out, following with his massive frame. He sported blue jeans, a dress shirt, leather tie, and motorcycle boots.

Fab made the introductions.

"You're letting the women listen in?" Gunz laughed, amused with himself.

"It was either that or tie them up and gag them," Creole said with a straight face.

"I like those kinds of games, but they have a tendency to get me in trouble." He flipped a chair around and straddled it.

I eyed the scar on the side of his nose where a stripper had taken a chunk out with her teeth. You'd think it would serve as a reminder when he looked in the mirror in the morning to avoid crazy women.

Gunz zeroed in on Didier. "Fabbie and I have been friends forever. Not quite, but a long time as real friends go. I made a promise not to knowingly put either of these women in danger. A time or two, events changed at the last minute, but that can't be helped. As always, they handled themselves like pros." He smiled at the two of us.

"I called this meeting," Creole said, returning the stare-down. "I thought it was about time we set some ground rules if you're going to use our wives on your cases."

"I gotcha. I've probably got that covered from the start. I'm upfront about everything I know about the cases. All involve family members. Occasionally, one goes off the rails, but that happens in the best of families." He flashed his signature smarmy smile.

"How many relatives do you have?" Didier asked.

"Hundreds. More than I can count. Grandma and Grandpa each came from a family of twenty. The siblings did their best to keep the line going, and on down from there. No one in our family talks about birth control." He flashed a toothy grin.

"You were chosen as the leader?" Didier wasn't completely convinced.

"Natural choice, since I *am* a leader." He took the cap off a silver bottle and downed the contents. "Take this latest fiasco." He shrugged. "If Jimmy and Roberta had called me, I could've fixed them up with a reputable contractor in one call, not some shyster that fleeced them out of their insurance money."

I kicked Fab, sending a "say something" message.

"Gunz looks after his family," Fab said.

"You're legit?" Creole questioned.

"Straight up. I'll admit I had a criminal tendency or two in the past, but my youthful indiscretions are behind me."

To my ears, Gunz sounded like a politician. "Everybody got their questions answered?" I asked.

"We're agreed then." Creole stuck out his hand, and they shook.

Gunz stood, turned to Didier, and did the same. "Let me know when the meeting is set," he said to Fab, then waved and left.

The door closed. Fab picked up the envelope and ripped it open, removing a sheet and pocketing the keys that fell out. She scanned the page and took out her phone. "In the spirit of keeping you updated..." She punched in a number and waited for someone to answer. "Mr. Wallis," she cooed in a sweet tone.

Didier's and Creole's eyebrows went up.

"I got your name from..." Fab paused and giggled. "I've forgotten. But I wrote your name first on the list." She went on to tell him that she'd gotten a house at a bargain, had been able to roll construction funds into the loan, and had a budget of a hundred thousand, managing to sound more and more ditzy as the conversation went on. "Tomorrow would be great." She read the address off the paper she'd gotten from Gunz. "So excited to get this project started." She tittered and hung up.

I clapped. "That was award-winning. You were so sweet, my teeth ache."

"Well done," Creole cheered. "I believed you."

Didier hugged her to him. "You two be careful. I'm happy that this job doesn't include you confronting him."

"Depending on how many people he's ripped off, the situation could jump ugly fast," Creole said.

"Here's the plan," Fab said. "I'm going to the property in the Porsche. Madison follows, parks one house down, and snaps pictures. When the meeting concludes, after he leaves, I'll get in the SUV and we'll follow him to his next stop, hopefully his office. If not, then we'll know who else to warn about his illegal practices."

"Let's hope you're not leaving your car in a terrible neighborhood." I made a face. "And it's still there when you get back."

Chapter Thirty-Four

The next morning, Creole was more than a little surprised when he answered the banging on the back door, expecting to find Fab, but Billy was standing there instead.

"Oops, I forgot to tell you," I said to his what-the-heck look.

Billy snorted out a laugh. He came in, and I offered him a beverage for the road.

"I called Spoon this morning and asked to borrow his star employee for a driving job. I know a couple of loose cannons that would jump at the opportunity to drive Fab's Porsche, but she'd kill me. She still might, as she doesn't know my Plan B... or C. It's hard to keep track of my brilliant ideas these days."

Creole shook his head. "The plan would be what exactly?" He wasn't happy with my lapse.

"I didn't think leaving Fab's sports car parked in the driveway of a vacant shack was a great idea no matter how good the neighborhood. It might disappear. Or attract the cops, thinking it's being used as a drug house. Hence Billy." I extended my arm. "He's going to drive it back here. Don't you dare eat in it," I admonished the man.

Billy grinned.

"Under no circumstances," Creole pointed his finger at me, "do you invite trouble. Got it?"

"We're tailing the contractor to his next location, which will hopefully be his office." I shrugged, as if to say 'what could go wrong?'

"That would be too easy," Creole said. "Keep in mind, the longer you follow the man, the greater the chance of him spotting you. If you make a living screwing people, like he apparently does, I'd think you'd keep one eye peeled over your shoulder."

"Most people don't know that contractors have to register with the county to do work," Billy said. "If they did, they'd go to the website, and these people would've found a list of complaints against Chester Wallis. He has a history of not doing the work and running off with the money instead."

Honk, honk.

"That's Fab," I told Billy. "She's ready to leave."

"I'll go out and say hello." Billy opened the door and waved to Fab, who was parked in front in her Porsche.

I put my arms around Creole. "You have a nice day, dear." I stood on my tiptoes and kissed him.

"Have an uneventful day." He walked me out

and waved to Fab, who was making a u-turn to head out to the highway. He opened the door to my loaner SUV, and I slid in.

"I take it you smoothed the rough edges from my plan, thereby saving me an inquisition from Fab?" I asked Billy as I followed her out to the road.

"Her only comment was, 'At least she chose someone who can drive.'" Billy snorted.

"Straight driving job," I said. "No surprises, or at least I hope not." Spoon laughed when I'd told him the same thing and warned me that I'd better send his best employee back in one piece.

"The boss is going to check with a few of his sources and see what he can find out about Wallis. He'd also like to see him run out of town."

Surprisingly, Fab didn't leave me in her exhaust fumes to find the property on my own. The house was located on the outskirts of town. Fab and I had been to the neighborhood before, but a few streets over.

Fab pulled into the driveway of a sad little one-story that had been ravaged by water damage and showed active signs of rot and mold. A real contractor would recommend raising it off the ground, stripping it to the studs, and basically starting from scratch.

I u-turned and pulled to the curb.

"You can get closer." Billy waved me forward. "Pull up behind the trailer, and you'll go unnoticed unless this Wallis character scans the street. We'll notice if he does that and come up with another of your plans."

"I've got Xander on standby to run Wallis's license plate. I'm hoping he comes up with an address that will cut our day short."

"The kid was super excited that you didn't dump him when he went off to finish college. He was stressing hard, no matter how many times I told him that you'd never do that." When Xander first came to town and needed a place to live, Billy had offered up a room, and they ended up becoming good friends.

"I'm just happy that he's still able to work for me and it doesn't interfere with his classes," I said. "He's every bit as good as that last so-called professional we used, and no snarky attitude to contend with."

A Ford 650 pulled into the driveway alongside Fab's Porsche. She'd gotten out and leaned against the hood and waved as he drove in. Wallis got out, clipboard in hand.

"You'd think the guy would show up in a work truck." Billy watched the man's every move. "It's hard to believe that truck's ever been to a job site. It looks like he just picked it up from the detailer."

"I'd like Gunz to turn him in to the cops. If he's run out of town, he'll just set up his scam somewhere else."

"A few years in jail would be good for a guy

like that. Better yet, force him to make the repairs he promised people and pay out of his own pocket."

Billy and I watched as Fab and the man disappeared inside. The two were in there for quite a while. Finally, they came out and circled the property, tromping through the weeds around the side of the house.

Billy rolled down the window, opened the door, and got out, standing close, shielded from view. I crawled over the seat. "I'll wait until you've cleared the block, then jump in the Porsche and get out of here." He looked up and down the street. "So far, we haven't attracted any attention. Wallis never even took notice of his surroundings."

Fab and Wallis came back and stood in the driveway, talking as he made notes. Eventually, he ripped off a sheet and handed it to Fab, then waved, got back in his truck, and roared away.

When Wallis was almost to the end of the block, Fab retrieved her purse, ran to Billy and handed off the keys, exchanged a few words, then jogged across the road, jumped behind the wheel, and took off in pursuit.

"Wallis is very professional, except the couple of times he leered at me when he thought I wasn't looking," Fab said. "He gave every impression that he knew what he was doing and was the man for the job. He said he'd get it done on time and not go over budget."

"How did you leave it?"

"Wallis quoted a hundred thousand for the job. I'd already told him that was my supposed budget, but it did surprise me when he quoted the entire amount. He asked for half up front. I told him I needed to talk to the husband and get back to him, but that said husband was always agreeable to what I wanted. The whole time, I batted my eyelashes and simpered." Fab gave me a demonstration.

I laughed. "I'll have to request a replay at a family dinner."

"Don't think I can't embarrass you back."

Fab hung back until Wallis turned onto the highway, then took off in hot pursuit. We followed him for quite some time without anything interesting happening. I was just about to whine about being bored when Wallis turned into a residential area and pulled up in front of a one-story conch-style home. The old house had been kept up but showed signs of wear.

"Cute neighborhood," I said, craning my head around.

Fab backed into the driveway of a house two down on the other side of the street with a For Sale sign stuck in the weeds. The uncovered windows showed it to be vacant and allowed a view through to the backyard.

We cooled our heels for a good thirty minutes. Wallis finally came out and stood on the porch, an older woman by his side. He took her hand in his and kissed the top of her head before jumping in his truck. The woman went back inside.

"Interesting way to end a business call," Fab said, and once again waited until he was at the corner before following him.

We followed him north out of town to a private airport. Once inside, he pulled up to a gate, inserted his card, and wound around and out of view.

"Lost him." Fab hit the steering wheel.

"Before you suggest hacking your way through the security gate, I feel compelled to remind you that it's not worth a trip to jail. You can bet this place has plenty of cameras monitoring our every move."

"I wonder if Wallis picked up his tail," Fab mused as she continued down the road and looped around inside the airport instead of exiting. "Now what? We can't sit out here and wait for him to leave. There's no parking and we'll be noticed in a hot second, and once we are, security will be all over us."

"If he's got an office in one of the hangars, I have no clue how we'd track him down." To my relief, Fab left the airport and got back on the main road. "Our other option is to go back and question the woman at the house we just left."

"You're nervy."

"Me?" I said in all innocence. "This is for *your* client. I'm along for the fun and games, which have been lacking thus far." It didn't take long for me to figure out she was going to follow through on my suggestion.

"What are you going to say when she answers the door?" Fab asked.

"Park where you did before, keep your hat and glasses on, and roll down the window. I want you in plain sight but not easily picked out in a lineup." I turned to the window. "I'll tell her that I'm interested in the house across the street and that the realtor pointed to the truck and said the man driving it was a contractor. Then ask would she recommend him, and oh yeah, does she have a number? That won't be particularly helpful, as we already have that. I know, I'll ask where his office is located."

"It's not your worst idea." Fab grinned at me. "Another option to lure him in is to call and let him know I'm ready to hand over a check for fifty thousand. When he arrives at the property, we're nowhere in sight and Gunz takes over."

"Skip the woman's house, and we'll go with your plan."

"Gunz is going to want an address. At the very least, he'll scare the you know what out of Wallis, and any smart man would relocate and not set foot back in this town."

"The scare wouldn't happen to include painfully squeezing the money out of the man, would it?" I shuddered. "If we set Wallis up for a few crushed bones or worse, we could be charged with a crime."

"You worry too much."

"You don't worry enough," I snapped back. "Here's plan whatever the letter—instead of Gunz meeting Wallis, how about Gunz turning it over to a cop friend? Having dealt with the likes of Chester Wallis in the past, newsflash: the money's most likely gone already. Then, once Wallis is arrested, Gunz gets one of his contractor friends to go out and do the rebuild."

"That's in progress."

"Let's go home."

That was promptly ignored, as Fab turned onto the woman's street and parked in the same place as before.

I got out and slammed the door, walking across the street and up the brick driveway. I pasted on my friendly face and knocked. The same woman answered the door, her hand fisted around the collar of a pit bull, who appeared calm, but I didn't want to test that.

I gave her the speech I'd run by Fab.

She gave me an unsettling once-over. "He's a nice man," she said vaguely, as though needing time to decide what to say next. "He's made a couple of repairs here and has always been fairly priced."

I looked over her shoulder and tried not to be obvious in checking out the interior. "Does 'he' have a name, and how can I contact him?"

The woman's benign smile was replaced by a less-than-friendly demeanor, the change abrupt.

"Would you like to come in?"

I stepped back, ignoring her question. At the same time, I noticed the Smith & Wesson on the table next to her easy chair. "Would you happen to have the address for his office or be able to give me general directions? I'm sure I could find it." I took another step back.

"It's Able's—north on the highway back towards town, a mile up on the right side." She waved airily as she lied through her teeth. Someone might want to mention that she wasn't good at it and came off as unbelievable.

I took one last look inside, and my eyes fell on a series of pictures hanging over the sideboard. "Cute house." I hurriedly added, "Thank you for your time," and hot-footed it off the porch. I waved to Fab, so the woman would notice I wasn't alone.

She stood and watched as I left her yard, walked across the street, and climbed in the passenger side of the SUV. She was still standing in the doorway when we drove away.

"When she first opened the door, she came across as the grandmotherly sort. The change in her when I asked for Wallis's contact information was sudden; her eyes turned cold, and her icy stare reminded me that I don't have old-lady rapport."

"Really, Madison," Fab chastised. "Your mother would be horrified at that reference."

"If my mother were to meet her, she'd have

been happy that I didn't come up with something less flattering."

"Did you learn anything?"

"I was impressed that she never let Wallis' name slip and ignored me when I asked. I got what I'm sure will turn out to be bogus directions to his office. Slow down on the chance she wasn't lying through her teeth." I repeated the vague directions. "Almost forgot. I'm not one hundred percent sure about this next tidbit, but there were some family group shots hanging on the wall, or so I'd assume, since random folks would be odd. I'd swear Chester's mug was smiling from one of them. It would take a closer look to make a positive ID, but I'm not going back."

My phone rang.

"Paydirt," Xander said when I answered. "The address you just sent over—the house was owned by a man who's since died, and it's now in probate. There's a lawsuit to get Myrtle Wallis out of the property. She's claiming rights as his widow, except they weren't married and it's unclear how long the two knew one another—a couple of months at best. She's representing herself, and that's not the best option."

"Good job. I'm tacking on a bonus for you, courtesy of the client." I hung up and gave Fab the news. "Looks like we found Chester's mother."

"I'll pass along the information, and Gunz can

deal with it. I wonder if the mother knows about her son's shady business dealings. Before you start with the warnings, this may be better for Wallis's health, as Gunz wouldn't hurt a woman. What he will do is use her to smoke old Chester out and send them both packing."

"Whatever Gunz decides to do, he has to be prepared. Let him know that she has a gun and a dog."

Chapter Thirty-Five

I decided that I wanted a couple of days of downtime but wasn't sure how that would work out, since what I wanted was to just sneak away to the beach. I was also tempted to put an out-of-order sticker on my phone, except I didn't have one and was certain it wouldn't stop it from ringing. As it happened, I got one day's respite from the phone. The following morning, it rang in my hand. Mac, hmm… I counted the rings and answered before it went to voicemail.

"Huge favor," Mac said breathlessly. She must not have heard my groan, as she rambled on. "My best friend from kindergarten is in town. Today only, and I want to show her around. I could leave Rude on lookout, except we have a check-in and she has no clue how to do the paperwork."

There went the fantasy of a quiet day sitting on the sand. "I'd love to fill in," I said grumpily.

"I know you wouldn't, but you're the best."

"Don't get carried away. When do I need to be there?"

"ASAP. You never know when these folks are

going to show up. I told them early was okeydokey."

"I'll be right over after I make an effort to pretty myself up." I hung up and frowned down at my bathing suit and sheer cover-up, not wanting to trade them for something less fun. I glanced up at the television, which was showing the feed from the security cameras, and caught sight of Fab walking down the street. I slid into a pair of flip-flops and went out to investigate.

I opened the gate. "What are you up to?" I asked when she was a foot away. "You never walk anywhere."

"I figured it would give me enough time to decide whether to pick the lock or knock."

I told her about Mac's call. "Come with me." Noticing that her nose was stuck in the air the whole time I talked, I figured the chances were nil.

"That sounds like too much fun for me." Fab turned and started to walk away.

"I go everywhere with you," I said in a huff. "You can't keep me company?"

She slowed slightly, half-turned, shook her head, and continued back towards her house.

"This relationship is over," I bellowed. "O-V-E-R."

She waved over her head.

I stomped back into the house and headed for the closet, changing into a red wrap sundress, accenting it with a shell belt and jewelry, and sliding into some sandals. I stood in front of the mirror, trying to decide if I'd perfected managerial, and realized I'd forgotten to strap on my thigh holster.

On the way out, I grabbed my purse and phone and made a mental note to find a new best friend. I jumped behind the wheel and flew over to The Cottages. I parked in front of the office, wanting to kick myself for forgetting to stop at my favorite coffee haunt.

I sat in Mac's chair and stared at the list she'd left me. At the top, she'd written, "Try not to shoot anyone." And added, "Although good for business, the boss doesn't like it." I groaned when I saw that we still had one empty cottage, even after the new guests checked-in. I made the executive decision that it could wait until Mac got back to be rented. Besides, walk-ins off the street were frowned on. They often came with "Trouble" stamped in the middle of their foreheads.

I swiveled in the seat and stared at the coffeemaker. How hard could it be? Choose one of the little cups in the rack, shove it in, and voila—something hot to drink. Oh yeah, don't forget water. Before I did that, I decided to make the rounds. It was mid-morning, but one could hope that everyone was still in bed. Halfway down the driveway, I stopped checking for drunks slumped in a stupor on their porches and instead followed the sounds of voices and laughter coming from the pool area, which got louder as I got closer. I rounded the corner and skidded to a stop. It wasn't goat yoga. It was alcohol-fueled yoga.

The guests were lined up on mats, a bottle of liquor and a shot glass at their sides. From what I could deduce, in this class led by Rude, if someone couldn't get the position right, they downed a shot. It was the wrong incentive, in my opinion. A few were in their cups already, and I'd bet they'd all be passed out in the next hour.

Not wanting to be a big meanie but also not wanting anyone to drown, I pushed open the gate and zeroed in on Crum, who was straddling a barstool in a pair of speedos with a mariachi band design. Probably a compromise between him and Mac, with Crum insisting on nudity, and the ugly bathing suit won. I waved to Rude.

She was a keeper and quite popular among the guests. She'd organized a bus tour to all the haunted spots in town, of which there was one, but she'd managed to make up another eleven. That had been a hit, and Mac and Rude had their heads together, coming up with other tour options.

I marched over to Crum. "What are you doing?"

"I've been hired as the lifeguard." He ran his finger down his hairless chest. "I get a hefty tip if no one drowns. That, dearie, ain't happening on my watch."

"It better not because I'll saddle you with the paperwork."

"Got it, girlie. If you wouldn't mind moving, you're blocking my view."

I turned to see where he was pointing, and he had a bird's-eye view right down the scant bathing suit tops of two of the female guests. "New rule for you: no tupping the guests."

"You still holding a grudge over Maricruz?" Crum grouched. "It's not my fault she went catting around in the middle of the night. I don't like sleeping with women after... you know... but she could've at least said good-bye."

"Have you talked to her?"

He snorted, conveying, *Have you lost your mind?* "Didn't think she'd want my condolences over her other date dying of a drug overdose."

"Make sure that everyone gets back to their cottage safely. I don't want them sleeping out here and rolling into the pool."

"Got it, General." He saluted.

"Keep in mind that the size of your tip depends on you re-homing these people safely."

I walked back to the office, where I kicked off my shoes and lay down on the couch. I'd barely gotten comfortable when the door flew open. Fab stood in the doorway in her sexy jeans and tennis shoes, gigantic cups of coffee in her hands. I licked my lips.

She handed me a cup, and I pulled off the lid and sighed at the big mound of whipped cream.

"I guess we can be friends again," I said, throwing in a little pout.

Fab produced a bag from behind her back and presented it with a flourish. I poked my nose inside and pulled out a small cup, popping open the lid and licking my lips. "Cherries." I beamed at her. "This seals it. We're friends."

"Have I missed anything?" Fab rounded the desk and claimed Mac's chair.

"Drunk yoga in progress at the pool. Crum in an obscene bathing suit that's clearly too small and barely covers his... is bodyguarding."

Fab made a face. "I offered to take him shopping once—outfit him and pay. He looked down his nose, per his usual, and said, 'Why waste the money?' Then proceeded to tell me that his closets were full. He hits up a store down the street and goes through the donation bags at least once a week."

"That's a good way to get arrested."

"He made friends with one of the women that mans the store. They both get their happy endings."

I came close to choking on my coffee. "So pleased you showed up, and with the secret sauce of life." I toasted her.

"My luck, I'd miss something good and Mac would trot out that gloaty smile of hers during the retelling."

The door blew open and Joseph barreled in, drunk, with Svetlana under one arm. "She's been maimed," he cried and held her out. One arm had gone flat.

"What happened?" I managed a shocked expression. I knew that in Mac's list of tricks, she had someone who fixed rubber girlfriends. Another item for the growing list of what she needed to deal with when she got back. Svetlana would take precedence over shutting down drunk yoga, as I liked her.

"Dickass wanted me to sell her to him. I tried to explain that she's my soulmate. So he stuck her with a knife. If I hadn't been at Custer's, I'd have called the cops. Didn't want to get arrested since I'd tipped a few and planned to walk home. This town needs a walking path through the bushes."

"Does Dick have a last name? I can sic my friend here on him, and I'm certain that he'd never assault Svet again."

Fab made guns with her fingers and shot them around the room, complete with sound effects, entertaining herself and me.

"Penn. I don't think it's short for pencil, although it's the only way I can remember his name," Joseph said with a straight face.

Before I could come up with a suitable inanity, the door blew open again. You'd think we were in the middle of hurricane-force winds.

A middle-aged couple pushed against one another to see who could get through the door first, tossing biting comments at each other that each ignored as they continued to talk over the other.

I stood. Out of options, since I couldn't maneuver Joseph around the couple, I led him over to the couch, shoving him down. Svetlana landed in his lap. I went and stood behind the desk. Did Fab stand so we could change places? Heck no. "How may I help you?"

"Where's Mac-y?" the woman barked. "Never seen you before."

I ran my finger down the list that Mac had left. "Are you the Tripps?" The man nodded. "I'm sure I can make the check-in process go smoothly."

"Just give us the key." Mr. Tripp snapped his fingers and stuck out his hand. "Mac-y's got all our information on file, *and* the credit card."

"I'll have to tell the owner how efficient *Mac* is."

"I've heard the owner's a flake." Mrs. Tripp sparked with interest. "You met her?"

Joseph snorted a laugh and rolled onto his side.

"I've never heard myself described that way." I reached in the drawer and pulled out the welcome envelope with the key attached. "You might want to ask my friend here; she'd be more objective."

Mr. Tripp relieved me of the envelope, and the two of them gave me a once-over.

"Madison's nicer than I am," Fab said. "I'd

kick you out and point you to the pay-by-the-hour motel."

Mrs. Tripp tittered. "You two are cute." They backed out the door and slammed it shut.

I turned to Joseph. "You fall asleep, and you're going to wake up when your butt hits the floor." I reached out and took Svetlana out of his arms. "I'll make sure she gets repaired. Just because she won't be around for a few days to keep an eye on you," I winked at her, "doesn't mean you can run wild. Don't forget I don't do jail runs anymore."

"I'm too old to be getting jailed in the hinterlands," Joseph lamented. "It's hard to get a bus or ride of any kind. Thumbs aren't reliable, and who can walk it?"

I circled the desk and opened the door since Joseph smelled and I didn't want it permeating the office. Furrball, Rude's cat, ran in and under the desk. Next, he hopped up on the bookcase and climbed to the top. He sniffed Kitty, shoved her to one side, and lay down.

"They're a couple now," Joseph announced. "You'd think Furrball would hook up with a cat that was alive, so he could get his kitty on, but guess not."

I covered my face and laughed. I didn't fail to notice that Fab had a huge grin on her face.

"Come on, old boy." I held out my hand to Joseph. "I'm going to escort you home. Don't want you getting lost." It took a couple of tugs to get him upright.

"It's just down the driveway."

I hooked my arm in his so he couldn't trudge off and end up in the bushes. I knew I wouldn't be able to haul him out and Fab would be zero help. I said to Fab, "You're in charge. This place better be standing when I get back."

"Leave the door open so I can see what's going on," Fab ordered.

"You ready for a nap?" I asked Joseph.

"What am I going to do without Svet?" he whined.

"You're going to have plenty of company. Crum's going to hang out with you." I didn't dare suggest Mac; she'd quit. Crum wouldn't be swell about it either, but once he heard 'money,' he'd get cooperative. "Don't worry about your girlfriend; I'll have a rush put on her. As for Dick, he won't be bothering you again."

"You're sweet. Sometimes, anyway."

"Great compliment." I opened his door and ushered him inside and over to his easy chair. "You need anything before I go?"

Joseph kicked back and closed his eyes. "Got it covered."

I reigned myself in from running back outside to suck in some fresh air. It didn't take me long after inheriting the place to figure out that I wasn't cut out to run the day-to-day operations. Days like this were a reminder and increased my appreciation for Mac, which was already off the charts.

A pickup truck rumbled into the driveway and screeched to a halt. A couple of bedraggled thirty-something men hopped out and headed to the office. They not only triggered my "trouble" warning but sent it skyrocketing to "criminal." I had plenty of experience and could easily pick them out.

When I got to the door, they were hovered over the desk, berating Fab. "What do you mean you're full up? That's not what the sign says," one bellowed in her face. I expected her to shoot him. Instead, she favored him with a crazy-girl smile. Stupid men didn't even back up.

"We don't have a vacancy sign," I said from the threshold. "Berating the help is not allowed, so hit the road. There are plenty of options out on the highway." I squeezed by the side of the desk.

"You can't refuse to serve us," the other gritted through his stained teeth.

"Get out." Fab leveled her Walther at him. "You test me, and you're not going to like the results." She lowered her aim.

They both bristled and backed through the door. "You're not getting away with this; we'll shut you down."

I closed and locked the door behind them and sat on the couch. "We've got an available cottage, but no one knows that. I'll get Billy to come and stay a few nights. That will lessen the chances of any excitement breaking out."

"I heard the truck shoot into the driveway. So

far, I haven't heard them leave," Fab said.

I got up and peeked through the blinds. "You're right; they're still sitting there."

It didn't take long before a police cruiser rolled up. "They must not be wanted," I said, and was happy to see Kevin get out. "We need to get the license plate number off that truck," I said to Fab. "As a precautionary measure."

There were two doors in the room, both of which looked like closets. One was, but the other led outside. Fab stood and went through that door.

The knock at the office door was unmistakably a cop knock.

"Come in, officer." I unlocked it and waved my hand. "Have a seat; help yourself to a soda." I backed up and claimed Mac's chair.

"After," Kevin huffed. "Give me the quick, short version."

"They wanted to rent a cottage. I told them we didn't have an available one. Unless you're moving out..." I smiled. "As far as their contention we have a vacancy sign, you know that they made that part up."

"I'm not going anywhere. You'd miss me, and you know it." Kevin smiled and walked back out.

I put together a small tote of soda and candy.

Kevin wasn't gone for very long before he stuck his head in the door. "They're gone. I vouched for your truthfulness. Also told them that a cop lived here, and if they had any intention of coming back and stirring up trouble, they'd be headed to jail."

I handed him the bag. "Return it for a refill."

As soon as Kevin pulled away from the curb, Fab walked back in.

"Good timing," I said.

"I read your to-do list, and you're done here. I told Rude to keep an eye out and call if there were any problems she couldn't take care of. Can't imagine what that would be."

On the paper that Mac had left, I scribbled, "Call me before you do anything else."

I locked up, and Fab and I went to our cars.

Chapter Thirty-Six

Fab and I decided to drop her car off at her house and go get our drunk on. The guys spotted us on the highway, followed us home, and invited themselves along to Jake's. We got into Creole's truck, and as we pulled out onto the highway, my phone rang. Xander's face popped up.

"I sent you a report about your friend," he said. "Fab's kind of interesting. Did you know she was charged with murder once before?"

"I did. We were friends at the time. In case you were wondering, neither of us did it." I wanted him to know, in case there was any confusion.

"I ran your background too, but you're kind of boring." Xander laughed. "I dug up as much I could on Fab's ex-husband, Gabriel Rochefort," he continued. "Now that was some entertaining reading, especially about his associates—nice name for criminal friends. I ran reports on every name associated with Gabriel and Fab; turns out that most are dead, but a few are still amongst the living. I figured you'd ask what those people were doing now and decided to have a ready answer."

"Reassure me that Gabriel's still dead." I sighed and leaned back against the seat. *That's all we need.*

"No worries there." Xander chuckled. "His family had him cremated and shipped back to France... for burial, I presume, or to have him hang out on the mantel."

I refused to laugh at the last part, not wanting to encourage the inappropriate humor that I enjoyed. "Good job. I'll start reading right now." I hung up and opened Creole's leather plumber's bag, which I'd bought him, and pulled out his iPad. "Is this charged?"

Fab pushed forward and hung her head over the seat. "Who was on the phone?" she demanded.

Didier reached out to pull her back.

"Xander, and most of the conversation was about you. A smidge about me."

"What are you talking about?" Didier demanded, abandoning the tussle with Fab.

"Xander ran background checks on Fab and me." I turned in my seat. "Sad to say, you were more interesting." I flashed a sad face at Fab. "He dug up info about Gabriel that he thought we should read. Just so you know, your ex was cremated, so there's no chance of him knocking on the door."

"Did you ask Xander to check us out?" Fab asked.

"He mentioned it, and I didn't discourage

him." I hadn't expected it to lead anywhere, but on the off chance... "I'm certain that every information person we used in the past ran a check on the two of us before doing any work for us. We may have a little color in our pasts, but neither of us has anything to hide."

"Since the report is about me, I should be the one to read it." Fab slapped her hand over the seat.

"Here's a lesson about possession—I've got the iPad and the file." I held it up and out of her reach.

Creole pulled into Jake's and parked. "Do you want to go home?"

"We can eat and read at the same time," I said.

Creole called for a vote, and it was unanimous, with no grumbling from Fab. We got out and went inside. Creole headed to the kitchen to place the order, Didier to the bar, and I went outside to claim the deck, Fab hot on my heels.

Fab put the "keep out" sign on the knob and banged the door closed.

We sat at the table, Fab next to me, and I opened my email account.

"At least Gabriel isn't coming back to haunt me." Fab shuddered.

"I'm happy about that too," I said. "Given a do-over, he'd probably shoot me on sight."

"I'd take the bullet over being tossed in the Atlantic to see if it was possible for me to swim back to the Keys."

"Didn't he decide that a bullet would be more humane, quicker?" At Fab's snort, I smiled. "I'm not one to speak ill of the dead, but good riddance." I knew the first time I looked into the man's cold and calculating blue eyes that he'd bring trouble, and only his death stopped him from causing more. "You speak to the Rochefort family after his demise?"

"I didn't have the nerve to call them and offer phony condolences. They didn't contact me either. That old saying about sleeping dogs is good advice."

"I wonder what Xander found," I mused, scrolling down the screen. "No hints. Just that it was entertaining reading."

"Let's hope that he's found another person of interest in Aurora's murder," Fab said. "I think it's weird that she was also involved with Gabriel, and now they're both dead."

The door opened, and Didier came out and served the drinks, followed by Creole.

I took a healthy sip of my margarita, wanting to guzzle it, but decided it wasn't a night for drunkenness. I pulled up the attachment and pushed the iPad into the center of the table so we could all see the screen.

Fab read faster than me, but I kept up with the gist and read the headlines of the articles Xander had included. Creole hung his head over my shoulder. Didier crowded in on Fab's other side.

"Pays to be rich in this town," Fab said in disgust. "Chrissy Wright murdered two people and got off. There wasn't even a trial; the charges were dropped."

"How is that possible?" Didier asked. "As I recall, she confessed."

"What I remember, still in vivid detail," Fab shook her head in disgust, "is the society maven and heiress, Chrissy Wright, standing at the top of the steps leading down into her basement, those beady eyes of hers trained on us, filled with hate, as she proceeded to gloat about committing double murder."

"Once Chrissy offed her pesky husband — alimony can be expensive when you're a zillionaire — Gabriel had to go," I said, recalling the same scene. "Besides the fact that he'd grown annoying, she couldn't leave a witness and open herself to a lifetime of blackmail. She knew that Gabriel would use that as leverage over her to fund a cushy lifestyle." I hadn't forgotten how that woman had had me and Fab trussed up in her basement. The only time she'd deigned to descend the stairs was when she informed the two of us that we had an hour or two left to live, and the only reason we hadn't been killed outright was she wanted to gloat over her murderous accomplishments.

"What surprised me was that she was going to let her lackey, Bruno, have the thrill of killing us. I get that she wouldn't want to dirty her hands disposing of our bodies, but after murdering two people already, what's two more?" Fab asked. "It was smart, though—then she'd have something to hang over his head. Chrissy was shrewd enough to keep her mouth shut when the cops showed up, and she ordered Bruno to do the same."

"After we were rescued, I didn't follow the case, figuring it was a slam dunk," I said. "That those two would rot in jail. I'm afraid to ask what happened."

"At the time, the Chief ordered that none of his officers were to speak about the case," Creole said. "By the time the order was lifted, I'd moved on to another case and never gave Chrissy Wright another thought. But I do know that she wasn't in jail long. In fact, a mere week later, she posted a cash bond and bailed out with a leg monitor. That shocked more than a few of the investigating officers in the department, as they thought they'd made a good case against her."

"What happened to greasy Bruno?" I asked. "It wasn't clear, when Chrissy was in the height of her boasting about the murders, whether he got his hands bloody in any way. I do remember her ordering him to dispose of our bodies by weighing us down and tossing us in the Atlantic, hoping the fish would eat us."

"Bruno confessed," Fab said in utter shock. She'd continued to scroll through the articles. "Says here that right before the trial was to begin, he withdrew his not-guilty plea and pled guilty, telling the court that he acted on his own out of love for Chrissy and that she didn't know anything about what he'd done."

"Why would Bruno confess to murdering two people when he didn't?" Didier asked. "Why not turn state's evidence against Chrissy in exchange for a lighter sentence or possibly even immunity? I'd think the District Attorney would offer up a sweet deal to get Chrissy."

"Shock waves rippled through the department on that one," Creole said. "I heard at the time that there wasn't a deal in place in exchange for the confession. Bruno just threw himself on the mercy of the court. Not even a half-assed lawyer would let their client confess to double murder."

"The ink was barely dry on the confession when he was found dead in his cell," Fab read.

"Isn't that convenient?" I said. "My guess is Bruno was double-crossed. I realize that I didn't know him well, but he didn't strike me as the type to sacrifice his life for Chrissy. Must have been something big in it for him. But what? And why was he killed, if he was? Even if he changed his mind, it would too late after a confession. I don't think he could even appeal the verdict."

"And Chrissy Wright?" Didier asked in disgust. "What happened to her?"

"All charges were dropped." Fab stared at the screen. "So sweet." Her voice dripped with sarcasm. "Chrissy was welcomed back into the bosom of society. Judging by the clippings that Xander included of her out and about, she's living it up. No low profile for her."

"The DA dropping the charges raised more than a few eyebrows at the time," Creole said. "There wasn't one officer that worked the case who wasn't shocked at the outcome. There was talk of an internal investigation, but everything quieted down overnight; even the news media dropped the story. It was like it never happened. As I recall, a couple of years later, the DA ran for re-election and won easily, despite other questionable decisions he'd made that his opponent did his best to exploit."

I continued to scroll through the report. "Lookee here. Chrissy recently made the news. The police report says someone tried to run her Bentley off the road, and she lost control and wrapped it around a pole. From the picture, I'd say the damage was overstated, but I'm certain she got a new one. Can't have a dented vehicle, even if it's been repaired."

"There was also an attempted break-in at her mansion." Fab tapped the screen.

"What sticks out," Creole said, "is that she's experiencing the same odd incidents as you."

"Coincidence?" I asked. "Or someone who has it in for both of you? Another of Gabriel's lovers? Business associates?"

"Do you know if any of Gabriel's friends are still around?" Creole asked Fab.

"Gabriel didn't have friends. He had relationships with people that had a talent he didn't, usually of the criminal kind." Fab leaned her head against Didier's shoulder. "I distanced myself from Gabriel, as he was in the habit of screwing everyone he knew, and that certainly included me. I wasn't the perfect wife, not even close, but I'd never have murdered him in cold blood like he planned to do to me. That's why it surprised me that he made me the beneficiary on a healthy bank account. It sat untouched for years before I turned it over to Caspian to investigate and invest."

"Possibly a family member holding a grudge?" Creole asked.

"Getting even wasn't his family's style; they just moved on to the next con. They lived for the thrill of the next payout—the bigger the better." Fab rubbed her fingers together. "There didn't seem to be an end game, as though there would never be enough."

My phone dinged, and I read the message. "You need to go pay Dick a visit," I told Fab. "The sooner the better. Can't have anything happening to our girl Svet. She'll be coming back from the blow-up hospital next week, and I want her to feel safe. I'm forwarding the information about the man."

"Dickass?" She smirked.

"Don't shoot him." I made a face. "Scare the bodily fluids out of him and issue an explicit warning that something grisly will happen if he ever thinks about touching Svetlana or looking in her direction again."

"Why is it that once again, Didier and I have to ask what the hell you're talking about?" Creole demanded.

"It's because I haven't had a minute to relay the details of my exciting day." I held up my hands, an innocent look on my face. "The one where Fab sat back and laughed at me the whole time, like the supportive friend she's not."

"I was this close," Fab held her fingers an inch apart, "to blowing you off completely." She blew out a big burst of air and smiled. "So happy I didn't. My idea of bringing you coffee was a stroke of genius, if I do say so myself. I paid for extra, extra whipped cream, so you know. Worth every penny. It got me back in your good graces as soon as your eyes landed on the cup. I knew the second the door was kicked open the first time that there'd have been no way to capture the madness in any kind of retelling."

"That's why you're on." I flourished my hand. "Since I'm certain that you didn't miss a trick, *you* can relay the day's events. And make sure you sauce them up the way only you can."

Fab stood and curtsied, then sat back down to the laughter of the guys. "Imagine my absolute shock when I drove up and could hear Madison screaming like a harridan from the middle of the street. What will the neighbors think?" She looked down her nose.

"I'll be sure and let you know if any complaints roll in. You can go scare the mollie out of them and disabuse them of any notion of calling the cops."

Fab relayed the details with exceptional flourish. When she was done, she half-stood and took a bow.

"No," Didier said adamantly and turned Fab to face him. "Being the great husband that I am," he grinned at her, "I'll take care of Dickass. You don't need to go looking for trouble."

"I'm thinking of another husband who's got you edged out of that 'great' business." I winked at Creole.

Didier laughed.

"Because it's Svet, I'll go along." Creole flexed his muscles. "When we're done chatting with Dick, that's the last Joseph will see of him."

Chapter Thirty-Seven

Fab had called earlier that morning. "Got a new client, Herman Frizzle, and he wants to meet this afternoon."

"Someone you know?"

"Cold call," she said hesitantly. "The address checks out — an office building in Homestead."

"I'm in. Unless Creole flips when I tell him I'm going."

"Creole probably already knows, since I was upfront with Didier and showed him a picture of the building I got off the internet."

"I'll be waiting outside. If not, honk." I laughed, got off the phone, and got dressed.

Work attire. Hmm... Fab did say office building, so I chose a full skirt and strapped my Glock to my inner thigh. After a quick kiss, Creole hooked his arm around me, and for once, I walked him to his truck and waved as he drove off.

"So how much fun is this job going to be?" I asked as Fab blew up the highway.

"As my trainee, you'll be hanging on my every word and maybe learn something about updating security systems. Mr. Frizzle claims that the building's system is sub-par, as he's had a couple of break-ins. He didn't get into details or say what, if anything, had been stolen."

"If there's a business office for the building, you should leave your card."

"Great minds." Fab tapped her temple and grinned. "I'll snoop around the property so I've got a general idea of their needs and stop in after the appointment."

"If you had more corporate clients, you'd be less inclined to handle the ones with personal issues."

Fab grimaced. "Update: the guys visited Mr. Penn, AKA Dickass, introduced themselves as friends of Svetlana, and told him that his grubby fingers better not be seen in the vicinity of her shapely form again, and if he was seen within several hundred feet, they'd be back to cut them off and shove them up his —"

"I'm certain the latter statement came from Creole. I'm surprised he didn't tell me."

"I asked him to let me do it. He laughed but agreed, commenting that I can't always take all the fun for myself." Fab's phone rang. She made a face at the screen and answered. "Mr. Frizzle," she said, after a pause amending it to, "Herman."

Problems with her new client already?

"Text me the new address. I'm about fifteen minutes away." Fab hung up and handed me her phone. "There's been a change of venue. Herman is in a meeting that's running longer than expected and wants to meet at another location. He said that he wanted it checked out as well."

Her phone beeped seconds later.

"I don't know Homestead well enough to know where this address is located," I said.

"When I ran a search on the other one, I found it's a high rise and part of a business park."

I entered the address into the GPS. Following its directions, Fab exited the highway and, several streets later, turned into a commercial area of one-story office parks intermingled with warehouse buildings.

She slowed at the address given. It was a rundown warehouse and the only neglected property on the block. The lower half of the building was aluminum; the upper half consisted almost entirely of broken windows. The parking lot asphalt was chopped up in places, and weeds grew out of the cracks. There was a dark blue truck parked in front of a set of roll-up doors.

"This smells like a setup of some kind," Fab growled and gave the building a closer once-over.

"Based on the condition of the rest of the buildings on this street, this one appears to have been abandoned a year ago at the very minimum and probably longer." I stared out the window. "It takes quite a bit of time to show this much neglect. It's also screaming creepy vibe to me."

"Write down the license tag as I pass." Fab pulled into the lot and around potholes, cruising slowly past the entrance.

I hung out the window and snapped pictures. It surprised me when Fab exited to the street and parked at the curb. "This doesn't feel right."

She picked up her phone and placed a call. "It's ringing. No answer."

"A supposed business, apparently with no employees and not answering the phone in the middle of the day? Unless Herman gave you his personal number."

"I'm not feeling adventurous today." Fab sped away, then slowed and pulled into the parking lot of an adjacent office park, cruised around, and parked behind a large portable sign where we had a view of the property across the street.

We didn't have long to wait. A blue-jeaned man, his baseball hat pulled down low, came around the side of the building and stood staring down toward the corner before getting into the truck and roaring by us.

"Would be hard to recognize him if we see him again," I said.

Fab, who'd sat idling, flew after him in hot pursuit. It soon became apparent that he was aware he was being followed, as his driving got erratic—speeding up, slowing, and weaving between cars. Fab maneuvered a few tricks of her own, ending up on his bumper. He slowed for a yellow light, then sped through after it turned red and blew down the road.

"That was dangerous. He ran the risk of being

t-boned by cross traffic." I pointed at the two cars that shot across the highway as soon the light changed.

Fab kept her eyes glued to the road ahead and, before the light turned green, announced, "He lost us." She slammed her hand on the steering wheel.

I picked up my phone and Fab's and texted Frizzle's number to Xander. My second message had the new address to check out, and I also forwarded the pic of the license tag. I called Frizzle's number, and once again, it went to voicemail.

"I'm betting it was another ambush," Fab said in disgust. "Xander won't turn up anything; it will all be a dead end."

"This trainee has a bit of free advice for you." I made a face, hoping she'd smile. Didn't work. "You're going to want to hear this. No more new clients until we figure out who's behind these phony setups and, more importantly, what they want."

"How long is that going to take?" Fab snapped. "I could go out of business. Probably won't matter; once Didier finds out about this latest whatever it was, he's not going to let me out of the house."

"I'm proud of you." I smiled. "Normally, you'd jump out of the car and investigate the warehouse on your own." I was so happy and relieved she hadn't done just that. "Then you know what would've happened? I can answer that. We would've been at a distinct disadvantage, entering what I'm sure is an empty building and walking into a possible trap."

The grim look on her face was my answer.

"What do you suppose was the purpose in luring us here?" I asked. "For us to end up dead? That could've happened today. As good a shots as we are, we would've been at a distinct disadvantage." I shuddered at the thought that we hadn't told anyone about the change of address; there would have been no help coming if things went south. "If it's the same person, and it must be, perhaps the plan is for you to get jailed on another bogus charge? That happened already, and so far, it hasn't worked out as whoever hoped, I'm sure. If it hadn't been for your alibi, you'd be in jail, and you would be if prosecutors had some kind of irrefutable evidence against you. Thank goodness this person didn't have any to plant; if they did, they surely would have by this time."

"Maybe it's all a game, and the fun is in tormenting me." Fab had u-turned and gone back to the warehouse.

"What are you doing?"

"Calm down," Fab said in a placating tone. "I'm going to cruise by for one last look before we head home. I'm not even pulling in the parking lot, if that makes you happy."

"It would make me happier if we were already

on the way home."

True to her word, Fab slowed and continued past the building. Hanging a u-turn, she rolled down the window and snapped pictures.

I breathed a sigh of relief when she turned onto the main highway and I didn't see anyone following us. We rode half the way in silence, and I was tired of the gloomy mood. "I'm thinking we should drag out that inflatable dock of yours and float on the water, guzzling something cold to drink."

"I like—"

The SUV lifted off the road and went airborne, twisting to one side as it flew through the air, and landed hard, ramming through a chain-link fence and hanging up, less than a foot from plunging into the water. The airbags deployed.

"You okay?" Fab whispered. "What just happened?"

"Accident?" I was slumped sideways after hitting my head, staring mindlessly out the window, waiting for a stiff wind to push us the rest of the way into the murky water, where we'd drown.

The silence from the driver's side was deafening.

"Talk to me," I said.

Nothing.

It was hard to know how much time went by. Approaching sirens permeated my consciousness. Then nothing.

The passenger door was pried open, and two paramedics lifted me out and onto a stretcher, which they loaded in the back of an ambulance. Fab was already there, eyes open, a weak smile on her face.

"What happened?" I asked the paramedic.

"You were rear-ended."

"Is the other guy okay?"

He paused for so long that I was certain the other person was dead. "Hit and run."

I squeezed my eyes closed. This was no accident.

We were close enough to town that we were taken to Tarpon Cove Hospital. We got the e-ticket ride into the emergency room and were ushered into our own cubicles.

A doctor came in and asked a few questions, and then I was rolled down the hallway for a couple of x-rays.

I'd given the nurse Creole's number, and when I was brought back, he was sitting next to the bed. He ran his hand over my forehead and kissed me. "You okay?"

"Other than all of my organs feeling like they've been rearranged, I'm swell."

"You listen to me." He cupped my chin and brushed my lips with his. "You two are going to be okay. A little rest, and under the care of your own personal nurse, you'll be back on your feet in no time."

"Not the same guy as before," I groaned with

a wink. "He's sooo bossy."

"Then you'll have to be extra cooperative and do everything he says. Any chance of that?"

"I'll do my best."

"I'm taking that as an emphatic yes." He grinned, but it was gone in the next second. "You want to tell me what happened?"

"I'm not sure, exactly; it feels like I have blank spots. We were headed home from Homestead. Fab was driving, no faster than usual, and then we were flying through the air and spiraling down to within a breath of the water." I closed my eyes and tried to recall the events. "I grasped the door handle, which might not have been the smartest thing, hung on tight, and tried not to move, wanting to prevent us from tipping over and disappearing. Then the paramedics showed up."

Creole leaned over and gently wrapped his arms around me. "You're safe now."

"I want to go home," I whined and, not wanting to cry, squeezed my eyes closed.

"That's a good sign." He kissed my forehead and dried my eyes with his shirt. "I promise I'm going to get you out of here as soon as I can."

I wanted to sleep, which probably had something to do with the IV attached to my arm. I opened one eye and stared at the bag of clear fluid; it unnerved me that I didn't remember when it was hooked up.

Kevin's voice permeated my brain; he was

talking to Creole. I opened my eyes. He waved.

"What happened?" he asked.

"Rear-ended. It happened so fast," I said. Why was he asking me? He probably knew more about it than I did at this point.

Creole filled him in on what I'd told him. "What about the other driver?"

"Got away," Kevin said with a sympathetic look. "According to witnesses, we're looking for an oversized blue truck. It should have severe front-end damage and therefore be easy to spot."

"Fab didn't do anything to incite road rage," I said.

"Got any enemies?" Kevin asked.

"No one that would run me off the road," I said. Truth was, I didn't do enemies.

Kevin asked a few more questions of Creole and left.

As I closed my eyes again, I remembered I needed to tell Creole about the warehouse. I couldn't help but wonder if it had anything to do with the accident as sleep claimed me once again.

I dozed on and off, thinking several times that it was a good sign I hadn't been checked into a room. Finally, I woke up feeling a bit more awake. Creole's head lay on my chest as he watched TV. I combed his hair with my fingers. "That meeting that I went to with Fab…"

He sat up and kissed my cheek. "Got the details from Didier. Also heard that the two of you decided on no more new clients, and both of us are happy about that."

"Me too."

The nurse came in with discharge papers and went over the instructions. She left and came back with a wheelchair.

"Freedom," I said.

"We're going straight home; you can see Fab in the morning," Creole said.

"No complaint from me there. I feel like I've been hit by a truck." I laughed weakly, which got me a frown in return.

Chapter Thirty-Eight

A week later, I went for a follow-up visit to the doctor and was told to take it easy, no heavy lifting, and to get up and move around. I saw that as an excuse to hit the beach by myself and pick up shells, filling the antique bucket that Creole had bought me.

Fab had called the day after the accident, furious because Caspian had informed her that he was hiring a nurse. I'd rolled my eyes and expressed it to her in my tone, telling her to tell Papa to save his money and not waste the woman's time, that Fab would run the nurse off in an hour. I'd suggested that we hire Rude to pick up lunches and anything else we needed, and Fab went for it. Rude was ecstatic. Caspian hadn't been happy, labeling her odd.

That night, after the doctor cleared me, Spoon brought the Hummer back when he and Mother came for a visit. We'd been invited to their condo, but I'd begged off leaving my house. Brad and Mila showed up right behind them. "I love that you always bring food," I told Mother. Which came with a hundred questions that I answered lamely but truthfully, so she wouldn't be annoyed with me.

I was happy when Fab and Didier showed up. There'd been daily phone calls, but no visits.

Creole updated everyone once we were seated around the outside table. "The loaner SUV was totaled," he informed us. "The truck hasn't been found, and it will be difficult to identify the owner, since the tags were stolen. Not a single lead on the driver."

"It's easy to switch tags," I said. "Maybe we'll get lucky, and it will turn out it was dumped somewhere, and it can be recovered and dusted for prints. I wonder if there's a connection to the warehouse; the truck parked in front was the same color." I didn't for a second believe that it was a coincidence.

"Your instincts on that warehouse were right on," Creole said to Fab. "It stood empty for a few years after being foreclosed on. Because of paperwork issues that took a while to get straightened out, it was only recently listed. Thus far, no takers."

"Cornered Kevin today," Didier said. "It's his opinion, based on witness accounts, that you were targeted. The truck ran up on you going well over the speed limit, plowed into you, and never braked. Whoever was behind the wheel knew what they were doing; after a minor skid, the driver regained control and sped off. He thinks that you were meant to end up in the water."

"Fab and I have been over every bit of minutia a dozen times and still have no clue as to what this person wants," I said. "In light of recent events, I'd say they want Fab dead. Or both of us."

"It's sunk in, and in a big way, that anyone could creep around the corner and do me in." Fab shuddered. "It's unnerving. I'm not going to give whoever this is a second chance. To that end, I'm going to run my business out of my house. Any new clients, I'll get Toady to take them."

"I'm going to keep a low profile myself," I said. "I don't want to unknowingly lead anyone back here."

* * *

Another week passed, Fab got another cold call that she turned down flat, offering to send her partner instead, but the man was only interested in dealing with her. Afterwards, Fab called the number back, and a woman answered with the name of a different company. A couple of days later, an old client called, wanting the security system at his home updated. He'd had it installed when he first moved in and wanted the latest tricks to protect his property. Fab called me about riding along.

"This client...?" I asked.

"Mr. Sanders," Fab said. "What about him?"

"Under normal circumstances, I wouldn't ask, but are you sure it was him? Did you talk about old times? Some kind of identifier so you know you were talking to Mr. Sanders and not some psycho."

"I did ask how long it had been since I did a job for him. He laughed, sounding embarrassed that it had been a long time, and offered his condolences about Gabriel." Fab anticipated my next question and said, "The last dealings I had with Mr. Sanders were pre-Gabriel."

As soon as I found out Sanders lived on Fisher Island, I knew the reason for the excitement in Fab's voice. I was sure that she planned to cruise past Chrissy's house and stop for a chat, and why not, since she was in the neighborhood? I'd make her triple-promise that she wouldn't set so much as a toe on the woman's property. Take a good pair of binoculars and get a good peep from the street and hope that a neighbor didn't spot her. It wouldn't yield any information, but maybe it would satisfy her curiosity, making her feel like she'd done something productive.

Creole hadn't been happy to hear about the latest client, and that was putting it mildly. It had mostly to do with where Sanders lived. He was only slightly less annoyed when he heard that it was an old client. He called Xander himself and had him run a check, verifying that the property was still owned by Mr. Sanders and his wife. The phone number that Sanders had called from was traced back to a landline inside the home and also in his name. Creole made me promise more than once that under no circumstance would I creep around Chrissy Wright's property, reminding me that I'd done so in the past and it was unlikely it had changed.

It was an easy promise to make.

I drove to Fab's and u-turned, getting out and going around to the passenger side.

Fab walked down the steps, giving me a once-over. "What do you have on?"

I looked down at my black leggings under a tennis skirt, lightweight long-sleeve crop top, and running shoes. Judging by the pinched angle of her nose, she hated my outfit. It served another function, which I wouldn't bother to enlighten her about due to her poor attitude. Ms. Snobby could wait. "It's designer and new." I preened, ignoring her eyeroll. "I'm surprised that you got permission to leave the house. You did, didn't you?" I only asked to irritate her, and it hit the mark… somewhat.

"Didier listed the don'ts for me and made me agree to each one." With no hesitation, Fab ran down the rules.

I was happy to hear that Didier had gotten her to agree to everything I'd planned to ask for; it saved me from having to argue with her. I disclosed my promise to Creole, in case she was about to ask me.

"Didier told me three times that I'm not to

even slow down going by Chrissy's house."

"You agreed?" I asked her.

"I was done with the promising—it was getting irritating—so I reassured him that I wouldn't take a single shortcut and sealed it with a kiss.

As Fab drove north, she went over how the job would go down. It was the same as when I'd gone with her to other new security clients—she'd make recommendations and, if they approved, schedule a later date to bring in the installer.

It wasn't until she turned onto the Causeway that my stomach churned. The sooner we got to Fisher Island and back on the ferry headed home, the happier I'd be. Gone were the days when we had to sneak over; she'd somehow secured a pass that never expired. There was no wait for the ferry; we drove right on and parked. Usually, I liked to get out, sit on one of the benches, and stare at the blue-green water. Today, I stayed seated and rolled down the window. Fab did the same thing.

We were silent on the short ride over to the island.

Once the ferry docked, Fab drove off and stuck to the main road around the island. True to her word, she didn't slow past Chrissy Wright's mansion, although she did loop around again before pulling up to a two-story Mediterranean mansion that was a popular style for the area. To my surprise, the security gate stood open.

Fab pulled in and parked. "Maybe you should stay in the car, since you're not dressed professionally." She smoothed down her black pencil skirt, worn with a white silk blouse and heels high enough to make your nose bleed, and got out.

"Not a chance." I got out and took a moment to enjoy the lush, tropical landscape. "Introduce me as your maid... or not at all. It's highly unlikely they'll ask once I don't pass inspection. Besides, it's popular to drag around the hired help; makes you look all richy."

"You behave yourself." She shook her finger at me.

"Yes, Mom." I followed her up the stairs to the massive front door. The bell could be heard across the waterfront.

The butler answered the door—forties, hot-looking, dark good looks, and wearing an expensive suit. The job must pay really well.

"Ms. Merceau." He flashed an ingratiating smile and opened the door wide.

I trudged in behind Fab and chose a chair off to the side, while she sat on the couch. The butler barely gave me a glance; he didn't so much as shift his gaze, staying focused on Fab.

"Mr. Sanders is finishing up a call and will be right with you. I fixed refreshments." The butler bared his teeth in a smile and left the room.

I stared around the cavernous room,

everything designed to be admired, with furniture not made for comfort. The view of the waters of the Government Cut took center stage. I could sit and stare out the window and watch the boats go by all day. Except this wasn't my house. I snapped my fingers at Fab, my code to her not to schmooze all day. Creole was waiting for a call that we were on our way home, and he'd griped more than once that it better not take all day. I'd agreed with him and told him so.

Butler dude was back, tray in hand, handing us each a cut crystal glass of iced tea and providing a matching crystal coaster. As I stared down into my glass, a fleck of white caught my attention, disappearing quickly. Lint? That made my skin crawl. Drinking my own lint, dust, etc. was one thing, though I probably wouldn't even do that, but another person's? Not happening.

The butler had his back turned, exchanging pleasantries with Fab and saying that Mr. Sanders was looking forward to the upgrade of his system.

In lieu of answering, she drank her tea. I shook my head to get her attention so she would see me pour half my glass on the carpet next to the chair. Fab was also averse to drinking dirt. The butler left the room.

Fab shot me a *what's going on?* look.

I stood and walked around the room, pausing to look at the knickknacks, and was about to tell her not to drink any more tea when I caught sight of the butler standing off in the corner, staring at Fab. It unnerved me. I went back to my seat and contemplated a fake barfing scenario. Fab would kill me if she lost her client due to my machinations, and I'd hate for him to never use Fab again because of me — or worse, spread the word — but I was ready to leave, and now.

Before I could do anything, a couple of things happened at once.

Chapter Thirty-Nine

Chrissy Wright stormed into the room, reminiscent of a gale-force wind, a manic gleam in her eye, waving a gun. Fab slumped back against the cushions, not passed out, but in a state that showed she didn't care what was going on around her. The butler stomped over and grabbed me out of my chair. Taking my cue from Fab, I forced myself to go limp, doing my best not to fight being manhandled. He ran his hands around my middle, front and back, relieving me of my Glock, then stuck his hand down the front of my sports bra. He then gave Fab the same intrusive examination. He took her Walther from her back holster and tossed it on a nearby chair, along with our phones.

"Now, now, Gregory. We don't have all day for an invasive feel-up." Chrissy laughed, sounding overexcited. "Got you now, bitch," she gloated and pointed her Glock at Fab, punctuating it with shooting noises instead of the real thing. "You." Chrissy turned her gun on me. "I'm going to blow your brains out, but not before you watch your friend die."

"Can you at least tell us why?" I asked, trying

to sound vague, so as not to tip her off that I hadn't been drugged.

Fab was struggling to sit up and fight the effects of whatever was in the drink.

"That bitch was supposed to fry for the deaths of my beloved Maxwell and Gabriel." Chrissy waved her gun around in a mad frenzy. "Instead, my dear Bruno paid the price."

"But Fab didn't murder either of those men." I closed my eyes and pretended a faint state. "You did. You probably also paid someone to kill Bruno."

"All charges were dropped," Chrissy said, as though that made her innocent. "I spent *days* in jail. I had to go to a spa to get rid of the ill effects." She shuddered. "I'm an heiress. I don't belong in jail when I've got the money to buy my way out of a mishap or two," she said, blowing double-murder off by making it sound like an unpaid parking ticket.

"If everything goes as before," I said to Gregory, motioning between Fab and I. "You will confess and conveniently hang yourself. And Chrissy here will be turned loose to run amok in Florida society."

"Oh shut up," Chrissy snapped. "Unless you want to die now."

Gregory shot her a questioning look.

"Before you kill us." Fab coughed. "Surely you want to brag? You went to a lot of work to torment me. Starting with the murder of Aurora Bissett."

"Aurora!" Chrissy sneered. "I hated her and would've gotten rid of her sooner, but it wasn't convenient. And who to frame for the crime? You were my first and only choice. But first, I had to do my research and not just get impatient and rid myself of her. That's where having money helps—you can buy whatever you want."

Fab went into another coughing fit, hanging her head and making retching noises.

Chrissy crossed the room. "Stop with the sound effects." She hit Fab in the head with the butt of her gun.

Fab groaned and went limp.

"Get her some water," Chrissy ordered Gregory. "She dies when I say she does and not a second before."

Gregory disappeared and came back with a bottle of water. He threw half in Fab's face, then tipped her head back and poured the rest into her mouth. She coughed, sputtered, and blew the rest all over his suit.

Chrissy caught his arm before he could backhand Fab. "You'll get your playtime." She walked around in circles, turning to stare at Fab, seemingly happy that she had her attention once again. "Aurora was an irritant. We were friends, or so she thought. I couldn't have cared less that she banged Gabriel. And then to find out that she'd invited Maxwell into her bed… That was another reason I wasn't going to shell out lifetime alimony by divorcing him. Maxwell had me and went for that simpering dolt." Chrissy wasn't the first spouse to think murder was a better alternative than paying alimony.

"Some friend." I struggled to sound sympathetic. My only goal was to keep her talking.

Chrissy ignored me, all her attention focused on Fab. "After their deaths, Aurora begged my forgiveness. She sobbed pathetic tears, needing to be close to someone who knew Maxwell and Gabriel. They were her whole life. Lucky her, my gun was tucked inside my purse. Had I had it in my hand, I wouldn't have been able to talk myself out of shoving it in her mouth. I told myself 'patience' over and over. It was a picture of you in the society section with your handsome husband that started me thinking that I could rid my life of two of the most annoying women I'd ever met, and at the same time. You being happy—no way was I going to allow that." Chrissy turned and flicked her eyes across my face; it was clear I fell short. "You actually got someone to marry you?" she said to me. "Look at you; you're a mess," she sneered, as her eyes went over me from head to toe.

"Sorry for the ugly outfit," I said to Fab. "I'll make it up to you."

"Your friend just lied to you," Chrissy mocked. "You two aren't going anywhere." She nodded at Gregory, who walked over, jerked me upright, and dragged me across the room, tossing me on the couch next to Fab. He went back and sat in the chair I'd occupied, training his gun on us.

"I must say, it was tedious planning the same mishaps for me that befell you, but what better alibi than to also look like a victim? It's been fun tormenting the two of you, but eventually, the fun and games had to come to an end. I was getting bored, but the biggest factor was wanting you dead. I made the mistake of not killing you quicker the last time; this time will be different." Chrissy zeroed in on Fab. "I'll wait until after your funeral, then get an introduction to your husband and offer a comforting shoulder. When I'm done, he won't remember your name."

Even if Didier had never heard the name Chrissy Wright, he wouldn't give her the time of day. He'd be polite, but she'd get a speedy brush-off. Fab wasn't the kind of woman men forgot. It obviously still needled Chrissy that Gabriel never completely got over his ex-wife. He'd never stopped wanting Fab, and when he'd finally accepted that a reconciliation wasn't going to happen, he'd planned to use her for one last job and then kill her. He wouldn't allow her a happy-ever-after with someone else.

"I'll give it to the two of you." Chrissy's annoyance was on the rise again. "It was costly to torment you. I had to hire two investigators to track you, and even then, you picked up the first tail. The dead flowers were my own idea." She laughed. "It gave me the perfect opportunity to check out your offices. It surprised me that you'd chose a dreary warehouse in a dreadful neighborhood. I knew you lacked style."

It was now a sought-after area, thanks to the Boardwalk project. But even if Chrissy had actually gotten inside the building, I was certain the woman would never have given design credit to Fab. I wasn't the only one who thought the offices could easily grace a magazine cover.

"*The* most fun," Chrissy clapped, "was telling you that Didier was dead. I spoke to you in my normal voice, a little simpering maybe." Her tone changed to a child's for that last part. "And loved every minute of your wounded distress. I made the call from the parking lot of the hospital, and you didn't disappoint, arriving distraught and racing inside. I fantasized playing that joke on you over and over but didn't figure you'd fall for it a second time. Too bad." She made a sad face. "I laughed for hours."

"Hilarious," I seethed.

Chrissy stood and came to stand in front of me, leaning down. "Shut up, you bland little nothing," she shrieked in my face.

I flinched away.

"The dead body?" Fab asked, showing signs that she was becoming more lucid again.

"Bought it." Chrissy wrinkled her nose.

"Another perk to having money. Gregory saw to the details. I wasn't about to get my hands dirty." She beamed at him, so absorbed in herself that she missed the calculating gleam in Gregory's eyes, which was growing in intensity. He wasn't as besotted as her previous goon, Bruno, or as easily led.

"So you went to all this trouble to get even with me? Why?" Fab asked. "For sleeping with my ex? We were married at the time. And I don't remember even meeting Maxwell."

"I needed someone to frame, and you were so convenient. Gabriel went on and on, extolling your virtues, how clever you were, how fearless. He changed his tune when you told him you were done. Knowing men the way I do, I knew it was only a matter of time before he turned on you, so I hurried him along by planting the blackmail idea in his ear. *Once she's been useful, kill her.* Worked like a charm, but then, I knew it would." Chrissy leaned back against the chair, laying her gun at her side, appearing exhausted from all her bragging. "Any more questions before I kill you... slowly, of course?"

"Where's Mr. Sanders?" I asked. "Is he in on your murderous plan?"

"The Sanderses go to their home in Vail for a couple of months at this time every year."

"That's convenient," Fab snarked.

"One more thing," I said. I turned to face Fab and scooted closer, holding my arms out for a hug, which was short. "Love you. I also want you to know that I made up my mind that I was tired of us ending up with the short end of the stick. Don't like it at all."

"Isn't that sweet?" Chrissy cooed.

I straightened to a sitting position. "I can't seem to find the right words to express how I feel about you and your latest lackey." I drew my newest purchase from a pocket on the side of my thigh and, without hesitation, shot Gregory, who slumped off the chair to the floor.

The revolver, a special-order Beretta, was small but deadly nonetheless.

Shocked, Chrissy hesitated a moment too long before reaching for her gun. My second shot ripped through her shoulder, and she screeched, the gun clattering to the floor. The only reason she was still alive was because she needed to answer the cops' questions. I knew it hurt like the devil, as I'd been shot in the shoulder before, and I couldn't work up a scintilla of sympathy.

Fab ran her hand down the side of my pants, sticking her fingers in the pocket, and grinned. "You better have ordered two pairs."

"And two guns. Because you need the right size." I winked and jumped up, going over to where Chrissy mewled, rolling on the floor. I tossed her cell phone across the room, smiling at the crunching noise it made.

Gregory still hadn't moved.

I walked over and toed him with my shoe. No

response. I grabbed my phone, pocketing Fab's, and calling 911. While I reported the shooting, Chrissy began screaming, "She's trying to kill me," over and over. I gave the information and hung up. "If I wanted you dead, you'd be on the floor with your henchman. I'm an accurate shot." I raced over to Fab and carded my fingers through the hair at the back of her head, where Chrissy had hit her. "No blood."

"It's going to take more than a hit from her weak-ass arm to hurt me."

"You should get that checked out. You also need a blood test to find out what Gregory laced our drinks with. It was a white substance, which I mistook for dirt or whatever. Thank goodness."

"Help me stand." Fab held up her arms.

"You're not going anywhere. That way, we don't have to struggle to remember what happened where." I crossed to the leaded-glass French doors, unlocked them, and pushed them open, resting them against the wall. "Fresh air." The Sanders were going to have quite the welcome-home cleanup; what was a few bugs in addition?

A security team showed ahead of the cops. Along with an ambulance. They threw a sheet over Gregory and attended to Chrissy, who was busy throwing out accusations that we were in a scheme to kill her. For what reason, she didn't say. She continued to scream as they rolled her out the door.

"Call our lawyer," Fab ordered.

"You'd think I'd know to do that right after 911." I scrolled through my phone and easily found Cruz's number. Susie answered, which shouldn't have surprised me, since it was his office, but that didn't mean I wanted to deal with her. I cut straight to the chase. "This is Madison Westin. Fab and I were involved in a shooting and need representation."

"Have Ms. Merceau call directly, since she's already a client. Mr. Campion won't be able to represent you both. It's against his rules." Susie's tone was gleeful.

"Do you have someone else in the office that's available?" I tried not to sound pleading, but when you need a lawyer...

"Sorry." She hung up.

I took out Fab's phone, scrolled through it and found the number, then placed the call, handing it to her. She gave me a quizzical look. Susie put her straight through. Fab told Cruz what happened, and he gave his usual advice: "Don't speak until I get there." Then added, "Thank goodness you're local; I'll meet you at the station." He wanted to talk to one of the security guards, and she handed off the phone.

I relayed how Susie had gleefully blown me off.

"My first request of Cruz will be a lawyer for you. You take the same advice I am." She zipped her lips. "I can imagine that Drama Bitch is filling the paramedics' ears with claims that we're serial killers."

"Do you have a hospital out here?" I asked one of the guards.

"We have a helicopter and ferry on standby for emergencies and will have Mrs. Wright back on the mainland in minutes."

"How are we going to prove our innocence?" Fab whispered.

"Well, we won't be using Mr. Sanders as an alibi, since he doesn't know what just went down in his house and won't be happy when he finds out. Wonder how Chrissy knew he was an old client of yours."

"They hobnob in the same social circles, so maybe my name got mentioned back when and she filed the tidbit away." Fab ended in a snooty tone that mimicked Chrissy and made me smile. She leaned over and fingered the pocket on the side of my pants again. "Love these pants."

"And obviously the smaller Beretta doesn't lack stopping-power." I picked up the phone again. "I'm calling Creole, in case we get hauled off to police headquarters."

Three of Miami's finest barreled through the door. One beelined for us and removed the phones from our possession.

"We've contacted our lawyer, Cruz Campion, and he's told us not to answer any questions until he arrives," I said.

"I got the call," the cop said. "I need you to

stand," he ordered us both. I watched Fab with concern, but while unsteady, she managed it. When we were both up, he read us the Miranda warning. "You're being taken into custody for questioning." He cuffed us, and another cop came over and walked us out to the waiting police cruiser.

Chapter Forty

When we got to the ferry landing, there was one waiting, and it whisked us to the mainland. I put my head on Fab's shoulder.

"You need to sit up," the officer ordered.

Hang in there, Fab mouthed.

It wasn't lights and sirens, but it didn't take long before the officer pulled into the police garage and helped us out. Once inside the station, we were separated. Fab was led farther down the hall—to where Cruz was waiting, I presumed—while I was ushered into a holding cell and the cuffs taken off. The door slammed shut with a resounding bang. "How long will I be here?"

"We can hold you up to seventy-two hours before charging you." The officer locked the outer door and was gone.

I eyed the bed, not finding it at all appealing, but since my choices were limited to it or the floor, I sat down and found it damn uncomfortable. I scooted back and huddled into a ball against the wall. I hoped that Cruz would come through with a lawyer for me quickly. If he weaseled, Fab would borrow his phone and get me representation. I didn't know how long I could hold out against answering questions, especially if I was waiting for a lawyer who never showed. Creole wouldn't let me rot in jail… if he could find me.

The door opened again, and a familiar face walked in, smug smile in place. I'd have rolled my eyes but didn't have the energy. "I see you're still bald," I said, peering into the face of Casio Famosa. Big deal or just a dick, depending on who you asked in the police department.

"Now Red, I'm here to help." Casio unlocked the cell door, came in, and sat down. "Tell me what happened and don't skimp on the details."

I didn't think what he was doing was legal, but as excessively flattering as he was, I trusted him. We'd had encounters in the past and had never screwed each other over.

"The *beginning* beginning or starting from today?"

Casio mulled that one over for a minute. "Today, and then loop back around if it's pertinent."

I gave him the detailed version and did my best not to leave anything out.

"You and I have something in common— neither of us are fans of Chrissy Wright." Casio flashed a grin that most wouldn't find reassuring; instead, they'd take a step back. "That woman belongs in jail, and it would please me ever so much to be the one to put her there and make sure she stays put this time." He went on to tell me that he'd been assigned the murder at the Wright mansion back in the day and it ate at him that the charges got dropped. He'd never bought that Bruno killed the two men and told the District Attorney so, and was more than a little annoyed to be discounted and shown the door.

"I'm going to need a favor. If you're inclined to say no outright, I'll remind you that you owe me." This close, I noticed his lack of eyebrows.

"You're going to owe me huge when you walk out of here a free woman," Casio boasted. "I know you and your friend didn't murder or attempt to murder anyone, and I'm going to prove it. If I have my way, I hope to get the old case opened, confession or not. Besides, Fab needs to get out of here and raise her baby."

I swallowed a snort. Now wasn't the time to fess up that the preggo story had been made up so Fab had a good reason for not working for his smarmier brother, Brick Famosa, anymore. She'd wanted a no-hard-feelings exit. "About my favor…"

"Can't wait to hear what it is."

"Call my husband, Creole. Your old partner in hunting criminals," I reminded him, in case he was going to claim amnesia. I'd guess not, judging by his smirk. "Tell him I need a lawyer and, if you're as good as you say, a ride home."

"I'll make that call right now." Casio stood.

"I'm on my way out to Fisher to prove your innocence on any accusation Chrissy levels. You hang in there."

I continued to huddle against the wall and dozed off. My eyes popped open when the door opened again. This time, an officer I hadn't seen before led me down the hallway and ushered me into a cold and dreary meeting room. Tank, AKA Patrick Cannon, waved from the other side of the only table.

We'd availed ourselves of his talents in the past, and if he couldn't handle it, he farmed it out. I knew he'd specialized in criminal law.

"Happy to see you," I said, and sat in the only other chair.

"Creole sends his regards."

"If I don't get to see him, tell him I regard him too." The mention of my husband's name had tears threatening to spill down my face. I sucked them back with a couple of short breaths.

"I may not be as arrogant as your friend's lawyer, but I'll get you out of here." The big man patted my hand. "Tell me what went down, starting with your arrival on Fisher. Creole gave me the backstory."

I repeated everything, in the same detail as I had with Casio, and told him about the detective's visit and his offer of help.

"I'll get with the detective. There are ways to prove your and Fab's innocence, and I'm sure he's made an extensive mental list on his drive over to the island." Tank opened his briefcase and pushed a bag of M&Ms at me, which I gobbled down. He got up and knocked on the door, requesting water, which appeared within a few minutes.

After that reprieve, I was led back to my cell for what seemed like days. In fact, it was only hours later—early morning of the next day but still dark outside—when Fab and I were released. Casio was in the lobby, standing next to Fab when I arrived, and he informed us that Sanders actually *had* an updated security system, which had caught everything on tape.

"I promise to make the case stick this time." Casio walked us to the exit. "Although, Chrissy probably won't get a life sentence, as she would have for the double homicide, which is the downside." He unlocked the door, and we scurried out with a backward wave.

Fab hooked her arm in mine. "I'd suggest we run, except someone might think we're escaping."

"A ride. That's what we need."

"There's the Hummer over there." Fab pointed.

Chapter Forty-One

Creole and Didier had been waiting in the parking lot for our release. It was a silent drive home. I was happy not to have to answer any more questions and leaned my head against Creole's shoulder.

When we arrived home, Didier scooped Fab into his arms and carried her into their house. Creole drove us back to our house and carried me inside. I insisted on a shower before getting into bed, where I immediately fell asleep.

The next morning, Creole brought me a cup of coffee and climbed in beside me. "How are you feeling?"

"Weirded out."

"Casio and I exchanged a few phone calls last night. I got your version of the story from him, and he updated me on his investigation. As you know, Chrissy and her partner planned for the two of you to never leave the house alive. It's unclear what they were planning on doing with your bodies. Leave them in the living room for Fab's client to find? That would've been gruesome for the couple."

"It was small comfort, but I knew that you'd never let Chrissy and Gregory get away with our deaths." I leaned over and kissed his cheek.

"Casio arrested Chrissy and placed a guard outside her hospital room. As expected, she lawyered up. We haven't heard the last of her, as she's screaming her innocence to whoever will listen, making the two of you out to be murdering thugs and saying that you lured her to the Sanders house and ambushed her."

"That's the reason I didn't kill her. Figured the cops would think just that." I handed him my coffee mug and leaned back against the pillows. "Wonder how Fab is doing?"

He grabbed his phone off the bedside table and placed a call, asking my question. The conversation was short. "Fab's still feeling out of it, not quite herself."

"I wonder what the heck Gregory put in our drinks. It only took a few minutes to make Fab lethargic. I spilled mine on the carpet. I'll have to tell Mother; it will be the one time she's not appalled by my bad manners."

"The cops had a blood test taken at the station. Should have the results of what kind of sedative it was fairly soon. The good thing is that there were no lasting effects."

There was a knock at the door. Creole and I exchanged looks.

"Why don't you answer it, since all I have on is your t-shirt?" I smiled at him.

Creole got up and crossed the room. "Do you want to place a wager as to who'd show up without a call?"

I laughed, knowing there was more than one choice, and jumped out of bed, ducking behind the screen to pull on sweats. My hair was sticking on end, completing my hot-mess look.

He opened the door, and Mother and Spoon came in with a couple of large shopping bags, followed by Brad, Liam, and Mila.

I craned my head around the screen and waved.

Mila ran at top speed in my direction, and I had just enough time to back up and crouch down. She took a flying leap into my arms, and I stumbled back and made sure we landed on the bed. It was clear she'd had practice. "You feeling better?" Her little hands cupped my cheeks.

Mother was right behind her and sat down beside us. "We brought groceries. Spoon's cooking." She enveloped us in a three-way bear hug.

I bit back tears. "I don't tell you enough that I love you and you're a very cool mother."

"Stop or we'll both start crying." Mother wiped at my eyes.

"Just the mention of food and I'm hungry." I slid off the bed and stood, Mila in my arms. I swung her in an arc, setting her on her feet, and she took off running. I hooked my arm under

Mother's, and we crossed to the kitchen, where I hugged Spoon.

Creole had opened the pocket doors to the patio and slid them back, and Brad and Liam were pulling out the table and gathering chairs.

The door opened, and Fab waltzed in with a grin on her face, Didier behind her, appearing slightly annoyed. I ran and enveloped her in a hug. "We won't tell Creole that you picked the lock," I whispered in her ear.

"You're no fun."

Mother came over and hugged Fab, holding her at arm's distance and giving her a once-over. "You okay?"

"I'm not complaining about anything for at least a couple of days."

I walked out to the patio and hugged and kissed Brad and Liam. "Thank you for teaching me to shoot and not giving up until I got good at it," I said to Brad. "Your encouragement is why I'm still around to annoy you."

Spoon took over the kitchen and, with the help of the guys, cooked breakfast. Mother and I set the table, while Fab played with Mila.

"I miss these family get-togethers." I looked up at Creole, who'd come up behind me. "We need more room."

"I'm going to leave telling Fab that we're moving to you." He smirked.

It was fun to gather around the table, watch as the pancakes, eggs, and bacon were devoured, and just be with family.

Chapter Forty-Two

It had been a long week, with both Fab and I expecting to get a call from our lawyers that the District Attorney's office would like a meeting.

Finally, Fab called Cruz and got brushed off by Susie, who said, "I'll have him call you."

My lawyer was so much more approachable that I didn't hesitate to call him and ask for an update. "You'll be the first to hear when they call," Tank reassured me. "Don't worry. Silence isn't a bad thing."

When I found out that Tank was attending Chrissy Wright's arraignment later that week, I invited him to Fab's house for pizza and beer, which he readily accepted. Then I called her and booked the patio, assuring her I'd bring the food and drinks. I also called Creole and Didier.

Tank showed up looking the antithesis of a lawyer—at least, I assumed he hadn't just come from the courthouse in shorts and cowboy boots—and I led him out to the patio, where we gathered around the table. "Can't say I've had any other client feed me." He tore off a slice of pizza. "Like it. Maybe I'll put it in my next contract."

"Hopefully, it won't become a habit, representing one or the other of us, but just so you know, we're big on food and drink around here." I laughed.

After scarfing down half a pizza and washing it down with a beer, Tank got started. "As expected, Chrissy pled 'not guilty.' The judge set her bond at a hundred thousand, which surprised me, since we're talking kidnapping, and attempted murder. Plus the death of Gregory while in commission of a felony, which is another murder charged against her. The prosecuting attorney didn't object."

Creole's hand hit the table so hard, the silverware rattled. "What the—"

"There's more," Tank said. "Chrissy came prepared, had a shyster bondsman sitting in the front row, right behind her slick attorney. I'll give them credit for being on their game. My professional opinion is that they knew the court date would end with her going home."

"Chrissy's out?" Fab asked incredulously.

The guys were equally stunned.

"At least, tell us she's on a leg monitor and her movements are restricted," I said.

"The prosecutor didn't ask for it." Tank shook his head. "I'm sure they've probably processed her by now. The only condition was to contact the DA's office before leaving the state. As far as bail hearings go, it went fast and the stipulations were cushy. The prosecuting attorney just sat on his hands."

I turned on Fab. "You just talked to Cruz; how could he not know?"

"Cruz wasn't in the courtroom and wouldn't have a reason to attend unless it was his client," Tank answered. "The only way he'd know is if he had someone checking on the outcome."

"So crazy *bitch* can send someone after us again," I said with a shake of my head. "It's the only way to make sure we don't testify against her."

"Even if you hadn't held out the enticement of food, I'd planned to call and schedule a meeting." Tank downed his beer. Didier exchanged the empty bottle for a full one. "I'd suggest that you two keep a low profile. Chrissy's probably not stupid enough to come after you; she knows she'd be a suspect and would have to be able to prove her whereabouts if something happened. But with psycho people, it's hard to know what they're going to do next. One would think they'd do the smart thing, but oftentimes, they don't; they act on emotion.

"Considering her past," Didier snapped, "who knows what she'd do. She could show up out of nowhere or hire a killer."

"Except she made it clear that she wants to orchestrate my death and watch while it happens," Fab said. "Chrissy has enough money to hire anything done. If the rumors are true, it's not going to run out in her lifetime. It's clear she has homicidal delusions and is arrogant enough to think she's never going to have to pay, even if she's caught with a smoking gun in her hand. So far, she's been right."

"You'd think she'd spend a few bucks to get mentally healthy," I said.

"From what we know about Chrissy, once she decides that she's going to try again to kill the two of you, she'll hire someone to find you," Creole said. "I wish I could say that she'd back off and we'd never see or hear from her again, but the chances are slim."

"You two need to be aware of everything going on around you when you leave this cushy compound," Tank reminded us.

"Agreed," Fab said. I nodded.

"Any clue if Chrissy knows where we live?" Didier asked.

"I'd say no," Fab said. "None of her so-called pranks happened here at the house. If she had the address, I'd think one of them would have."

"We know she has the office address, so all of us will steer clear of there," Creole said.

"You can both work from home," Didier suggested.

"Just thinking the same thing." Fab smiled at him.

"During the day, the two of you should stay together at one house or the other," Creole said.

That sounded good to me.

Chapter Forty-Three

My eyes flew open and I looked over at the window where the sun was streaming through. It took a few moments to remember that I'd decided to grab a nap and make use of the ginormous bed in the guest bedroom of Fab's house, which had been designated as mine and Creole's as soon as it was furnished. Fab had wanted Creole and me to move in, but I'd reassured her that we'd still have coffee in the morning while living just down the street.

I struggled to shake off the tiredness from not being able to sleep the previous night after hearing that Chrissy Wright was on the loose. Worry gnawed at me about the waiting game of when and where she'd strike next. There was a slight chance that she'd go away, but no one believed that. We'd decided that I'd spend the days at Fab's until we figured out a game plan for dealing with the crazy woman.

The bedroom door was ajar, and voices traveled down the hallway, sounding like they were coming from the kitchen. Didier must have come home early, and it was time for me to leave and give them some alone time. It wouldn't surprise me if Creole had left at the same time, in which case, he'd be showing up any minute, if he wasn't already here. Then it dawned on me that for me to be hearing voices, someone had to be yelling, and I'd never heard Didier do that. The last thing I wanted to do was interrupt a fight. I sat up, tossed my feet over the side of the bed, and slid them into a pair of slipper shoes. I tugged down my t-shirt dress and gathered my things, stuffing them in my bag and leaving it on the bed. When I crept halfway down the hall, I realized that the loud voices were Fab's and another woman's. Actually, the other woman was doing all the talking. It took a minute, but I recognized the voice, and my neck hair danced.

There was a frantic sound to Chrissy's ramblings. "I hate you... bitch... why can't you die?"

I hurried back to my bedroom and fished the Beretta out of my bag. Creole and I had discussed whether to wear it around Fab's house, and he didn't think it necessary, as long as it was within reach. I slipped out of my shoes and tiptoed back down the hall, pasting myself to the wall.

"This time, you're going to go to jail, and you're going to stay there," Fab told her in a calm voice. "Kill me, and the cops' first stop is going to be your mansion, where you'll be led out in cuffs. No designer clothes in jail, and the food's terrible."

"There's proof I already left the country," Chrissy gloated. "It couldn't possibly be little ol' me."

"You're not getting out of this alive, I promise you," Fab said in a cold, hard tone. "You'll end up like your friend, Bruno—remember him? You and I know that he didn't hang himself. Your death will also be ruled a suicide, but it won't be. If you do make it out of the country, my father will hunt you down, and your demise won't be pretty or painless."

Chrissy laughed. "Empty threats."

"You kill me and then what? You drive off into the sunset?" Fab asked.

"First stop is down the street to blow your friend's face off. I don't get you two; you couldn't do better? She's so beneath you."

"I couldn't have a better friend. Apparently, you've never had one, or you'd know that. Oh that's right, you killed the last person who thought she was a friend."

Chrissy ignored Fab. "Then I'm gone. Out of here."

"How did you find out where I live?" Fab asked.

I knew Fab was buying time and I needed to make a move before crazy-woman shot her. Forget jail or anything else if that happened; I'd blow *her* face off. I inched forward carefully until I could see into the room without being seen.

"Your office was closed up like a tomb. So

what's a smart girl to do? Have your husbands followed. Now that was easy. They led me right here." She half-laughed, clearly not believing her luck. "It surprised me when I got the report back and saw you both live on the same street. My investigator was thorough and got me a layout of the street and who lives where."

"How did you get past the security gates?"

"Haven't you learned anything from me? Anything can be bought, and that includes your pool boy. I sold him a lie about having a surprise for you. Although not completely a lie, now was it?" Chrissy's right shoulder was still bandaged, but she managed to keep control of the gun with the use of her left hand as she waved it around. "Go sit on the couch. How fabulous will it look when your husband finds your body lifelessly staring at him and the blood has seeped through that cheap fabric? Have I already told you how much I'm going to enjoy this? Because I am."

The element of surprise was called for. If she turned and saw me, she might shoot wildly. "Hey Chrissy," I yelled.

Chrissy pivoted around and, as anticipated, pulled the trigger. I'd crouched, and it went over my head and into the wall. I returned fire and hit her in the vicinity of her heart, if she had one. She dropped with a surprised look on her face.

Fab rushed over to Chrissy and peered down, nudging her with her foot. She rushed around the body and threw herself at me. "You okay?"

I nodded into her shoulder. "Your turn to call 911," I said in a faint tone.

"Thank you. For saving my life. Again." Fab walked me over to a barstool and had me sit facing away from the body. She retrieved her phone and made the calls, first to Didier, then the lawyers, and then the cops. That done, she led me into the living room, shoved me down on one of the couches, and sat next to me, arm around my shoulders. "This is getting to be a habit that we need to break. We need to start protecting ourselves before things go awry."

The guys burst through the front door a nanosecond ahead of the cops. Right behind them was Kevin, who'd once again drawn the short straw. He didn't seem to mind.

Creole and Didier took charge and ordered us out to the pool area, walking us out. We chose a double chaise to sit on, and they went back inside to deal with the cops.

"Once crime-scene-cleaner dude is done, you'll never know that...well, you know," I said to Fab. "Sorry for shooting her inside, but I didn't know how to get her outside."

Fab wrinkled her nose.

"Just think how popular I'll be once word spreads at Jake's. Customers will be lined up to see me. They don't need to know I don't hang out there." I huddled close to Fab and laid my head on her shoulder. "I owed you from before. If I hadn't screwed it up the first time, Chrissy wouldn't have gotten a second attempt."

"You know what I thought about, staring down the barrel of her weapon once again? That it wasn't ever going to end until one of us was dead. Even if she got jail time, which based on previous experience wasn't likely, it wouldn't be near long enough. I'd have to move far away and leave no forwarding address… or look over my shoulder for the rest of my life."

"I'd have had to tag along. She hated me, and I think it's because we're such good friends and that bugged her," I said.

"Do you know how badass your reputation's going to be when this gets around?" Fab tugged on the end of my hair. "Wait until I trot out my rendition. People will see you coming and run the other way, like they do for Spoon or Gunz."

"That would be kind of cool. Don't tell anyone I said that." I crossed my lips with my finger. "Besides, it's not appropriate talk when you have a dead woman in your house."

"Old Chrissy was going to blow me to bits with a smile on her face. I'm feeling little sympathy here. It was clearly her or us, and that, my friend, is self-defense."

"Remember when I first hit town and I was the incarnation of Dorothy, fresh from the corn field? What happened to that innocence?"

"That was stupidity." Fab sniffed. "You kicked naïve Madison to the curb and let it be known you were no one's doormat. Good thing. I was opposed to having a friend from the beginning. And a sissy one? I think not. I'm happy with how everything worked out, and as we both know, that's all that matters."

"So what you're telling me is that you're okay with loosening your standards and allowing a friend into your life?"

"Yep." Fab grinned and hugged me hard.

PARADISE SERIES NOVELS

Crazy in Paradise
Deception in Paradise
Trouble in Paradise
Murder in Paradise
Greed in Paradise
Revenge in Paradise
Kidnapped in Paradise
Swindled in Paradise
Executed in Paradise
Hurricane in Paradise
Lottery in Paradise
Ambushed in Paradise
Blownup in Paradise
Psycho in Paradise
Overdose in Paradise
Initiation in Paradise
Jealous in Paradise
Wronged in Paradise

Zuma Seals Series:

Malibu Hills Murder
Mission Paradise
One For The Team

Deborah's books are available on Amazon

amazon.com/Deborah-Brown/e/B0059MAIKQ

About the Author

Deborah Brown is an Amazon bestselling author of the Paradise series. She lives on the Gulf of Mexico, with her ungrateful animals, where Mother Nature takes out her bad attitude in the form of hurricanes.

For a free short story, sign up for my newsletter. It will also keep you up-to-date with new releases and special promotions: www.deborahbrownbooks.com

Follow on FaceBook: facebook.com/DeborahBrownAuthor

You can contact her at Wildcurls@hotmail.com

Deborah's books are available on Amazon

amazon.com/Deborah-Brown/e/B0059MAIKQ

Made in the USA
Columbia, SC
16 July 2020

13013771R00205